Treasure Key

Too Close to Key West
Too Far From Reality

Wayne Gales

ISBN-13: 978-1482707984

ISBN-10: 1482707985

To Captain Robert Moran – The Real Deal

Table of Contents

Acknowledgements

My late father, Frank Gales, reminded me several years ago to "write about what I know." I've been writing most of my adult life, mostly travel stories with a few stabs at some fictional short stories. I've always felt I had a book in me, and the concept of this story, about living on a houseboat in Key West, has been rattling around in my head for years. The true definition of fiction is a story about things that *could* happen. Everything in the novel definitely could happen, and in fact, much of it *did* happen. Fiction is blurred by truth in much of this story, both the historical part and the contemporary story. There *was* a fleet of Spanish ships sunk in 1733, and there are several stories about a large horde of gold and silver that was hauled off and hidden by Jefferson Davis and his Confederate cabinet at the end of the Civil War. Greek spongers did invade the Keys and were not welcome, and there was an attempted coup in Grenada. Look it all up.

Personally, I lived in Key West off and on for nearly seven years in the 90's, and the last year I was there I lived in the exact houseboat that I write about. I do play music, and I'm an avid snorkeler, if not diver, but my son is an experienced diver and is accurately portrayed in the story. Both my kids are black belts in Tai-Kwan-Do. Virtually all the remaining characters in the novel are real people, or based on real people. My friends in the Keys have learned to be kind to me to avoid being killed in the sequel. I guess the only truly made-up person in the book, is me. But then again, who gets to live their life vicariously through themselves? A true paradox.

I released this book through a publishing company in 2010 under the title *Doorstop on a Houseboat in Key West.* While it did get my book published, it was full of typos and errors, and the publisher did diddly squat to market my product and then added insult to injury by putting it on Amazon and Barnes and Noble at highway robbery prices. My last royalty check was a dollar eighty four cents. I got the publisher to release the book back to me early in 2013. Now it has a new name, fewer mistakes, a much better ending and leads well into the sequel, "Key West Camouflage."

Thanks to Karen Thurman for her help in developing both of our characters. Thanks to Stumpy (Rumpy) for *being* a character. Thank you Lisa Owens for the non-stop patience it takes to edit my poor punctuation. And of course a special thank you to my lovely wife Tina for enduring endless hours of my reading phrases, snippets and chapters while I tried to turn an idea into a novel and taking the remarkable photograph we used for the cover.

I want to give special thanks to my ex landlord (the houseboat owner) and very good personal friend, Bob Moran, former Vice President of Treasure Salvors, Inc, the late Mel Fisher's company. Bob was part of the team that eventually discovered the most famous shipwreck in history, the *Nuestra Senora de Atocha*. Bob was able to provide both technical assistance and some great anecdotal stories about diving for treasure in the Keys.

I dedicate this book to Bob.

Wayne Gales
July 2013

Starry Starry Night

I'm getting too old for this shit.

Don't get me wrong. I love the ocean, diving, treasure hunting, getting rich and all that. But when you're putting on your third tank in one day and dropping over the side to suck the bottom of the ocean up with the likelihood that all you are going to go home with tonight is wrinkled fingers, it can get you down.

But here I am, six years into a project that could last twenty, which means somebody else will probably find the mother lode after I spent half a decade scouring every other inch of the sea floor.

But that's the way it works.

My name's Russell Bricklin Wahl, "Bric" for short. I'm a native Key Wester, called "Conchs" for the big sea snail that was a staple of the Bahamian diet two hundred years ago. Like my ancestors, going back over ten generations, I make my living in the ocean. Some were fishermen, some spongers, but most of my family were wreckers, people that made a living salvaging the countless shipwrecks that have run aground on Caribbean reefs since European ships found the Americas. At one time it was hugely profitable to be a wrecker, then the government ruined a good thing by putting up a series of lighthouses on all the Bahamian islands and down the keys. The wreck business slowed substantially after that, unless one of my uncles blew the candles out of the lighthouses and rigged decoys to confuse the sailors. One of the more inventive ploys was to string a series of lanterns on a rope between two mules and walk along the shore. To a sailing ship, it would appear that another ship was safely much closer to the islands, and would change course, running aground on a reef. The call "Wreck Ashore!" would go out throughout the village, and boatloads of Conchs would race to the foundered vessel to claim salvage. It was a true grey area - defining the difference between wrecker and pirate.

Holding my hand over my mask, I flipped backwards off the dive platform of the salvage ship *La Brisa,* a converted World War II era tugboat. *La Brisa* isn't a perfect dive platform, but it ran (most of the time) didn't leak (much), and it was bought for pennies on the dollar out of an auction in Tarpon Springs, so that made it a perfect dive platform for Harry Sykas' dive operation. We've been looking for a wreck, thought to be one of the ships belonging to the Spanish silver fleet that was caught in a hurricane in 1733 that sunk or damaged most of the fleet. While the famous wrecks found by Mel Fisher, like the *Nuestra Senora de la Atocha* and the *Santa Margarita* that sunk in 1622, created massive publicity and fabulous wealth to Fisher and Treasure Salvors, Inc, those 1622 ships had not been successfully salvaged just after sinking. The galleons of the 1733 fleet were quickly salvaged within months or at most few years after the hurricane. They had also sunk in shallower waters, their location carefully logged, and most of the treasure removed by the Spaniards quickly within a few months or years. Without dive gear back in those days, the common method was to burn the wreck to the waterline, and then they would use grappling hooks to pull up lower deck boards, and then send down slaves to get the gold and silver below. But some of that treasure had been missed by the Spaniards and was then rather quietly gathered in the sixties by local treasure hunters in the Keys.

Records say that all of that fleet sunk in the reefs between Marathon and Key Largo, or even further north. It was strange that the wreck we were working was well west, at least sixty miles, off the next nearest documented 1733 galleon. It was likely this site was not one of the main merchant ships, and the treasure was probably not a giant treasure, but still had enormous profit potential to Harry's operation. We were chasing a debris field, odds and ends of treasure and clues that scatter along the sea bottom as a galleon slowly comes apart in a driving storm. Thus far, we had only found a few small congregates of silver "Pieces of Eight", six emeralds and a small gold cross with an inscription on the back that suggested it was worn by a clergyman. Enough to keep us searching, but far from enough to live on. Six years into the search and Harry was deep in debt. Not from a global standpoint. His Greek family operation in Tarpon Springs was flush, but this was his personal baby, and he had to fund it out of his own pocket. We weren't even positive there was a wreck down here, except that Harry's grandfather hooked a gold chain when he was sponging off Boca Grande around the turn of the century. It funded his grandfather's sponging company up in Tarpon Springs, and left his offspring with a fable that Harry had always wanted to explore. We keep finding a few items here and there, just enough to keep us going, but hardly enough to keep us fed.

I wasn't getting too rich, or any younger, for that matter, either.

We were hunting in about fifty feet of water. Instead of the "mailbox" that some treasure hunting ships use, we were using an airlift that sucked up the bottom and blew it onto a big net at the back of the boat, depositing rocks, mud, shells, the occasionally genuinely pissed-off Moray eel, and, sometimes, maybe a little treasure. Mailboxes consist of massive curved tubes that hang off the back of a ship and, when dropped down in the water behind the running twin screws literally blew the sand out of the way and exposed the sea bottom and possible sunken treasure. Airlifts are a little less efficient and more work, but also less damaging to the environment. They merely mess up the environment instead of destroying it like the mailboxes do. Besides, below fifty feet, mailboxes don't work that well. That being said, I don't recall dumping three hundred thousand gallons of half-treated sewage every hour into the ocean like most cities do, so my conscience wasn't too clouded by guilt today.

The airlift is a multi-person project. One guy hangs at the bottom sucking up sand, rocks, and everything else not stuck to the bottom while a crew on top sorts the junk, sifting the sand, throwing bulky stuff back overboard (hopefully not on my head) and looking for any silver, gold or jewelry that goes up the chute. The guy at the bottom, namely yours truly for this dive, looks for things that get exposed, silver bars, encrusted coins, or other artifacts. Running the operation topside today was Mike "Doobie" Hunt, not my favorite person in the world, but more or less marginally occasionally reliable. Sometime. Some days he works the lift and sometimes I do, and he's on the bottom. Both jobs sound glamorous and aren't.

Pay was enough to get by, but not exceptional, and it was hard, hard work. Six years of work on the site had yielded hardly enough treasure to fill a five-gallon bucket. Things had better start happening pretty soon, or the checks would start bouncing. I've been through this before, and I know now that, as a single dad with two teenage kids, I couldn't afford to miss a paycheck. The tide-enhanced current was ripping through the site, and even though it was good that the water was being constantly cleared of sand, I had to hold on to the airlift nozzle for dear life just to keep from being washed away with the debris. Suddenly, I saw a glint on the bottom. I shut off the airlift, dropped it and dove for the shiny spot. Digging my hand into the settling sand where I last saw the glimmer, I was rewarded with a thirty inch length of bright gold chain. Silver turns black and encrusted in salt water, but gold, even though it can get encrusted a little with sea life, always shines forever. Holding the chain up in admiration, I forgot the current and was whipped ass over teakettle out of the hole and away. In just seconds, I was fifty feet away from *La Brisa* and, with no chance of making it back, surfaced and started yelling at the boat. "Come get me!" I yelled. The noise of the airlift drowned out my voice, and Doobie was plugged into his iPod as normal and, yes, I saw a little puff of smoke that was more than likely a cigarette without a label or a filter if you get my drift. After all, his name ain't Virginia Slims. Doobie and the rest of the crew was not that alarmed that I had shut off the sucker, assuming I was checking something out. Eventually, they would decide something was amiss and come looking; I figured I would be halfway to Fort Jefferson in the Dry Tortugas before then. I looked around and saw that the nearest land was the south shore of Boca Grande Key, just about 400 yards away.

With the current helping me, I reached walkable bottom in a half hour, where I pulled my tank, weights and fins off. Happy that I always wore walking booties inside my flippers, I worked my way to the shoreline to wait. At this point, the day was pretty well a bust. Slogging through knee deep water and dragging all my gear, I tripped over something, stubbed my toe, and did a rather unceremonious face plant in shallow water. Looking at what I fell over from about three inches away, I came face to face with the unmistakable outline of an old cannon. Cannons ain't pieces of eight, but have immense value and can truly help date and identify a wreck. Maybe this day wasn't going to be a bust after all. I dropped my gear on the shore and gave the big gun a cursory inspection. Crusted with sea-life and partially buried, you could tell it was likely Spanish, probably an eight pounder, (meaning the cannonballs it shot weighed eight pounds) and decidedly old. I was puzzled how a four hundred pound iron cannon could wind up in just a few feet of water, and if it has been here since 1733, global warming meant it was likely a half dozen feet or more above the waterline when it first came to rest here. Cannons don't float – somebody had to put it here, or part of a wreck washed up on shore. It made sense to move *La Brisa* over to see if we could get it aboard. That hulk needed almost nine feet underneath her, and even with a high tide, it's likely we couldn't get much closer than about sixty feet.

Back to more pressing matters, I looked out to the boat to see if anyone had decided to look for me. It was on the outside edge of my fifty year old vision, but it appeared I had finally come up missing. I waved my hands over my head, and if someone had the intelligence to think I might still be alive, a pair of binoculars would have spotted me easily. I finally gave up and started thinking about spending the night.

I'm sure they would eventually find me or my crab-picked body.

Depending on whether or not you're one of those "half - full or half-empty" kind of people, Boca Grande is either one of the most beautiful places on the planet, or the loneliest, most God-forsaken two acres of sand and bushes you have ever seen. The highest spot on the key is about six feet, and other than some scrub, small mangroves and one lone palm tree, it's devoid of any food or water. Most of the island is a shallow marshy lagoon, good only for nesting water birds, and anything resembling a tropical system will submerge it. That being said, you can stroll a beach that hasn't seen footprints for weeks or months, sit in the sand and not see or hear anything manmade, and see more stars filling a non-light polluted sky at night than you can ever imagine. I had parked on this exact beach numerous times in my careless youth, usually doing things my parents would not approve of, but the beach always survived, as did I.

As the light began to fade, I settled down for the evening. No food, no water, no way to make a fire. I know you have seen the survival guy rub two sticks together or get some matches out of his handy dandy survival kit, along with a hook, fishing line, compass, SAT-phone, and plasma TV. I was working all day twenty feet below a floating hotel and didn't need any other gear. Perhaps I could tell myself some bad jokes and rub two dry clichés together. Oh well. It was a warm evening. I kicked back, used my tank for a pillow and looked at the heavens. In the middle of nowhere, without light or air pollution, you could see maybe a thousand times as many stars as are visible in the city. Late summer constellations, Andromeda, Pegasus, Pisces and others shone so brightly you could read a book, if I had a book. My friends from my childhood, winter images of Orion, Perseus and Taurus, with the fabled Pleiades in its midst, would not be around for a few more months. I finally drifted off to sleep, silently bitching at myself for not following rule number one, to never, never dive without a buddy.

My dreams, like always, were wild, vivid, manic and in color. A storm was raging in the middle of the night, and a small ship was tossing in the waves like tennis shoes in a dryer. I watched main mast snap off, and crew members were being washed overboard. The captain was standing on the forecastle, laughing at the storm and wearing a large gold chain around his neck. He was loading gold bars and jewelry into wooden chests. Then, he waved his hands over his head, and the wind stopped, calming the wild seas in an instant. Clouds parted and a million stars shown through, but these stars weren't twinkling, they were all falling into the ocean in a brilliant shower of sparks. More and more fell, closer and closer, and I was afraid one would hit me. The sparks were piercing my eyelids, and I woke with a startled yell, came up to a sitting position, and then back down on the scuba tank with a clang, knocking myself silly. It took me a second to remember where I was and get the stars out of my head and then realized that it wasn't all a dream. The sky was ablaze with shooting stars. One or two every few seconds, leaving vivid colored contrails. "That's right!" I exclaimed to no one. It's mid-August. The Perseid Meteor Shower. Just like the rest of the night sky when you're out the middle of nowhere, I could see probably ten times as many meteorites as the normal eye could pick up in town. Such brilliant and breathtaking displays made the mind invent sounds. I could swear there was a hissing sound every time one of these specs of dust emerged into the atmosphere. I've heard other people talk about this phenomenon and I could tell how real it felt. I lay back down and watched the free show for another hour, and drifted back again to, for once, a dreamless sleep.

I woke to a false dawn and the sound of an outboard approaching the beach, the summer Key's waters phosphoring the bow wave with a dull green glow. The Zodiac slowed as it approached the shore. Theodore "Tack" Morgan was coming right toward me. Tack is my friend Bo Morgan's son. Tack's in his late 30's and as much of a fish as my son Broderick. He grew up on treasure ships, and was aboard with his dad when they found one of the greatest treasures of all time. Currently he was co-running this dive operation.

"You decide to camp out last night?" Tack called out. "It might have been nice if you had filed a flight plan."

"Ah, you know, just needed a little 'Me' time. What made you look over here?"

"Dimwit radioed that you had drowned, and they couldn't find the body, so I came out last night in the fast boat, and happened to bring my infrared binocs. I could see you were alive and toasty warm on the shore and didn't want to wake you up." He tossed me a bottle of Zephyrhills water.

I waded out to Tack, pulled the Zodiac to shore and then showed him what I found. As soon as it was daylight we went back out to the *La Brisa* and after making sure Doobie saw his life flash before his face a few times, I grabbed a camp shovel and jumped back in the Zodiac. The crew weighed anchor and started to see how close they could get to shore. Digging under the big gun, we ran the ropes under it and looped it around the winch line from the *La Brisa*. The crew fired up the winch, and the cannon began to move from its 250 year old resting spot. As the big gun started to move, I caught the unmistakable glint of gold underneath. I started to reach down, and then, on an impulse, quickly kicked some sand to cover the object.

It was time to stop being a wage slave and start becoming an entrepreneur.

Back on the mother ship, we pulled the cannon on the deck and sat it on some wooden blocks. I had totally forgotten the other gold discovery from earlier in the day until Tack popped off with "you gettin together a Mister T starter kit?" Sheepishly I pulled the gold chain over my head and took it below. We measured, weighed, cataloged and photographed the chain before dropping it in the ship's safe. It was thirty-two inches long, nearly a pound in weight, make that fourteen troy ounces. The big, crudely made links were designed to be used one at a time for payment. Possibly hanging around the neck of a clergyman or rich merchant, the chain had likely hastened the drowning of a man that probably couldn't swim anyway. Value in gold, say around fifteen grand, and in

15

historical value say ten times that. The cannon was worth maybe another five grand. More if it had historical value and provenance.

Everybody gets paid this week. Everybody gets laid next week.

Flashback - May 24, 1733. Vera Cruz, Mexico

The New Spain Fleet, commanded by, Lieutenant General Don Rodrigo de Torres y Morales, departed Vera Cruz Mexico for Spain. The fleet made a stop in Havana to pick up last minute provisions and a few dignitaries that were returning home to Spain. The fleet was comprised of seventeen ships; the three principal ones being the Capitana El Rubi, the Almiranta El Gallo Indiano, and the Refuerzo El Infante. Each of these three warships carried 60 cannons, and their combined registry of treasure was in the neighborhood of thirteen million pesos in gold, silver, and copper. The rest of the ships all carried some amount of silver along with other valuable commodities, and some armament to aid in fighting off pirates and privateers. Along with the registered treasure, there was perhaps another two million pesos in "non-registered" gold, silver, and jewelry.

Once out in Gulf, the ships slowly worked their way north to the 25th parallel, where they took advantage of the westerly winds to push them eastward. As the lower Florida Keys were sighted, they positioned a sailor at the bow to sound for depth along the treacherous reefs. At this point, the navigators knew they were off the southwest tip of the Florida Keys in a place called Sonda de Tortuga. From here it was an easy 30 league tack south to pick up the Cuban coast and Havana. Eighteenth century Havana was the center of commerce for the Spanish in all the West Indies. Merchants came here from all over the Caribbean provinces to trade and load goods aboard ships bound for Spain. The day prior to departure, the harbor was buzzing with activity, and the great ships were packed to capacity with last minute treasure and provisions. Great quantities of salted meat and biscuits were lowered into the holds, and the water casks were all filled to overflowing.

On the morning of the 13th of July, the fleet sailed out of Havana for Spain with the tide. A brilliant yellow sunrise greeted the ships as they worked their way into the Florida straits, where a fair southeast breeze met them. The flagship

El Ruby was swathed in red paint, and cross-emblazoned sails, led the fleet up the Straits. They planned to turn eastward for Spain, and this swift waterway, known today as the Gulfstream, would give the ships an extra four knots speed. Unfortunately, an approaching weather system a few hundred miles to the southeast had other plans for them.

The Gulf of Mexico, Florida, Cuba and the entire Caribbean Sea is always dangerous in hurricane season, and the following day disaster hit. Sailing near present day Key Largo, the fleet ran directly into a major storm and, save one lucky vessel, all were mortally damaged and lay at the bottom of the Florida Straits or hard aground on the coastal reefs.

The salvage of the wrecked ships began within a few days after the storm. Three of the ships were re-floated with little difficulty: the Murguia (Nuestra Senora del Rosario y Santo Domingo), the Sanches Madrid (El Gran Poder de Dios), and a small ship; bound for St. Augustine under the protection of the convoy.

Two of the ships of the Flota met absolute disaster: the San Ignacio and the Fragata which was bound for St. Augustine with the payroll for the Presidio. The San Ignacio came apart out in front of present-day Marathon, and only 12 or 14 of those aboard survived. The El Floridano crashed across the reef known today as Coffin's Patch and only one man lived to tell the tale.

Blonde Obsession

There was no other way to get the cannon back to port other than to pull anchor and drive the lumbering *La Brisa* back. A fast and nimble tugboat sixty years ago, the twin diesels were tired, and the boat was heavy with gear and extra structures that had been built on the back, including a large shade over the deck that doubled as a second-story bedroom for outdoor nighttime snoozes. Ten knots was about the best she could do. That translated into a two hour trip. I normally commuted back and forth on the shuttle boat, but it was called off today as the big boat was coming home. Time to fill and fuel, stock up on basics and let the mechanics breathe a little more life into the tired engines anyway. I took advantage of the time to call the boss, and let him know of the day's take. Harry Sykas was more than pleased to hear about the gold chain. He wasn't thinking of bigger paychecks. He would use it to fend off the wolves, and maybe generate enough publicity to lure some more investors.

"Any word on the research with the cross?" I asked. "A little," replied Harry. "Likely non-documented personal treasure, maybe worn by a monk or a ship's officer. Who knows? All the coins were minted before 1732, so I think we may be right in thinking it's an undocumented wreck from the 1733 fleet. Get that cannon in the truck tonight and send it up to me. We will see if we can cross-reference it too."

Spanish Silver "Flotas" or Flotillas carried treasure from the Americas to Spain between 1550 and 1735. The typical fleet consisted of several types of ships. Heavily armed galleons served as protection for the bulk of the fleet, the heavily loaded merchant ships. The only difference between the merchants and galleon was the amount of armament carried in one and the amount of treasure in the other. There was also a fair amount of gold, and semi-precious and precious stones, including emeralds. While all the "official" cargo was carefully and meticulously documented, there was a lot of non-documented treasure too, contraband, bribes, all incredible wealth, and all being taken home by individuals.

This undocumented treasure was often some of the items

that brought immense value well beyond their weight in precious metal. That was the cross that had been brought up before, and likely the gold chain that I had found today. (And, I would guess, probably whatever I saw that was shiny under that cannon too). Fifteen million bucks in documented gold and silver on the ship could be possibly doubled with this contraband. It was a valuable unknown.

Harry promised to get back to me soon. I was not the leader of the project, just the senior diver and usually served as "straw boss" when the big guy was up at his offices in Tarpon Springs. Harry couldn't dive for rubber duckies in a bathtub, but liked to think he knew how to run a business.

As the *La Brisa* motored across the channel into the harbor, the right diesel started to overheat, and then quit. Another water pump broken, and who knows how much downtime until a replacement could be fixed, found or even fabricated. I changed out of my boat clothes, swimsuit, dive booties, a torn tank top and fisherman's hat with a pair of Costas, into my more presentable shore side attire, a Guy Harvey t-shirt with a fish printed on both sides, khaki shorts and topsiders. For a hat, I donned my favorite, a weathered blue cap that my son found lying on the bottom in ninety feet of water, crusted with sea life. I ran it through the washer a dozen times and the words "Old Guys Rule" emerged. The bill was studded in rhinestones with the words "Rock Star." I loved that hat. My only piece of jewelry, a four Real coin from the wreck, surrounded by a custom-made bezel created by my friend Cindy in Colorado, hung from a thirty-inch eighteen-carat gold chain around my neck. The gold bezel design features three dolphins and a naked mermaid and looks a little flashy, but it's the only keepsake I have of true value.

My mode of transportation for the last three years is a 1978 Volkswagen "Thing." Modeled after the Nazi German personnel cars in the 40's, the Thing was so ugly it was cute. Google one up sometime. They were simple, cheap, and they wouldn't break down. In proper pseudo-army/conch cruiser disguise, my Thing was painted in a camouflage and decorated with a lot of rust and air where much of the body and fenders used to be. The passenger side floorboard was made out of a hammered-flat cookie sheet that I found on Mount Trashmore that was pop-riveted to the floor. The current gearshift knob was a fake shrunken head I got from a voodoo store in New Orleans. The radio didn't work, the rag top had rotted away when Jimmy Carter was president and the brakes barely worked when I bought it. There was a faded "Free the Watergate 5000" bumper sticker on the back bumper. The key was broken off in the ignition, so you started it by jamming a dime or a quarter in the ignition switch and turning it hard to the right. I sometimes used a guitar pick since there was always one in my pocket or slipped into the windshield rubber. On more than one occasion, a friend, knowing my car was rather security challenged would jump in my car and use it for a grocery run or such. Most of the time it came back, sometimes I had to go hunting for her. Nobody ever stole her, as there was little faith in it being able to get more than twenty miles beyond Big Pine without self-destructing. But, you know, hey, it was mine, it was paid for, and that was good enough for me. I bought the car from a local entrepreneur, Karen Murphy when we were dating. She was upgrading her lifestyle, and I was on my way down. Price was right, and the product both didn't fit her long-term goals, but was perfect for me.

Karen and I had skirted the edge of being an item since the day we met. Actually it was the second time we met. The first time I saw Karen I was barging into the lobby bar in a little motel on a small island in the Caribbean as the advance party of an American invasion. I was wearing camouflage, combat boots, green/black face paint and holding a Heckler & Koch P11 underwater handgun, cocked and ready. She was calmly sitting at the bar in a remarkably small string bikini top and some sort of sarong. Her bare, sandy feet were up on the table, and she was trying to flag down a server to order another rum drink. Karen was the only person in the lobby and laughed her ass off at the Rambo act. You see, she didn't know she needed to be rescued. The insurrection and subsequent "invasion" by us rugged types was going on at the other end of the island. "Are you okay, ma'am?" I asked.

"No," She replied. "No, my glass is empty. And I was seriously hoping for a ride to a nice restaurant. Apparently, that is out of the question, but I'll still need that drink." You could dive in deep and swim around those blue eyes, and I just stood there, looking stupid with no snappy response. "What's with the getup?" She asked. I explained that the Cuban government had decided to help fund a little coup, and we had been deployed to put down the insurrection. "Stay put and don't go outside till you get the all-clear." I told her with as much authority as I could muster. She just swirled the ice in her empty glass with her pinky, smiled and nodded her compliance.

I took a pad and paper and took down her personal info, then backed out of the bar/lobby looking like I was ready to protect her with my life. I pocketed the notepad for safekeeping, but by the time I got home it had been hammered into Kleenex at the bottom of my duffel bag by four MRI's, (Meals Ready to Eat – eat these for three days and you won't be able to shit for a month) a Speed Stick underarm deodorant and two spare clips of ammo, but I had already memorized her name, and those eyes. That was 1983, and it was nearly twenty years later that I ran into her again, right in Key West, sitting at the bar at Schooner Wharf. I recognized those eyes and instantly remembered her name.

"Karen! You probably don't remember me, but I saved your live once on Grenada." She dipped her finger in her beer, stuck it in the ash tray and smeared cigarette ash on my face before I could pull away. "Yes! It is you!" She said. "You were a little heavier on the makeup that day." We laughed, and I bought her a few more beers, and we kinda started dating off and on, but she saw right through me. She had me figured out better than I had me figured out, so it never developed, but it never diminished. We parted friendship over a slight scheduling mix-up that got her ticked off, and we haven't spoken since.

Anyway, she's living with some charter fisherman now, and I seem to be married to a Spanish galleon. When she owned the car, it was fondly known around town as the Bitch Box. It's a guy car now, but I like the name so Bitch Box she remained. Today, when I got off work, it was parked where I had left it, on the side of the street behind B.O.'s Fishwagon on Caroline Street. As long as the day had been, I decided a grain-based, well chilled five-percent alcohol reward or two was in order. B.O.'s is the kind of place locals are drawn to and tourists veer away from, until they get a tip from a local, and then it becomes a must-stop on any Key West trip. It epitomizes the official term "Hole in the Wall." It actually doesn't have much in the form of walls to have a hole in, just a small central building that houses the kitchen and bathrooms, and a scattering of haphazard chairs, tables, barstools and rough board walls to comprise the rest. An old Chevy pickup is more or less built into the decorations, and various signs, posters, photos and other flotsam and jetsam complete the rather rustic decorations. On a slanted, cramped corner is what passes for a bandstand, and on frequent occasions you can find any number of musicians providing music noise to the background noise. Tonight it was Barry Cuda and the Sharks. Barry is the certified Key West "Pianimal." He has a fairly large upright piano that has four large rubber wheels bolted to the bottom. He rolls it from gig to gig with his stool and tip jar riding on top of the keyboard. Barry can play three or four places a day. Lunch at Sloppy Joes, afternoon at the Hog's Breath, twilight at B.O.'s and an evening gig at Buzzards. He's good enough that I have followed him to all venues on a lazy summer afternoon. His music is excellent, jazz, blues and old ribald bar songs. I've sat in with him more than once, and it's always a treat.

B.O.'s has certifiably the coldest bottled beer on planet earth. They must have a scientist on payroll that can make that refrigerator hover a nano-degree above absolute zero, and there is nothing like the first sip of a beer that cold after a day on the water in ninety degree heat and hundred percent humidity. I hated to drink alone and rarely had to, but the hair, what little of it that was left on the back of my neck stood straight on end when I spotted Karen sitting on one of the rickety park benches in the corner near Barry's piano. It was ninety degrees at eight pm, and I still broke into a cold sweat. She lifted her bottle, tipped it in my direction and motioned to the unoccupied seat across from her, an overturned ice chest with a cushion. I went to the counter, bought two cold Bud Longnecks, ordered a grouper sandwich and turned to face a situation which had the potential to be either a pleasant encounter or a poorly planned impromptu homicide.

I decided to open the conversation. "What brings you to this neighborhood? Not your normal stomping grounds," and dropped one of the chilled Buds in front of her while still standing.

"Thought I'd go slumming," She answered, taking a long pull on the Bud. "Actually I had business over on Eaton and parked in the pay lot here. Anyway the beer is cold, the music's decent, and all you have to do is tolerate what might crawl out from under a rock."

She finished her second beer and a raised eyebrow sent me scurrying to the bar for another round, handed one over and clinked bottle necks. I felt like a cobra being toyed with by a mongoose. "Pax?" I ventured.

"Bric, I never hold a grudge. Sit down. Hell, I've almost totally forgotten your no-show at the airport. You remember though, right? That seven day, prepaid by me, all expenses trip to Aruba?" Seriously Bric, I had almost forgotten until you walked in. No biggie. How could I still be mad over something that happened three years, seven months, eleven days and three hours ago?" She raised the bottle and again motioned for me to sit and I did. I joined her at the spool stolen from a long-forgotten electric company that was now serving as a wobbly table. But, I stayed out of her reach. I made a quick mental note that I was still likely within throwing range. "Those headlights on the Bitch Box still exploding?" She asked sweetly. "You truly need to figure out what makes that happen. I bet there's some kind of recall with Volkswagen. You should check it out." I had suspected for a long time who was hammering my headlights. The mystery was apparently solved.

"Sweetie, I've tried to explain that a hundred times. I ……"
"Buddy boy, don't 'sweetie' me and there's no need to spin another yarn. I told you, I'm cool, it's over. No biggie and I got me a nice strapping real live man now that knows the way home, cooks,

cleans and does dishes. Hey, good sex and half the utilities were all I ever asked for. I'm not a hundred percent sure you wouldn't be oh-for-two on that kind of arrangement anyway." She finished her first beer and then tossed the fresh one down in four swallows, and then Karen pulled her keys out of her purse and stood up. I couldn't help but flinch, but she slid around to my side of the table, pulled my hat off and gave me a big kiss on my bald spot. "You take care of my car, Bric. It's a classic." I flashbacked to a scene from Jurassic Park "*freeze, don't move, and maybe she won't know you're there.*" I stared at the ground and noticed the attractive, open-toed robin's egg blue pumps she was wearing, and tried to not show tears as she ground my foot into the floor with her one inch heels. She walked out the side exit into the dark. A few seconds later I heard the unmistakable pop and tinkle of another headlight being sent to high-beam heaven.

Thank God I always kept a few spare lights in the trunk. And besides, she's downright wrong. I'm very talented in bed. I think.

After Two more beers and my fresh grouper sandwich I was nurtured, both in body and soul, and the trauma had almost washed away. Almost. The crowd grew and shrank over the two hours or so I was there, and at least three "bar dogs" paid a visit to mooch a handout. Key West has a large supply of these happy canines, identifiable by the bandana that has been tied around their neck, officially signifying they belonged to someone. In the evening, usually before their master gets home, they make the rounds looking for a handout. Buddy Owen, AKA "B.O." had a supply of hot dogs in the fridge, and on more than one occasion I have seen him scold a dog, tell him to go away, get the hell out of here, then throw the dog a dog. It was mostly an act and both the staff and the dog knew the drill. Usually the dog would catch the wiener in the air, gulp it down, and then head off toward Schooner Wharf for the next handout.

Ah, to be a dog.

I paid my bill, tipped the band and wandered out to my

Thing. Happily and surprisingly, it started on demand, taking me home.

Fhashback - September 1734, near present-day Marathon Key Florida.

The salvage ship El Arco approached the hulk of the Capitana

El Ruby. The El Arco was an Xebec, a small three masted ship, flying triangular sails and built much lighter than the lumbering galleons. Its sail configuration made it nimble in light winds, and the light draft and weight gave it an advantage in the treacherous shallow reefs that the 1733 fleet had foundered on. On board was a crew of forty seamen and a squad of thirty soldiers, along with twenty black Caribbean slaves that were utilized as divers. Don Diego Morales deSilva, the captain of El Arco, directed the crew and soldiers to put the Capitana to the torch, burning the wreck to the waterline, making access to the treasure much easier directly through the deck. The El Arco tied up to the wreck and the crews, using grappling hooks, tore bulkheads and decks apart until they could reach the storage areas where the gold and silver was locked. After exposing the decks, they started sending the slaves down into thirty feet of murky water with ropes tied around their waists, holding heavy weights to get them to the bottom quickly. The slaves were sent down repeatedly and forcefully under threat of death if they failed to return with treasure. The salvage ship often used up all the slave labor by the time they had recovered a shipload of treasure.

The risk was worth the reward. (But only to the Spaniards) Literally millions of Pesos (billions in modern day wealth) lay under only thirty feet of water. Much of the treasure would eventually be recovered. The El Arco spent nearly six weeks tied to the Capitana, successfully pulling over two million pesos in silver "cobs" or pieces of eight and silver bars, fifty five gold bars, each over five pounds, nearly three hundred gem-quality Columbian emeralds, three small eight pound iron cannons, several personal items, including emerald crusted gold crosses and jewelry. By late October, the El Arco cast off from the Capitana and set sail for Vera Cruz. With the strong gulfstream moving in the wrong direction, the El Arco ran before the Easterly winds inside of the current, and outside of the reef, mostly in sight of the Keys. With luck, the nimble El Arco could make Vera Cruz in a little more than a week.

Stopping at night to anchor, the ship spent the second evening off the lower end of the Isla de los Martyrs, now called Key West while the crew rowed into shore to get fresh water, a rare commodity that could always be found there. The soldiers shot at, but missed a diminutive Key Deer, but did gather three loggerhead turtles found in the shallows.

The following morning the El Arco resumed the voyage, making decent time in the strong breeze. By late afternoon, the wind came around to the northeast and rose to near gale force. While the string of islands kept the waves from getting too large, the strong winds alarmed Captain deSilva who ordered the little Xebec in tighter to the low lying island as he planned to make anchor in the lee of the last of the Marytres, now known as the Marquesas Atol, hopefully safe in the channel between the two Keys. As dusk approached, he ordered the crew to make anchor and ride out the storm. The tropical storm raged through the night, and, although the fury never reached hurricane strength, the El Arco drug her anchor through the sandy bottom until it caught on the reef, breaking the anchor line. Adrift in the storm at dawn, mainmast gone, the ship bounced twice off the reef at two fathoms. With several hull timbers cracked, despite the waning storm, the ship started taking on water and slowly sinking.

Don Diego told the crew to put the rowboat over the side, and then directed them to throw anything that would float, then jump in and start paddling toward the shore. The captain loaded the lifeboat with food, some water and the highest valued items, contained in two heavy chests of gold, emeralds and some silver coins, on the boat. He knew the remaining treasure was safer on the bottom than on the island.   He also instructed the crew to remove one of the 8 pound cannons from the deck and place it in the boat too. Most of his officers and crew used flotsam to work their way to the shoreline, but several, including the first officer, who was hindered by several pounds of contraband gold around his neck perished. The only person among them that could swim was the lone surviving black slave. The tide was turning, and to keep the fatally damaged ship from drifting any farther into deeper water the Captain decided to scuttle it. He set a charge of gunpowder *below decks before retreating to the rowboat. The muffled explosion was not large, but guaranteed the ship would not stay afloat much longer.*

The crew rowed to the shore of the low island and beached. They were followed by thirty other surviving crewmembers who dragged themselves on shore, wet and exhausted. Within the hour, the little El Arco sank. The captain instructed his crew to remove the iron cannon from the rowboat and, with difficulty, sat it on the beach, the barrel pointed at the last tip of the sinking ship's mast as it slipped below the waves some two miles away. As an afterthought, he pulled his cutlass and scratched a long line on top of the cannon and drew a rough arrow to point to the direction of the sunken ship and its treasure. When they returned, they would at least have an idea where the wrecked ship lies, although he feared it might be too deep to salvage much.

Aside from fish and birds, the island now known as Boca Grande had no food and more importantly, no water. Well distanced from the trade lanes of the Gulfstream, the captain knew he and his crew could likely perish before help might show up. His best chance was to put out for their previous anchorage, where ships often stopped for water, and wait for help. The captain and a crew of twelve departed the following morning, fighting headwinds and arriving back at the island called Cayo Hueso (Island of Bones) now known as Key West the following afternoon. Nearly six weeks later, another Spanish salvage ship, Merced, anchored at Key West, finding five surviving seaman, starving and weak from dysentery. Captain DeSilva was not among the survivors. The remaining crew directed the salvage ship to where the rest of the crew was stranded on Boca Grande. They anchored and rowed ashore. The cannon was still there, but there was no sign of the remaining crew, the soldiers or the chest of gold and jewelry. Hopeful that another ship had discovered and rescued them, the salvage ship set sail again for Vera Cruz. The rescued crew from Key West was too weak to even suggest where the sunken ship lay. They resolved to give a full report

29

and organize a recovery mission when they got back to Vera Cruz.

The survivor's joy in their rescue was short lived. Halfway across the Gulf, the ship was set upon by an English Privateer, its salvaged treasure plundered and the crew murdered.

Dead men tell no tales.

Finder's Keeper's

The next morning I motored ten miles up A1A to Big Coppitt Key, where my fishing buddy John "Rumpy" Rumpendorfer lived. Rumpy makes a living doing various promotions, fishing derbies and the annual Miss Wild Key West beauty pageant. The rest of the time he fishes, works on his events, his latent heterosexual tendencies, and enjoying the Key West lifestyle, whatever that means. Today, I found him relaxing on a lounge chair on his back patio, wearing proper Key West camouflage, a tee shirt with a fish on it, khaki shorts and topsiders, sipping a rum drink and listening to Buffett on US1 Radio.

"Hey Rumpy, can I borrow the *Wave Whacker* for a few hours?"

"Sure. Bring it back full of gas and it's yours for the day."

"Sounds like a deal. Just running out west for a little ways to do some exploring."

Rump's eyes narrowed a bit. "Pal, you spend every day of your life out west exploring. I'm not sure I want to know more than that."

"Want to come with me? I'm just scouting some fishing areas. Little island I call Treasure Key."

I knew that Rumpy was likely far more interested in the next boat drink than the next boat ride, and I knew this offer would calm any suspicion of what I might be genuinely up to.

"Nah, I'm happy here. Ah, I think I know the name of every dry spot of land between here and Fort Jefferson. Treasure Cay is East, in the Bahamas, so that's not your destination. Like I said, I'm not sure if I seriously want to know what you're up to." And with that he sat down in a chair on his back patio, lit his twelfth cigarette of the morning and went silent behind his Costas.

I eased the 26 foot twin Yamaha powered twin-hulled *Wave Whacker* out of the canal on Big Coppitt and brought the boat up to plane. This part of Florida Bay is the perfect

31

description of "skinny water", and you have to know where you're going or you risk your boat, (or in this case, someone else's boat) becoming another notch on Davey Jones' six shooter. Despite the glare, I knew this route well, and, noting a few sticks thrust into both sides of the channel, I aimed for a tiny cut to the right of Half Moon Key. At high tide this was challenging, at low tide, inches could mean the difference between safe passage and buying a new lower end for your motors. Of course, it was low tide. Three feet to the right of me I noticed a great white heron that was not much more than ankle deep. As I got to the thinnest part, I slowed and tipped the engines up as much as I could to avoid dragging. Holding my breath, I cleared the thinnest and narrowest part without any crunching sounds. Clear of that and still cruising at 22 knots over water barely knee deep, I cleared past the harbor Keys and slid around the Ship Channel near Pier House, then between Wisteria and Tank Island. (I'll never get used to calling it Sunset Key. It's now a mega-expensive resort, and I mused what the guests would feel about being housed over what was more or less a toxic waste dump since shortly after World War Two).

The heading was due west, to the south of Man and Woman Keys, toward Boca Grande. It's just east of the well know Marquesas Atoll and a few dozen miles from the site of the *Atocha* and *Santa Margarita* wrecks, about an hour's boat ride from Rumpy's.

The highest spot on Boca Grande was about five feet above sea level and, other than a few lovely white sand beaches that were popular for fishermen to stop and eat lunch on and sunbathers looking for that perfect no-line tan, the island has few redeeming features. It's part of a national wildlife refuge and a nesting spot for birds. The *Whacker* has state of the art Garman GPS equipment, but I left it off, mostly because I knew every inch of the Keys, and also because I didn't want to leave any evidence on a device that was designed to track every move you made. Rumpy is as much of a pirate as I am, and it's best to keep one's secrets close to the vest, especially when those secrets were big, golden and shiny.

Approaching the destination, I eased off on the throttles,

trimmed the motors up and slid on to the sandy beach. Nicely grounded in calm waters, I dropped over the side and started working my way down the beach. With very few landmarks to go on, it was just dead reckoning and a lot of island experience that told me where to start looking. The cannon had been salvaged only a week earlier, but the sea bed can heal itself remarkably fast. I pulled a dive mask over my face and started cruising back and forth in ten inches of water. After a half hour, I began to get a sickening feeling that I would not get to see what caught my eye for a few seconds last week. Then I spotted a depression on the bottom, and saw there was no turtle grass growing. That looked like the spot. I started digging and felt something large and smooth, and extremely heavy. Planting my feet on the bottom, I got both hands under the object and pulled it out of the water. Amazed at the size and weight, it was a massive gold bar, well more than fifty pounds. Let see, 14.5 or so troy ounces to the pound, fifty pounds, and gold is currently about sixteen hundred per ounce. Hmm. Rounds out to maybe a million and a half bucks give or take a few Shelby Cobras. Wow. I looked down and saw the bottom was still showing "color." More than one? I dug a second identical bar out of the sand, and then a third. Triple Wow.

It dawned on me that my life was about to change big time, but I had to get this treasure home and then someplace far away from Key West, so it doesn't get caught up in the politics, much less the federal tax laws. I lugged them up to the beach and sat down in the sand for a closer look. The bars had a little sea life encrusted on them, but the end was bright on one and you could see a stamp. The only markings were the letters "CSA" stamped in an oval, with the "C" and "A" smaller. CSA? Confederate States of America? Where did they come from? How did they end up under a cannon from a ship that sank 130 years before the Civil War?

After digging all around the depression to see if there were maybe a couple hundred other gold bars, (not), I carried the three bars back to the *Wave Whacker* and placed one of the ingots in a small ice chest under some water bottles and two beers, and the other two in my dive bag. Okay, now only one beer as the hot July sun and a sense of celebration caused a Bud Longneck to go away in four quick swallows. Pushing the *Whacker* back into deeper water, I re-started and headed back to Key West, stopping at Oceanside Marina to fill up the *Whacker*, per the deal. A hundred twenty bucks and that pretty well cleaned me out till payday. Here I was, sitting on like four million dollars and I wasn't sure I could put food on the table for the rest of the week. Hopefully my son Brody could shoot a hogfish or catch some lobsters to put on the table till then. After fueling, I cruised back under the A1A Bridge and around Rockland Key to Big Coppitt and up the canal to Rumpy's house. I wasn't looking forward to acting nonchalant in front of a guy that could nearly read minds.

"Have a fun boat ride?"

"Yep. Found the most incredible honey hole. We can limit out in fifteen minutes next mini-lobster season."

"Since when have you ever stopped at a limit?"

"Yeah Rump. You got me there."

"We going fishing tomorrow? After all you got a full tank of gas," I pointed out.

"I hear it's gonna blow some. You're the weather genius. What do you think?"

On this, I had him. As an amateur meteorologist, I've consistently been more accurate than the weather channel when predicting hurricanes and storms. I could tell Rumpy that it was going to snow on Sunday, and he would go buy a parka and shovel. Actually I thought it might be a tad breezy, but I genuinely wanted to go fishing, and besides, other than the church channel, the news, and watching some grown man kiss largemouth bass on ESPN, there just ain't much to do on a Sunday morning. The only options I could see was to either start my own TV show or go fishing, so I fibbed just a little.

"Smooth as a baby's ass. Let's go find some tuna," I answered back.

"The Bucs are playing the Eagles tomorrow." He was starting to soften up.

"Look," I replied. We hit the water at oh-dark thirty, boat

some food and be back for the pre-game show."

"Not many tuna out there this time of the year but if you want to go drown some pilchards, I'm good with that. See you at oh-five thirty."

I picked the Igloo chest up like it was empty and flipped the backpack over my shoulders like it was full of feathers. As casually as I could manage I tossed Rumpy the keys and strolled around the side of the house to my car, nearly blowing a testicle in the process. If Rumpy's eyes were lasers, I'm sure they would have burned through my back.

Flashback - April, 7, 1865 – Lincolnton, Georgia

Lieutenant Albert Sawyer lay quietly on a bluff overlooking the road between Lincolnton and Irwinville Georgia. Below, he watched a company of Union Calvary move past. The war was over, but he truly wanted no contact with what he still called the enemy. As they moved out of sight around the bend, he motioned behind him for the ex-Confederate soldiers to move up with the horse drawn wagon. The wagon appeared to only have a load of hay, but the horses strained up the low hill, and the wagon tracks bit deeply into the thick red Georgia clay. They eased the wagon back onto the road and quietly drove toward the Mumford ranch in Brantley County.

Arriving near dusk, Sawyer pulled the wagon into the old livery stable. The elderly black attendant unhitched the horses, pulled water from the well and tended to the team. Slavery was over, but there was still a definite line of served and servant in the south. Under lantern light, the soldiers unloaded the hay and removed the floorboards of the wagon, exposing several heavy canvas bags full of gold and silver coins. Six large lead ingots also lie at the bottom of the wagon. The lead ingots, which were likely originally destined to be melted into bullets, weighed over 50 pounds each, and were topped with an oval design with the classic "CSA" emblem, denoting the Confederate States of America.

"What are we doing with those?" asked one of the sergeants. "That wagon is heavy enough." "They were all around President Davis' mansion," replied Sawyer. "They were being used for doorstops. I brought them along because I think they might have some value because of where they were during the war."

Choosing a place in the corner of the barn, the soldiers dug a deep hole and dropped the bags in. The coins, valued at over $200,000 US dollars, were part of a cache that had been traveling with Confederate President Jefferson Davis and his cabinet when they fled Richmond ahead of advancing union troops earlier that month. Davis had entrusted Sawyer, a Key West native and loyal confederate, with a good part of the half-million dollars in gold and silver. Some of this had come from banks in Richmond and the remainder was on loan from England. Part of the gold bullion was *comprised of treasure captured from Spanish salvage vessels by English Privateers over 100 years earlier. This gold, identifiable by their rough cast and Spanish "chop" marks, was not with the wagon and had seemingly vanished months earlier. After covering the bullion, they erased signs of their work and covered the corner in hay and straw. Exhausted, the squad bedded down for the evening.*

The following morning, leaving the lead ingots, their pistols, rifles and a small leather bag of English gold sovereigns in the bottom of the wagon, they replaced the false-floor, hitched up the team and headed due-south for a four day trip to Savannah. Now dressed in civilian clothes, they successfully gave the impression to any union troops that they were ex-soldiers and poor farmers making their way toward the city. With all arms hidden beneath the floorboards with the lead ingots, and carrying nothing of value, they were able to successfully talk their way through any Union opposition. Only once did it appear they might be arrested, and they averted it only when Sawyer quietly pressed an English Gold Sovereign into the palm of the Union Lieutenant. The last night before arriving in Savannah, they camped well off the road, ate in silence and bedded down for the night. Well before daybreak, the quiet was broken with the sound of four quick pistol shots.

We Should'a Been Here Tomorrow

About four thirty the next morning, I kicked Brody awake and had him run me over to the dock, and I fired up the Bitch

Box and headed for the I-Hop for a healthy Rooty Tooty Fresh 'n Fruity breakfast and still made it to Rumpy's house well before sunrise. The house was dark and quiet, no smell of coffee, and the Wave *Whacker* looked like it did when I had left yesterday afternoon. It would appear that the Rumpster had either A) blown his alarm clock, B) been blown by the neighbor, C) blown off the trip, D) none of the above, E) All of the above.

Fortunately his sliding glass door was open, and, had I been a thief, could have made off with forty grand in rods and reels, but if I took them, then I would have to store, clean and maintain them. It was so much easier to let him do all that, and then borrow them as often as I want to. Once inside, waking Rumpy up should be no issue. I merely picked up a cast-iron skillet from his sink and an aluminum meat tenderizer, peel a day old, (or week old) glazed Dunkin donut off the counter, and walked into his bedroom. You can't believe how loud a cast iron skillet can be when pointed in the right direction. After about twenty swats, I flipped on the light to see how I was progressing. Rumpy lay face down, butt naked and sound asleep. However, the young, attractive, tender, slightly over nourished and marginally illegal blonde was cowering in the corner under a bed sheet, trembling, a huge mop of blond ringlets surrounding a cherub face, her eyes the size of saucers. I nodded her presence, sat down on the corner of Rumpy's bed and whacked him soundly on the foot with the meat hammer.

That seemed to do the trick.

"So", I asked, munching the donut. "How was she?"

"Mr. Wahl, I never discuss the personal attributes of any of my constituents, in or out of their presence. If, perhaps, you could afford us a moment of privacy, I will bid the lass a proper good-bye and join you on yon boat."

Rumpy never talks like that, unless he's been recently laid by someone still in his presence.

I turned my attention to the little trollop under the sheet. "I bet you would love to hear how Johnny got the nickname 'Rumpy'."

She sniffed. "I believe I already know that."

"You know Rump's sodomy is illegal in 31 states, including Florida."

"Were not in Florida," Rumpy answered. "Remember the Keys seceded from the Union thirty years ago, and we don't have any rules. Besides, you can't rape the willing. Enough banter! Leave this room and give the girl some dignity. Oh, there's a gallon of Appleton's in the cupboard. Grab that and a six pack of cokes in case we get marooned. Or thirsty."

The good news was that we were still early enough to get where we wanted to go at a reasonable hour. The bad news was that while Rumpy was accomplishing a tender send-off, complete with possible carnal perks, I was shagging fifteen fishing rods, an ice chest with eight bags of ice, assorted tackle items and a day's worth of beverages out to the boat. Magically, just as I finished loading the last rod in its rod holder, you-know-who wandered out his back door, Marlboro in one hand and a large cup of black coffee, spiked, no doubt, in the other.

Gunther, Rumpy's next door neighbor, apparently came instantly awake with the sound of two very quiet outboards firing up, popped out his door with a hopeful expression. "Let's take him along," Rumpy suggested. "He's good with a cast net, and we need bait."

"Yeah." I responded. "You looked like you were doing pretty good with Annette this morning yourself."

"Rachael. Her name is Rachael, Audrey, or Sonja, or Betty, or Lisa something. One of my recent swimsuit models from the pageant."

"Good lay?"

"The best. She could suck the chrome off a trailer hitch."

Two miles out of the breakwater I was pretty friggin sure I had perhaps miscalculated the weather. I was hanging on for dear life as the bow of the *Wave Whacker* lurched at the sky another time and came hammering down off the swell, driving me into the boat seat like a tent peg and likely shortening me about a quarter inch per hour. At this rate, I would get back home and not be able to reach the pedals on my car. The weather report said two to four foot seas outside the reef, but we were plowing through a six foot east blowing swell that was very confused with a brisk north moving tide. It would bring to mind the wave pool at Wet 'N Wild on steroids, or dropping twenty bucks worth of quarters in the big washer at the Laundromat, climbing in, and having your buddy push the "on" button. Rumpy lit his third Marlboro and gave me a squinty-eyed look that distinctly indicated his regret to succumb to my desire to go fishing, and quickly moving his opinion of me from friend to chum.

The kind of chum you use to attract sharks.

Of all the advantages there are to living in the Keys, arguably the top of the dance ticket is this open air aquarium that surrounds us. I'm not sure there is any place on this planet you can seek such a diverse array of fish in such a concentrated place. Whether you are a snorkeler, diver, catch and releaser, or a fridge fisherman, like I am, you can view or catch Tarpon, Bonefish, Snapper, Grouper, Marlin, Sailfish, Dolphin (That's Mahi Mahi, not Flipper) several species of tuna, kings, wahoo, cobia, permit and pompano, tons of reef fish, not to mention lobster, and all are within spitting distance of Key West. It's a fisherman's dream, and supports a tidy sport and commercial fishing economy here. At somewhere around six to eight hundred bucks a pop, sport fishing is a little outside of my budget, so I have to either live my life vicariously through my son's experiences since he can seemingly bum a ride on the fanciest sport fishing boat at a whim, or go fishing with Rumpy. The *Wave Whacker* is a dandy boat, all equipped with depth finder, GPS, and tackle that would make most charter boat skippers green with envy. Rumpy knows these waters and always puts you over fish.

You often envision people that work in Key West spend all day on the gulf and every night on Duval at Buzzards, but we are working stiffs like everyone else, and the opportunity to get out on the water for play comes far too rarely, but when we do, it's a true treat. I've never been skunked with Rumpy, but today might be a first with this weather.

Before we could fish, we needed bait. There seems to be a rule that, on days where you can sink the boat with live bait, you can't get a single fish to hit one, and when you can't find bait, big fish are hanging under your boat, begging for a handout. Maybe this might be a good fishing day because we couldn't find bait anywhere. We had no problem getting out of the heavy weather into the lee of Man Key, but our normal hotspots for bait were dry. We moved farther and farther east till we pulled up to Boca Grande. Sheesh seemed like I couldn't keep away from this area. "This is where you guys are hunting for that galleon, correct?" asked Rumpy.

"Yep, just a few miles from here out thataway. We drug a cannon off the beach a few days ago. Don't have a clue how it got there." I felt it was an excellent moment to change the subject. "Rumpy, cruise over to the right. I saw some lovely shallows with lots of eel grass the other day. It could be Pilchard heaven."

Rumpy nodded acknowledgement and tilted the twin Yammie outboards up for shallow water operation, sliding the big twin hull boat into about 18 inches of skinny water. Gunther stepped up on the bow with the ten-foot cast net and watched the bottom carefully for the flash of silverside. He motioned the skipper to idle and made his first throw. He grunted with satisfaction as he pulled in the purse net, hauling it overboard and about fifty nice fat Pilchards. We scooped them out of the net and into the live well. Two more casts and we were good to go with ample bait.

We stored everything away and headed back out into the maelstrom. In a few minutes, we were back in six foot seas but were running more or less with the wind so not terrible, just brutal. After a half hour of slogging through this, I felt the *Whacker* slow as we approached the target area, a WWII U-boat sunk in 1943 by a US Army Air force PBY Sub-hunter in 240 feet of water. At wreck level, snapper and amberjack hang out. Near the surface this time of the year, you might find blackfin or yellowfin tuna, maybe even a sail or even a marlin. Or at least there were supposed to be. In these conditions, we chose to throw an anchor out to try and keep in place over the wreck. Otherwise, we could end up someplace east of Cancun later that afternoon. We began throwing all those baitfish that we dearly netted an hour ago back in the ocean, with the hope we could lure some tuna near the boat. I baited a hook with a live one and dropped the line overboard. There were a few boats nearby, some private and some charter.

Rumpy's boat does not have any seats, unless you count the ice chest. You stand and fish. Today we were just standing. It was just about all you could do to stay upright in this sea, and the thought of trying to remain standing while battling a monster tuna in this Cuisinart was not being met with relish. As it was, we did not appear to be in jeopardy of swamping the boat with fish carcasses. I had just about given up when I got a hard strike on the spin tackle. I was surprised and overreacted, pulling the bait out of the fish's mouth.

Fortunately for me, it was not a tuna but a respectable size and fairly stupid bull dolphin that had been attracted. He was hungry and I don't think I could have pulled the bait away had I wanted. The dolphin crashed the bait again; this time I set the hook, and was rewarded with an ESPN quality aerial show for about five minutes, at least ten frantic jumps. I boated the dolphin without much other excitement; it appeared the fish had tuckered itself out in acrobatics. Rumpy gaffed the dolphin and put it right in the ice chest like he always does. I would guess it was a good 45 pounds and the tail was hanging out of one end of the ice chest. Well, this fish did not appear to mind being speared by Vlad the Impaler, but he took immense exception to being dropped on a bed of ice, and we had to quickly close the ice chest and sit down on top of it, giving a masterly rendition of Debra Winger riding the mechanical bull in Urban Cowboy. In the midst of this, he broke his gaff in two, a handmade wooden gaff that he had owned for years, which put his opinion of me down even another notch.

With the tuna not showing and the dolphin few and far between, we decided after a few hours that we had enjoyed about as much of this as we could stand. The ride back was about as brutal as the ride out, only more into the wind, so a bit rougher and bit longer. By the time we got back to Big Coppitt, we had just about lost our lunch, our lust for outdoor sports, friendship of each other and our love of the ocean. I filleted the dolphin, thanked Rumpy for again being a dedicated skipper and gracious host, and headed home to count my bruises and try to get the planet to stop rolling around under me.

The next morning I looked out the window of my boat to a calm and smooth gulf. The strong winds and high seas were gone, and fishing would doubtless be better today. Problem was, it was Monday, and if I went fishing today, I would likely be wearing a paper hat and asking my clients if they wanted fries or rings with their order by Tuesday. All those boats were rigging up to head out for a day of tuna-filled action.

Them but not me.

Man, I should'a been there tomorrow.

Flashback - Savannah, Georgia, 1865

Sawyer drove the wagon alone into the city of Savannah Georgia. William Tecumseh Sherman's army had occupied Savannah until January of 1865, when they moved north in to the Carolinas. They had treated the city mildly when it was occupied a few months earlier. The city and infrastructure remained fairly intact, despite the port being closed during the war due to the blockade, and all rail lines in and out of the city were destroyed. Shipping was beginning to resume in the port as the trade-starved city started to come back to life. Sawyer found his uncle's house, and, after unhitching the wagon, lead the team to a livery stable and boarded them. He advised the owner they were for sale. That night he quietly pulled the boards from the false bottom on the wagon, hid the firearms under the house and stacked the six lead bars in a corner of the kitchen.

The following morning, Sawyer walked to the industrial part of town near the river. After some searching, he found the building he was looking for, a former button factory that was, in all appearances, closed down. Pushing open the unlocked door, he saw a single kerosene light toward the back of the building. "I'm looking for Hans Kraker." Sawyer called out. "I'm Kraker," a voice responded in a thick German accent. "What is it you want?"

"I heard from a mutual friend you can plate things with gold," Sawyer replied. "Who told you this?" Kraker asked. "Let's just say Mr. Davis sent me."

His eyes narrowed, and he answered slowly. "Yes, I have a small foundry, and I plated buttons and buckles with nickel for the Confederacy," said Kraker. "I can plate with gold too. What do you need me to do? I still have the chemicals, but little material."

"I have some lead bars that I need to turn into gold bars, with no questions asked," Sawyer replied.

"Hmmm. This is not easy to do. Gold does not stick to lead, so you have to plate the lead with something that will stick to lead, and use something that will stick to gold. For that, you use nickel, which I have some of, but I have no gold."

"I can provide the gold, and you can keep whatever you don't use for plating as payment. Is that acceptable?"

"How much gold do you have?"

"Thirty English Sovereigns."

"And how much lead do you need to plate?"

Sawyer held out his hands to indicate the size of the lead bars. "Six bars, about this size." Kraker thought for a moment, knowing he wouldn't need the gold from more than three of the half ounce gold coins to effectively plate the bars, but it's likely Sawyer wouldn't know that. "I need forty coins, nothing less," responded Kraker. "Okay, replied Sawyer. "I'll give you five more if you can get it done by the weekend. I need to ship them someplace."

"Very well," replied Kraker. *"Bring them to me tonight with your gold. Use the back door through the alley. Make sure no one follows you."*

Later that evening, Sawyer made six trips to the foundry, carrying one lead bar at a time. The last trip Sawyer also brought the bag of English coins and handed them over to the metal smith. The plating area smelled strongly of chemicals, and Kraker worked with large leather gloves and a heavy apron. *"You had best leave,"* Kraker said to Sawyer. *"These chemicals are extremely strong and dangerous unless you are careful and wear the correct clothing. Come back Friday with a wagon and we will be done."*

Metal electroplating had been in existence for nearly 2000 years. Using a substance like potassium cyanide that creates weak electrical current, metals can be plated. The chemicals are poisonous and harsh, and the lung damaging fumes can result in a short lifespan. Kraker had learned from his Russian *"Volga Deutch"* Jewish ancestors and worked with a heavy mask over his nose and mouth. First placing the lead bars in the solution, he dipped the nickel anodes in the bath and left them to soak for two days. Cranking them up out of the vat, the lead bars had transformed into the bright silvery color of nickel. This *"strike"* would enable them to now accept a gold finish. He then attached three of the gold Sovereigns to wires, and replaced the nickel-coated bars into another chemical bath. This time the bars were left in the solution for four days as the coins gave up metal volume and the bars slowly turned gold. Late Friday morning, he pulled them out of the solution a final time and rinsed them in a bath of fresh running well water. The lead bars were now gold bars. They would pass even the most careful examination, and the plating was thick enough that it would not flake off. The lead bars were heavy to start with, and it was likely no one would have ever picked up a lead or gold bar of that size, so the illusion was believable. Kraker carefully hid the remaining gold coins, and when Sawyer arrived that afternoon in his wagon, he accepted the bonus solemnly.

"You can promise nobody has seen you plating these bars?" Sawyer asked. *"I live alone, and I work alone," Kraker replied. "I have had no employees for nearly a year."*

As Kraker turned to go back into his foundry, he never had a chance to react to the butt of a .36 caliber Navy Revolver. He slumped to the ground unconscious. It took Sawyer some effort, but he was able to drag Kraker back into the plating room, and, being careful not to create a splash, rolled the body into the vat of potassium cyanide, where his body became unrecognizable in minutes.

Dead men tell no tales.

Cash In On the Dream

The CIA hasn't got a thing on the Coconut Telegraph in Key West. There are no secrets in this little town, and even though I had made a secret solo trip to a secret spot in a borrowed boat from a private dock on a Tuesday afternoon, I just felt these gold bars would not be a secret much longer if they hung around town and they needed to leave this rock in a hurry. The Bitch Box was barely safe to drive much beyond Stock Island, much less to Miami, so I had a double challenge. Get someone to hang with the kids and also loan me a car. Unlike most locals, I was a fairly honest, fairly hard working, fairly responsible single dad, didn't take drugs, smoke funny cigarettes, or drink too much. Well, not that much anyway. I do like the occasional beer or two. So the chance to borrow decent wheels wasn't out of the question. I figured the best chance would be my first, and maybe only try. Maggie Jones was always a soft touch, loved the kids and was as close as I could identify as a love interest, but being a single father living on a forty-foot derelict cabin cruiser permanently anchored off Hilton Haven drive, it was not like I brought a lot to the party. But Maggie often showed up when I was playing with the band, and I occasionally got to snatch a kiss in the parking lot, and on uncommonly rare occasions, vice versa.

As it turned out today, the salvage boat *La Brisa* needed some more major medical (or minor miracle), so I jumped in the Bitch Box and headed for the Casa Marina. One of the oldest resorts in town, it's now a Waldorf Astoria and has truly returned to its rightful place as the *Grande Dame* of the island. I pulled the Thing up into the circular driveway in front of the resort and tossed the keys to the Valet, warning him to not put any new scratches on it. Since the fenders were more rust than metal that would have been a tall order to prove. The seat covers had long since rotted away with only a beach towel sitting on exposed springs, and the valet stood perplexed at how he might park the hulk without covering his white shorts in rust. He chose discretion before valor and just decided to let it sit there in front of the five star resort, hoping the attraction of the car portraying local color eclipsed the very evident eyesore.

"Can I help you?" Lilly, the admin asked.

"Why, yes, young lady. I'm Rufus T. Cecil Beauregard Jones from the Immigration and Naturalization Service and I would like to see your employee records for the past twenty years."

Lilly eyed me up and down, noting the attire, khaki shorts,

aloha shirt, worn topsiders and long billed fishing cap with a pair of Costas hanging around my neck. "Excuse me?" she responded, not buying my line. "All of them?"

"Yes, and I'd like to start with your HR Director."

"Miss Jones, can you come here for a moment?"

Maggie walked out of her office, saw me, caught the act and hardly showed emotion. "Yes sir, can you step in here please?" With my best shit-eatin grin, I brushed past the admin and into Maggie's office, where she closed the door. Two minutes, or four days later, the kiss ended, and Maggie stepped back. "Where the Hell have you been?" She whispered. "The band sucks without you, and you haven't played with them for two weeks."

"Been busy," I answered. "We actually found some stuff on the wreck I've been working on and it's kept me busy. Sorry. Maggie, I have a big favor to ask. I need the kids to stay with you Saturday while I go to Miami." "Sure," she replied. "We can kayak out my canal to the backside of Boca Chica and have a picnic. What's up?" "Just some legal stuff I have to work on. Nothing big, but I have a second part to the favor. Can I take the Firechicken?" "Well, that will really cost you," she replied, smiling. "I'll let you know when I want to collect."

Mags was somewhat enigmatic, but that's not all that rare in Key West. She's had the same good job for over a dozen years, drives a classic immaculate muscle car 1972 Firebird Trans Am convertible, and cleans up nice in a windblown sort of way, but she lives in a single wide off a canal on the ocean side of Big Coppitt Key. I'm sure her house cost less than her car did. At home, she doesn't use air conditioning and can be found hanging around her place after work in ragged short cutoffs, braless in a cutoff tank top, or less. On weekends, she's out doing the Duval Crawl, especially on Friday nights after payday, and the song "Tequila Makes Her Clothes Fall Off" must have been inspired by her. I can't count the number of nights that I've had to drive her home at two am, watching half of her garments float out on A1A as she celebrated life to the fullest. Unfortunately by the time we got to her place she was either snoring or running into the house to drive the porcelain bus, and my amorous intentions were often delegated to the role of holding her long blonde hair out of the way while she yakked up her transgressions. So, my good deeds often went unrewarded, but she was a good person, and she always came right back into focus by the next morning.

I tooled the Firebird up the Keys from her place and jammed a CD in the player. I couldn't help but smile as the *words "I want money, lots and lots of money, I want a piece of the pie, I wanna be RICH"* played. I could also feel my palms start to sweat as I drove northeast up A1A. I hated leaving Key West these days. In the water of the Florida Keys, or anywhere around town, I'm at home, comfortable and at ease, but anything beyond mile marker 25, it's enemy territory, uncomfortable and uneasy. The further from the rock, the more foreign it feels. I passed Sugarloaf, Big Pine, Marathon, Tavernier then Key Largo. I opted for Card Sound road because of the incredible view over the bridge and drove past Alabama Jacks. With luck, I might stop by there on the way home for a beer and a burger. Hell with real luck, I could stop by there in the way home and *buy* Alabama Jacks.

From there, it was through Homestead and then slog up US1 (no way would I take the Turnpike) past Coconut Grove, to downtown Miami. Parking in the garage on Brickell Road, I hefted my little over-stressed backpack and walked across the street to an exceptionally non-descript building, leaving the other two bars in the trunk. Taking the elevator to the fourth floor, I entered a buzzing mayhem of activity. The entire floor was broken up into tiny offices, each owned by a Hassidic Jewish family who worked in the diamond or gold business. I had been there years before; brought along as a "bodyguard" by Harry Sykas to sell a few dozen loose gold chain links we had dredged up. Mordecai and Yehuda barely acknowledged me when I walked in. "What do you need?" One asked, bent over a loupe and not even looking up. "I have something that might be of interest to you," I answered. "Can we close the door?" "Close the door? No, we don't need to close the door. Nobody steals here. What is it you wish to show me?" I hefted my backpack up on the desk and opened the top.

Moredecai took a look in the pack, flipped open the towel it was wrapped in, and turned to his partner. "Yehuda, please close the door," Mordecai said quietly. "This item we may not want to share with everybody."

Mordecai grabbed the bar and removed it from the pack. "Six hundred, maybe seven hundred Troy, Yehuda. We don't have a scale large enough to weigh this." He turned to me. "You have this legally my friend? "Yep," I responded. "Did you buy it? How much did you pay?" "No, I found it," I answered. "Look, you might remember when I was here before that I'm a professional salvage diver. I found three gold bars in the ocean. Nobody else can lay claim, but there are some grey areas when it comes to treasure and salvage. It's kind of like finders, keepers, losers wind up wrapped in bricks and fishnet at the bottom of the Gulf. You can show it to the cops. It's the reporters I want to stay away from." "Not a problem my friend," Mordecai shrugged. "They're fake anyway."

I felt that sinking feeling I had felt before. If it's too good to be true, it's too good to be true. "How do you know so fast?" I asked. "I will prove it to you in a moment, but there are two very easy ways to tell just by looking at it." Mordecai went on; "first, the color is wrong. Gold bars are twenty four carat, or nearly so. This is plated or coated in an alloy, most likely melted gold coins. The color is subtlety different, but enough to spot if you have been doing this as long as I have. Secondly, look at the Confederate mark. Gold bars are either stamped after they have been cast, or the mark, like this one, is cast directly into the bar. The imprint is crisp with sharp edges. This one is rounded and smooth, which means it's plated. I have heard of but have never seen gold bars from the Confederate States and have never heard of any this size. From what I remember, most Confederate gold was acquired from English sympathizers, and at least some of that was Spanish treasure that had been captured hundreds of years before the Civil War." Next, Mordecai picked up a sharp scalpel and gestured to me for his ok. "Sure, go ahead." I know by now that staring at something won't change what it actually is. Moredcai flipped the bar over and started digging at a corner. In a moment, a flake

50

loosened and fell to the table. Underneath was a silvery color. "Probably nickel," Mordecai mumbled. "You can't plate lead with gold so you plate lead with nickel, then plate the nickel." He dug again with the scalpel, and a flake of the nickel popped off. The dull patina of lead now showed through. "We can flake the gold off the bars, and we will buy that from you. We don't have an interest in the lead. Bring us the other two, and if you want to come back in a little while, we will pay you for what we recover and give you your souvenirs back. If that CSA stamp can be shown to be genuine, there may be some historical value. I will remove the nickel too. It's worth a few dollars."

Four hours later, I walked out into the Miami sun in a daze. This morning I was a zillionaire. Now I'm not sure I have much more than enough gas to get Maggie's car back to Key West. Well, my Jewish friends would pay me fairly, and that would make it worth the trip.

An hour after that I was on the A1A back to Key West. My prize lead bars carefully hidden on the way up the Keys were occupying a very un-ceremonial place of honor on the passenger side floor. Hey, I got $220 dollars for the thin plate of gold and the nickel and had just acquired some darned nice doorstops.

If I had a door to stop.

Bric's Bricks.

Steak yesterday, steak tomorrow. Top Ramen today.

I drove past Alabama Jacks with hardly a look. I wasn't in the mood for beer and it appeared a cash purchase of the bar was not in the immediate future. A few hundred yards beyond Jacks is a toll booth and then over the Card Sound bridge for one of most spectacular views, and also the highest point, in the Keys. The right front tire gave me no warning at all and just let go with a bang. I didn't want to mess up her Firebird so instead of driving to a spot where I could pull off, I just stopped on the bridge to change the tire. Fortunately the spare was good and full of air. I got out the tire and the jack and then looked around for something to chock up a wheel, so we didn't roll backwards. My luck I'm on only one of two places in the entire Florida Keys with any kind of slope, and I need to find a rock. Ah, just the ticket. I reached back in the floorboard of the car and grabbed one of the lead bars and shoved it under a rear wheel. Changing the tire, I put the bad one back in the trunk and got underway.

I was a half mile down the highway when I remembered the lead bar. Oh well, still have two. Nah, better go back and get my souvenir, and anyway, somebody will run over it and have a wreck. After retrieving it, I mused that this drive home was likely the end to the strangest mystery possible. How the Hell did three gold plated Confederate lead bars end up buried underneath an eighteenth century Spanish cannon on an uninhabited island in the middle of nowhere?

Flashback, Savannah Docks - Albert Sawyer returned to his wagon and removed the tops of two wooden kegs marked "nails." Dumping out the contents onto the *floor of the wagon, he placed three of the plated bars in the kegs. Then he covered the bars with a burlap sack, and re-filled the kegs with the loose iron construction nails, hammering the tops shut. As dawn neared, he drove the team down to the Savannah Docks, where the St*

Augustine, a union-flagged, former Confederate blockade runner rested. Supplies and freight were being hauled aboard as he arrived. "Here's the order of nails for my uncle in Key West," He advised the dock master. He provided a bill of lading, and, again a few gold coins changed hands to ensure nobody would question the surprisingly heavy kegs. As planned, a boy from the livery stable showed up to take the team and wagon away, and Sawyer walked up the gangplank, paid the captain steerage fare then moved below to clear a personal spot in the cargo deck for the nine day trip. If all went as planned, he would return to that barn in a few months and recover all the silver.

The ship sailed under steam with the tide, heading for Key West with planned stops in St Augustine and Nassau. Both a large steam driven side-wheel and two sailing masts powered the ship St Augustine. Grossing 474 tons, the iron sided steamship had been an active Confederate Blockade runner from the beginning of the war, running cotton out of Mobile to Havana until she was captured by Union ships in 1863, and used to patrol the Atlantic coast. With the war over, the ship had been sold to the Georgia East Coast Shipping Company, and now hauled small freight throughout the Caribbean. Dry goods and cotton to Nassau, rum from Nassau and dry goods to St. Augustine, flour, beans, other foodstuffs and building supplies to Key West, cattle from Key West to Punta Rasa, near today's Fort Myers, then back to Key West for a load of sponges and turtles to take back to Savannah then transfer to New York. The war had interrupted most of this commerce and the industrial north was in need of products and raw materials.

Nine Days later, the St. Augustine pulled into Mallory Docks in Key West shortly before sunset. While unloading the cargo usually waited till morning, Sawyer was met at the dock with a wagon, and, again with some money changing hands, the two nail kegs were offloaded in the twilight and driven to a barn just off Caroline Street.

Sawyer knew his uncle Broderick Sawyer had too much money, and an equal amount of greed to pass up what he thought was a potentially profitable, if unscrupulous opportunity. Albert Sawyer had no ties to his island home, no qualms about cheating a relative and no plans to ever see Key West again.

He approached his uncle with the parts of his story that fit his needs. *"I led a company of soldiers that helped Jefferson Davis and his cabinet make off with millions in gold and silver ahead of the advancing Union army,"* he explained. *"We hid most of it in Georgia, but I kept six large gold bars, each about fifty pounds, and hid them in two kegs of nails. At twenty dollars per ounce, that's nearly ninety thousand US dollars,"* Sawyer continued. *"If anyone traces the gold to me, I'm a dead man many times over. But you could melt it down, call it Spanish treasure, and get rich."*

"And you want how much for this stolen gold?" Broderick asked. *"Just ten thousand Yankee dollars."* The elder Sawyer raised his eyes. *"Are they here?"* *"Yes, hidden nearby,"* Albert replied. *"I can take you there tonight, but my ship sails early tomorrow, so I need assurance you will buy them if they are as I described, and I will need to be paid in full before I depart. There's a feed scale in the barn, and you're welcome to verify the weight."*

"You're my brother's son, God rest his soul, answered the old man. If I cannot trust you, whom can I trust? What of the rest of the money you have hidden. What's to be done with that?"

"Oh, other people are now responsible for it," replied Albert, offhandedly. *"This was my payment for following their orders,"* He continued; *"They knew how difficult these gold bars would be to sell, so they gave me a large reward with an equally large risk."*

"I understand. All right, I will meet you at eleven o'clock. Tell me where."

Albert Sawyer gave his uncle directions and suggested they bring a cart or wagon, and they parted for the evening.

In the dark of night, Albert stepped out of the shadows behind a building on Caroline Street and waved down the horse-drawn wagon. Somewhat dismayed that, along with the old man, five of his watermen, two with Navy Colt .36 caliber revolvers in their belts, were also along, presumably to help haul the gold laden nail kegs and provide security. Albert approached the barn and was pleased to see the padlock was still secure. With one of the sailors holding a kerosene lantern, he pulled a large skeleton key out of his pocket and unlocked the ship's padlock. Stepping inside, his heart sank as he saw all at once, the missing boards at the back of the barn and that one of the kegs had been opened, and the nails were strewn over the floor. "We've been robbed!" he turned to his Uncle. "There's still three more bars in the other barrel, but three are gone."

"Well, let's look at what's left," The elder Sawyer replied. "I can still pay you half if they are what you have promised."

Albert turned to the remaining barrel, and, turning it upside down and using a crowbar, pried it open. The three large bars spilled out, gleaming gold in the lamplight. Sawyer picked one up and showed it to his Uncle, then motioned toward the feed scale. "That's not necessary. I trust that you know what they weigh." The old man reached in his satchel and pulled out several bundles of US currency. He roughly divided it in half and handed the portion over to Albert. "I can't say I find this tasteful, but the Confederacy is dead, and better I have this treasure than a bunch of Yankee carpetbaggers. Albert, I'll trust that you will keep this transaction quiet. Safe trip, and know you have a home any time you happen to be in this town."

Sawyer shoved the bills into his bag and walked away from the group without as much as a wave. The elder Sawyer waited till he was around the corner, and nodded to one of the sailors, who waited a few more moments before disappearing into the dark. Knowing Sawyer would cut over to Front Street and head toward Mallory Docks, the waterman walked straight down Caroline at a brisk pace and turned right at Simonton. It was easy to see Sawyer walking toward the docks, and easier yet to step behind him as he walked by, clubbing him hard on the back of the head with a lead filled sap, crushing his skull. Sawyer went down in a heap. The waterman quietly picked up Sawyer's satchel and melted back into the darkness.

And again, indeed, dead men tell no tales.

Looking For a Home in this
Open-Air Asylum

I brought the car back to Maggie's house and picked up the Bitch Box. I'm sure she was glad to be back driving something with seat cushions. I told her about the flat tire and offered to replace the tire. She told me she would call tomorrow and give me the damages. It would probably take most of the cash I had in my pocket I would guess. Gracie was there, but Brody had bailed on the hormone squad and gone fishing. We headed back to the dock to drive my little skiff out to our live aboard boat. As we walked out on the dock, Bo Morgan, who owned the dock where I tied up, stuck his head over the sundeck of his houseboat. "Bric got a message for you to call Harry. You can use my phone." Bo was a genuine treasure hunter, literally famous in Key West and had worked on some of the biggest and most famous shipwrecks ever found. You envision swashbuckling treasure hunters to be big, muscular, with a flowing mane of hair, six feet tall and omnipresent. Bo was about five foot seven, with a small mustache and light frame. Put a tie on him and set him behind a desk and he would look more like a CPA than a treasure hunter but looks can be deceiving. Bo had known me when I was a kid and got me a job as a deckhand on a treasure boat until I got certified as a diver. I quit and left the Keys a few years after that but stayed in touch with Bo over the years. When I returned to the Keys six years ago, penniless, jobless and out of hope, it was Bo that fed me, clothed me, found me a place to sleep and eventually got me hooked up with his son Tack to go to work for Harry Sykas.

Bo was good people.

I told Gracie to wait outside. She shrugged, sat down on the dock and put her Ipod headphones on. Stepping into Bo's living room was like walking into a museum. Autographed photos of Mel Fisher the man that found the *Nuestra Senora De Atocha*, the biggest and most fabulous treasure in history, with his arm around Bo, were on the wall. Leaning against the front porch was a large copper ingot salvaged from a Spanish wreck. Priceless to a museum, it's only true value to Bo was that it kept his floating dock more or less level by providing weight on the right side. Other maps, artefacts and memorabilia adored tables and walls, and a stack of deep sea fishing rods that belonged to Tack leaned against one wall while dive gear hung under the stairway to the roof. Bo didn't fish. Those were Tack's. Bo preferred to shoot his dinner with a spear gun.

Even though Bo's place is technically a "houseboat", it looks much more like a real house, except it was built on a barge and it floated in the bay. Securely attached to the shore, it gently rocks with the waves, rose and fell with the tides, and otherwise met the legal description of a boat. Just across the dock was another houseboat, also Bo's property. This one was larger, a true four-plex, and a positive income rental unit for Bo. He pointed to his phone on the table, and I dialed the number in Tarpon Springs. "Bric, I have good news," Said Harry. "That gold chain is worth a ton and I'm sending you a couple of grand for finding it. The State's not interested in it from a historical standpoint, so all they get is their twenty five percent. The cannon is unquestionably eighteenth century and Spanish, but there are no specific identifying markings that tie it to the Plate Fleet. I think we're in the right area," Sykas continued; "I have a hunch. While the *La Brisa* is in repair, I want you to tow a mag around that area. Create a grid and 'Mow the Lawn' for a while. But here's the deal. I know it's been a few weeks since you found that cannon. Do you think you can find the spot again?" I blushed and was glad I was on the phone and not face to face. It hadn't been two weeks but two days since I was standing on that spot. I stammered back that yes, I thought I could probably find the spot, but why? "Harry, that beach had been a popular party beach since the days when the most frequently caught fish in the gulf was 'square grouper'. I can't believe someone didn't find it before. Hell, I've sat on that beach myself in my early years not ten feet from that spot with a joint, a bottle and a blonde."

"I bet that cannon has been buried in the sand and exposed a dozen times over the years, probably every time there's a storm," Sykas went on. "I think that gun was put there purposely, and that someone aligned it, so it's pointing directly at the wreck, so they could return later on and recover the loot. When we cleaned up the gun, there was a deep scratch in the top with arrow points on the ends. I think it's pointing at the wreck. You know it's only about two miles from where my great grandfather found that chain a hundred years ago. Mark a line along where cannon was laying, start searching and I bet you will find that ship. I'll send the electronics down to you. Find a boat and someone that knows how to use a towed magnetometer, and let me know the cost."

I hung up the phone and knew I wouldn't have to search far for such an expert. Actually I wouldn't have to leave the living room I was standing in. "Bo, is the *Captain Morgan* up to a little side work?" I went on to explain the project. Having been the person to actually mark one of the biggest sunken treasures ever found in the Keys using a magnetometer towed underneath the forty-five foot *Captain Morgan*, which was still tied to Bo's dock, there was no better qualified person on the planet than Bo. He was in his seventies but still young enough for an adventure, given the challenge was great and the reward greater. He listened to the story, raised his eyebrows a little when I gave him the short version of the "gold" ingots, and then closed his eyes for a moment. "Two hundred a day, plus fuel, Tack's current full wages, and two percent of the gross if we find it." I whistled at the proposition. I wasn't sure Sykas would go for, or for that matter, could afford the rate. "It's gotta be worth my trouble," Morgan stated. "This couch is a helluva lot more comfortable than the captain's chair on the *Morgan*, and that's one big friggin ocean out there. That hunch might be good, or that wreck might be thirty miles away from there. For that matter, it could be lying on the other side of the ledge in nine hundred feet of water, or salvage crews in the 1700's or even in the 1960's could have cleaned her out. You're a good kid Bric, but business is business."

"Let me use your phone again."

I called Sykas back, and he was both surprised that I had found someone so quickly and then his Greek temper rose to the top at the proposition. Morgan could hear Harry yelling from his couch when the proposal was given. He clearly could hear that Sykas wouldn't be held hostage no matter who the fuck I might have found. And anyway who the hell came up with this outrageous number?

"Bo Morgan."

Silence on the phone for a few seconds and then some quiet words. I put my hand over the phone and turned to Bo.

"Harry wants to know if a check's okay."

Bo doesn't use contracts or lawyers. It had burned him more than once in the past, but the last time he had signed a piece of paper was a marriage certificate and that ended up costing him a ranch and millions in treasure. A handshake cemented the deal, and Bo told me he would start scraping the cobwebs off the engine room in the *Captain Morgan* and get her seaworthy. "One more thing Bo," I said as he walked toward the door. "I need to get the kids off that live aboard. It's tiny, has no sanitary facilities, no shower, and no privacy. It's not the place for a fifteen year old girl. Brody doesn't care. He's half fish anyway and turned half native and half caveman three days after he got back to Key West, but my daughter deserves more than this. I've got a two grand bonus coming. Do you have a unit on the houseboat that I can rent?" Bo's kind heart turned businessman in an instant. "Sure. The guy upstairs is two months behind, and he's moving Saturday. He doesn't know it yet, but I promise you it will be vacant Sunday morning. You can move in after I paint it, or paint and clean yourself and I'll just charge first and last. Nine hundred a month, and don't be late."

Nine hundred a month was exactly nine hundred a month more than I was currently paying, but child support was gone now, and I felt good about finding more treasure, and, either way, I seriously didn't have a choice. For the second time in two minutes, I shook Bo Morgan's hand.

I emerged from Bo's house, and Grace stood up. She didn't acknowledge my presence but stated walking toward the Zodiac. "Gracie, I know how hard it's been for you since you came back. I know you hate me, hate Key West and hate living on that derelict boat. So day after tomorrow, were moving in there." I pointed to the second floor of the houseboat.

"Really? Does it have, like, electricity and a real toilet that flushes?" She asked sarcastically. "Yes, baby, it's got that, and a TV. The couch is a sofa bed, and I'll try to get a laptop for you soon." "I get to have a dog," Grace replied. "And I get to pick, no questions asked." And she turned and walked away.

At that moment, I figured that I could have moved her into a mansion in Beverly Hills with Orlando Bloom as a butler and it wouldn't have created much of a reaction. Well, it's not always about making everyone happy. It's about moving in the right direction, and being the best person you know how to be. Brody hadn't shown up yet, but I wasn't that worried. When he made his way home he would whistle for me, bum a ride from Tack, or if no other way found itself, just jump in and swim to the boat.

I fired up the little three-horse Johnson and pulled away from the dock to the boat, anchored a few hundred yards away. As we tied up and boarded the derelict cabin cruiser, I became painfully aware of the bleak accommodations. Everything felt like dirty salt. Mattresses, sheets, pillows, bedspreads were all damp and crusty. A two burner propane stove sat on the counter, and a large ice chest served as a chair, table and refrigerator. Despite weekly trips to the Laundromat, keeping close to clean was an impossible task. Brody and Grace would both used the P.E. showers at school for a daily shower when school started, and right now borrowed Bo's shower every day or so, swimming in the ocean the rest of the time. Brody didn't care, but for Grace, it was truly a living Hell. I think that she probably didn't run away only because she wanted me to see just how much I had ruined her life. Four months ago, this was the ideal place for a single, broke part time treasure diver, part time bass player in a bar band. For a family of three, it was a disaster.

Just after we got home, I noticed Florida Fish and Wildlife boat approaching our boat. The boat eased up on the throttles and slowed to a stop. Brody was sitting in the right seat. This is never good. Brody stepped out of the twenty three foot Key Largo FWC boat and tied it to a cleat. He reached into the back of the boat and pulled up a lovely stringer of Hogfish, and Officer Joe Clark handed him his dive bag.

"Everything okay, officer?" I asked.

"Yes, I just found your son out past the channel. He had his dive flag up, was fishing in perfectly legal waters, and had a perfect limit of perfectly legal sized fish. I felt the least thing I could do to celebrate this event was to give him a free ride home."

Wonders never cease. At least we had fresh fish for dinner, and there is nothing better than fried hogfish. We waved bye-bye to the FWC guy. Brody stood and waved till he was out of sight, then turned around, reached into the bottoms of his half-wetsuit and pulled out six "short" lobster tails. "Dummy must have thought I was hung like a donkey," Brody muttered. "Man, if he had not shown up we would have been eating fresh Jewfish for dinner."

"Yeah, and if he had caught you with a wetsuit full of short lobster tails and a jewfish on your spear you would be a guest of the state tonight."

"Sure dad," Brody said with a grin. "The keyword there is 'if'."

Flashback - Key West, 1865

Johnny Pinder Russell wasn't a Union or Confederate sympathizer. All he really cared for was Johnny Russell, his scrawny, raw-boned 17-year-old pregnant wife Nellie, and a termite-ridden rundown shack they occupied on a large lot on Fleming Street in Key West. A self-described seaman, Johnny's 34 years had been spent mostly on the shady side of the law, joining wreck salvage teams when possible, but, not beyond helping the occasional boat accidentally sink, blurring the fine line between salvage and piracy. Johnny's father, grandfather and great grandfather had all been wreckers, emigrating to the Keys from Marsh Harbor on the island of Eleuthra, when he was just a teenager to be closer to the only legal salvage port in the Caribbean. The Russell family, along with several other English loyalists, had immigrated to the British held Bahamas shortly after the end of the Revolutionary War to avoid becoming American citizens. Taller than most people in those days, his spare frame, burned where uncovered by constant exposure to the island sunshine and salt air, was clothed in tattered rags and a ragged leather hat. Johnny nervously patted the heavy weight hidden under a gunnysack sitting on the bottom of the small sailboat he had "borrowed" from his uncle Joe. With luck, he would return from his mission before Joe discovered the boat missing, thereby avoiding a thrashing by his muscular relative. For that matter, the treasure at his feet wasn't his either. He had watched longshoremen carry two heavy kegs off a former confederate blockade-runner the night before. He could tell at that time, whatever they were carrying was exceptionally heavy, and he quietly followed them and the small cart down Caroline Street, where they were unloaded and brought into a barn behind one of the brothels that lined the street.

Johnny had waited patiently until it appeared nobody was watching, and slipped over the wooden fence, prying a few boards from the back of the barn and, once inside, lit a candle to look around. It didn't take him long to find what he was seeking, two wooden nail kegs resting in a corner. He examined the kegs and noticed immediately when he rolled one over that it was substantially heavier on one end than the other. Using a crowbar, he tipped a keg over and caved in the bottom of the keg, spilling the contents out on the straw. Even with the dim candlelight, it was easy to see the unmistakable shine of gold. Three large, oval shaped gold bars lie in front of him. Johnny was looking at riches far beyond his wildest dreams, if he could only figure a way to get them someplace else. They were large and oval, over nine inches long and about four inches thick, with a pronounced "CSA" emblem cast on top, and when Johnny tried to pick one up, he judged it weighed well over fifty pounds. Moving them would be tough, but not impossible. *Wrapping three in a burlap sack and fashioning a makeshift loop, he started dragging them out of the back of the barn. Shoving the bag under the fence and climbing over the top, Johnny picked up the heavy burden and headed toward his house down a back alley, stooped over with the weight. Key West on a hot summer night in 1865 was a quiet place, and he managed to get home with his prize unnoticed. He hid the sack underneath the shack and headed back for the rest. Approaching the brothel, it was apparent his efforts had been discovered and the barn was well lit, with several men with guns standing on Caroline Street. Well, three were better than none, and Johnny slinked back into the shadows and headed back home. The Civil War had ended a few months ago, and the town was overrun with Union troops, Yankee carpetbaggers and suddenly unemployed Confederate Soldiers. Johnny couldn't think of a single place that he could hide the gold in town, so he decided to hide them where nobody would ever find them.*

Hoisting his plunder again, he headed for the harbor and his Uncle Joe's little sloop. He figured he could take the boat, accomplish his mission and be back before his uncle discovered it had been "borrowed." Slipping out of the harbor with the tide at dawn, he was sailing west through the gulf by sunrise. Johnny couldn't swim a stroke, but he was more at home on a boat than he was on land and, despite a strong September Southeast fetch, he felt comfortable in the sixteen-foot sailboat.

Landmarks in the low lying keys were difficult to recognize for the inexperienced, but Johnny knew every rock, current and wreck in the area, and expertly guided the boat through the shallow reefs to a place he had found once before. Moving to the south side of Boca Grande by late afternoon, he lowered his sail in the gathering storm and switched to oars. Knowing he would not find what he was looking for in the gathering dusk, he beached the boat and huddled up for a fitful night's sleep.

The morning broke windy and gray. Johnny's seaman eyes told him this might be more than a fall thunderstorm, but he was alone with no other options than to complete his task and work his way back home best he could. Despite the rough water around the island, it only took him about 20 minutes to find what he was looking for, an ancient Spanish cannon that he had seen once before when stopping on the island to camp, almost totally buried in the sand. Johnny didn't care about history or where that cannon might have come from, but he knew it wasn't ever going to go anywhere, and would be a perfect landmark to hide his gold bars. Hoisting the heavy bars out of the boat, he lugged them over to the cannon, which was sitting in about three feet of water. Scooping the loose sand under the barrel, Johnny shoved the bars one by one, as far as he could underneath, and packed the sand and rocks back in until it was covered.

The weather was going steadily downhill, and Johnny didn't want to be caught on this tiny island in a storm. He knew if he worked his way back to Key West in the lee of low mangrove islands he could take advantage of the breeze without being swamped by high waves. He could plot the route in his sleep. Johnny sailed north of Boca Grande, Woman Key, Man Key, Crawfish Key, then edged out into Key West roads towards the north side of Key West. Johnny knew he'd make it. He always had before. The fast moving scuddy clouds, foam whipping from the whitecaps, and every increasing wind spoke to Johnny's worst fears; He was sailing into a tropical storm – maybe a hurricane and he had a good five miles of open water, almost upwind, to negotiate. The hard east wind meant the storm center – or, if it was a hurricane – the eye would be someplace to his south. Not likely to get stronger, but this was the right quadrant of the storm and thereby the most dangerous. He eased through the slot near Mule Key and was immediately slammed by six-foot waves and wild winds. He knew he couldn't make it across the straights, and turned the little sailboat to run back to safety, but it was too late; a massive wave crashed over the boat, rolling it over and throwing Johnny into the wild sea. Johnny couldn't swim, and his last thoughts were not of his wife or his house, but the gold fortune that he would now never get to recover and that nobody would ever find ...

Roots

This lifestyle wasn't in my master plan.

I married Wendy Sawyer a long time ago, right out of high school. Both of us were Key West natives and true Conchs, with over 150 years of combined island heritage between us. Wendy's family, the Sawyers, blended with my Russell bloodline for the umpteenth time. We joked in high school all the time about being kissing cousins, and then ended up falling in love. Of course, there weren't that many people in those days that you were *not* related to in some fashion on the island.

The ceremony was an island event, with relatives up the Keys as far north as Tavernier, both black and white, in attendance. Wendy's family had money, while my side of the aisle were poor fisherman, "wreckers" and watermen, not much different than they had been when they first arrived in Key West in the 1840's. All I had to my name was the old family Conch home on Fleming Street, over 120 years old and in dire need of either fixing up or tearing down. Work was scarce in Key West in the late seventies and I had no choice but to join the Navy.

A few years later, I put in for underwater training at the Naval Diving & Salvage Training Center (NDSTC) in Panama City, Florida and then started all over with a two-month boot camp at the Basic Underwater Demolition/SEAL training in Coronado, Calif. SEAL boot camp makes regular training feel like milk and cookies with Aunt Martha.   Don't get me wrong. I was in decent shape. Hell, I was in *GREAT* shape, and they still managed to break me down into babbling Jell-O in three weeks. As far as diving, free diving, underwater rescue and things like that, it was fairly effortless, and I was pretty well at the top of the class, but on dry land, (or more often, soggy mud), they managed to reduce all of us to our lowest level. They had two missions; get two thirds of the class to DOR (Drop on Request), and then turn the rest into a finely honed fighting machine. Out of a hundred twenty recruits at the beginning of the class, we lost forty in the first three days, and another twenty by the end of Hell Week. One even died by being a little too enthusiastic going over the top of a wall and broke his neck on the fall.   Twenty nine of us graduated, and that was a gang of genuine tough bastards. Like I said, I was pretty well at the top of the group in or underwater, and I could definitely hold my own in the fitness courses, running the one and a half mile course with a full pack in less than nine minutes.   That being said, I was not an inherently violent guy and even though I could kill or hospitalize about any human or three with my bare hands, my defensive posture in hand to hand combat earned me the nickname of "Kitten." Everybody has a nickname, but most were things like "Animal", "Bigfoot" or "Crush."   I just always assumed my middle name would earn me "Brick."   I got Kitten. Oh well. After graduating I joined the SEAL team at the Joint Expeditionary Base Little Creek in Virginia Beach and eventually did advance training right back in Key West at Truman Annex, which meant I got to sleep at home for a few months.

Hoo-Yah!

Being a Navy SEAL in the eighties was kind of a "tweener" existence. After Viet Nam and before the Gulf Wars, you spend days, weeks and months in training, with the chance of combat more or less out of the picture. More Seals died during this period from training than combat. I honestly expected to live out my Navy career in relative peace.

Then one night, we were kicked awake, geared up and got orders to help knock down an attempted coup in Grenada. We were ready for combat but not for this cluster fuck. I came very close to buying the farm. We were given two tasks, neither which I thought seriously matched our training, but looking backwards that pretty well described the whole three day war. The SEAL's missions were to protect, recover and extract Grenada's Governor General and then capture and control the only radio tower. Other than knowing vaguely where the Governor and the tower were, we didn't have much more info. It started off bad and went worse. We were in two transport planes and the one I was in completely missed the drop zone, kicking us out in the middle of a screaming rain squall a half-mile off shore. Four of my buddies drowned, and we never found their bodies, and I breathed more water than air for two hours. We finally dragged our wet asses on shore and regrouped, split into two teams and headed to our objectives. The squad that was supposed to rescue the Governor discovered they had drowned their SAT-phone. They were surrounded by Cubans and Grenadian troops and ended up using the local phone service to call a base in the US to call the commander on the ground in Grenada and call in fire support from an AC-130. Get this; the Chief had to use his MasterCard to get long distance. Don't you love technology? A squad of Recon Marines had to eventually fight their way up the hill and rescue them, which undoubtedly chapped their butts.

My squad didn't fare any better. We got to the radio tower and couldn't raise the command post. We took a lot of fire from opposing troops and some BTR-60's, Russian armored amphibian tanks, and starting taking casualties. We finally decided we couldn't hold the ground, blew up the station and fought our way, one foot at a time, back to the water. History books and news reports gave the impression that us high tech Americans more or less ran over the locals, but a target rifle in the hands of a nineteen year old kid in sandals, shorts and a dirty Che Guevara tee shirt can kill just as dead as regular Army soldier in full pack with a Kalashnikov. I was almost to the beach when I got creased right across both cheeks of my ass by a bullet. It stung like hell, but I knew it was too far from my heart to kill me and gave me good reason to get that much closer to Mother Earth. Hell, I would have cut off my dick and the buttons on my shirt if I thought it would make a lower profile. We waited till dark and then swam out into the bay, carrying the wounded, where we were eventually spotted by a reconnaissance plane and picked up by a chopper later that night, exhausted, wet, shot-up and unhappy. The next day I found myself on the other side of the island in relative peace with bandages on both sides of my ass, going from door to door looking for bad guys. That's where I met Karen. Two days later the "war" was over, the bad guys were dead or in jail, and we went home.

Despite that little interlude, I really enjoyed the service, and came out six years later as a certified Master Diver with experience in underwater demolition, and a good grasp of playing rock and roll bass guitar. I put the dive ticket to good use, working for several treasure hunters over the years, making a decent living during the day and playing music on weekends at local bars. Wendy worked as a waitress on the Sunset Pier, and we enjoyed the island lifestyle that will consume you, immerse you, or run you off. Then I went to work for a big treasure company, working for six years looking for an old treasure galleon that we could only find bits and pieces of. I was gone from home for days at a time, pay was spotty, and the strain was taking its toll on my relationship with Wendy. Finally, in 1985, I realized I was better off staying home, tending bar and playing music, and walked away from the organization. Three weeks later, they found the main part of the wreck and cashed in millions. I was left without a dime of the bonus.

On the other hand, back at home full time, the relationship got better, we were making ends meet, and then she got pregnant. Broderick Charles was born, and three years later, Grace Alice Wahl came along. I gave Brody a mask, fins and snorkel on his third birthday. He put his face in the water and hasn't come up yet. Brody seemed to feel his Conch roots and fell in love with Key West. Gracie, even from an early age, didn't care much for the life and the lifestyle. She wanted bright lights and big city, and wanted to move away and become a singer. Wendy was starting to long for something more too, both for her and the kids. Then one day when everyone was at work and school, an electrical short started a fire in that old, tinder-dry home, and it burned to the ground in minutes. Wendy took it as an omen, and left the following day, taking the kids with her to relatives in Sandusky Ohio. She filed for divorce a few months later, and there I was, homeless and with a massive child support payment due every month. I left my beloved Key West for a job as an underwater welder for an oil company in Brownsville, Texas. That job lasted for several years, but I seriously longed to get back to Key West. Finally, through Bo, I connected with Harry Sykas and moved back. With all my money going to child support, the abandoned old cabin cruiser and a dilapidated VW Thing was about all I could manage.

It wasn't all that bad, I guess.

Then I got a letter from Wendy, delivered to me in care of Bo Morgan, it was the first communication in a few years. It was less than a page short and to the point; she had ovarian cancer, six weeks to live, her family couldn't take care of the kids. Come get them now.

Life was about to change again.

Digging into what little savings I had, I flew to Cleveland, and took the bus to Sandusky. I stayed at the "Y", seeing the kids every day and Wendy in the evenings. I took their mind off what was going on by taking them to Cedar Point a few times, and once out to

Put-In-Bay, where some of my Key West chums spent the summers playing music for the tourists at the Round-House Bar. It was terrible to see her laying there, hair gone, the disease ravaging her body. I never stopped loving her, and was holding her hand when she took her last breath. The Ohio family loved their niece, but declined taking care of the kids any longer. We came back to Key West after the funeral.

Being a tenant in Bo's houseboat might have been the perfect solution, but it wasn't my first attempt. Even before I had the financial solution, I had started looking for a better place than my live aboard boat. Key West tends to polarize people - either you love it, or you hate it. To some, it's cramped, dirty, too far out of the way, uncivilized, un-cultured, too hot, too humid, too gay, too weird and too strange. To others it's paradise fulfilled - the end of a string of pearls in the middle of a multi colored ocean, full of flavor, excitement, and surprises. I think I lay somewhat between those two poles, but I lean enough toward the latter that I can ignore enough of the former to let me live here.

You can think of Key West in two manners, it's either that cream rises to the top, or shit falls to the bottom. I mean, I have traveled around the world, and I have seen boys kiss boys, girls hold hands with girls, a man running in nothing but short shorts and a straw ladies bonnet the size of a trash can lid. I have seen men in dresses, and old women with more tattoos than teeth. I have seen dogs in sunglasses, and cats jump through burning hoops, women exposing their breasts in public, drunks sleeping with the curb for a pillow. The only thing is I have seen all of that in Key West on two blocks of Duval Street on a Tuesday morning. It's truly a town where the bars have no windows and the windows have no bars.

For me, I was born and grew up here.

My childhood home was the family heritage home. The lot was first built on about 1855, and, from what we know, wasn't much more than a little shack with an outhouse on Fleming Street in old town. Built of scrap wood and ship timbers from salvaged wrecks, it was likely not much to look at. It burned, was rebuilt, burned again, rebuilt, damaged in the 1909 hurricanes, and then re-modeled with a second floor and an attic in the fashion of many Conch family homes, two story, wooden, living room downstairs, bedrooms upstairs, couple of small rooms in the loft with outside staircase so they could be rented out, and a little carriage barn in the back with an enormous Ficus tree shading the whole yard. If the place had ever been painted, there was no indication of it when I was a kid, but the house held many wonderful memories of kitchen smells and tons of little nooks and crannies that you could hide in and lots of nighttime creaks and squeaks that let you know this old house was alive and breathing. Either that or that some of my ancestors still lived there, and occasionally strolled the halls at night. It was enough to keep an imaginative six year old kid in bed and under the covers every night for sure.

I came late in my parent's life. Dad married mom in 1939 and had two kids quick like, then he joined the Navy after Pearl Harbor and served in the Pacific. Mom and my brother and sister moved out to San Diego to be a little closer to his home port, and mom and her sister worked at Consolidated Aircraft as real "Rosie the Riveters" for most of the war. They built B-24's and I think they had a heck of a good time, making money and dancing with the sailors on weekends. Mom never said anything, but she had this little metal jewelry box made from aircraft rivets and hinges that she said someone made for her. There was always a little smile on her face when she talked about those days, and I always wondered if she did more than dance with some of those sailors.

Mom and dad moved back to Key West after the war and I came along six years later. I was young when they both died, just a few years apart, of emphysema and pancreatic cancer. The only memento I have from my mother is that little metal jewelry box. I use it today to keep some of my keepsake Spanish gold and silver coins. Funny, there's probably five grand worth of collectables in that box, and I never think of them as capital, even when I have to use a fishing pole to catch dinner or go hungry. If it wasn't for the fire, I would probably still be rattling around in that old mansion today, but one afternoon, a rat probably gnawed through an electrical cord, and the house went up like a match. I had to sell the lot for back taxes and, with the wife booking out of town and no place to live, I bailed off the island for a while too.

When I came back, the option of buying a house was out of the question, and even coming up with first and last was nearly impossible. I ended up on a derelict abandoned boat in the bay for a long time, and it wasn't till I became a single dad that my hand was forced. It was time to become a legitimate tenant. Like I said, for a while before I shook hands with Bo, I started house hunting. Key West is one of the most expensive places to live in the country and, as the old saying goes; you either have three jobs and two roommates or two jobs and three roommates. As a single father with two kids, neither was an option. Now that I think of it, my pay wasn't that dreadful, but, that being said, spending seven or eight hours a day underwater, relying on a mechanical device to keep me breathing air, the pay *should* be good. If I squeaked and stretched, maybe I could afford to rent something decent enough for my family and me.

As a renter, there's that "in town, or out of town" decision. And if you decide to live in town, then you have to decide if it's New Town or Old Town. Decisions, decisions. Rentals in the Keys are directly proportional to the distance you are from Duval Street, which is Old Town. I think you pay about a dollar more per month for every inch closer you are to Duval. New Town, which is anyplace above White Street, about seven blocks from Duval, consists of houses that were mostly, but not entirely, built after World War II. Very typical track style homes, some apartment buildings, even a few mobile home parks, but by and large pretty ratty neighborhoods. Old Town offers tree-lined streets and rustic homes, many of them well over a hundred fifty years old, and most look like they were assembled from wood off the Ark. You can rent one of these homes, but a two story, three bedroom "Conch" home in decent shape can cost three million dollars to buy, and well over three grand a month to rent. Built in classical antebellum fashion, many of these homes are easily large enough to divide up into houses for two, three, or four apartments. Unfortunately, since the housing in Key West is sooooo tight they put six or seven or eight apartments in them. What you end up with is tiny little rooms with low ceilings and microscopic "kitchens", which often means cooking facilities that would probably downgrade a Barbie dream house. Parking is usually on the street, and thusly a direct target for local thieves looking for anything they can sell to buy that next hit of crack.

By nature, I'm not a shopper but a buyer. I have been known to go Christmas shopping for my entire family and friends after breakfast and be home before lunch, stopping on the way home to buy a car. At the same time, I'm picky and particular as to what I might want, or in this case, tolerate, to live in. I took the normal path, searching the Key West Citizen, affectionately known by the locals at the Mackerel Wrapper, identifying its most functional role in the community. I started about a month before my actual search, perusing the Sunday classifieds to get some sort of idea of what was on the market. I figured that if I was incredibly lucky, I could find something in old town for $750, and might go to $950 a month for a real peach. Problem is, as I mentioned before, $750 will hardly raise you above the homeless that sleep under Garrison Bight Bridge and roast squirrels on a stick for dinner, and $950 just creeps into the realm of the habitable. But there were a few in the paper that fit the criteria, and after a few weeks of reading, I started getting a little closer to action.

Armed with a Sunday paper and a cup of coffee, I started cruising the classifieds, circling those that were promising and crossing out those that were out of the question. Out of the four columns of "Apartments - furnished and unfurnished." I found about four possible candidates. Now comes the second problem - It's Sunday in Key West, and you dare not call anyone before eleven or you might endure the wrath of Sunday's hangover after Saturday night's revelry. The problem is the good stuff doesn't hang around much, so I pushed the envelope and started calling at ten. My first call was promising. In downtown, close to work, high ceilings, rustic location, upstairs, large rooms with wood floors. The visit was not quite the visual that I had in mind, but the place still had possibilities. It was at that point that I started my glossary of Key West Classified Rental terms as I found that rustic meant the building was over a hundred years old, upstairs meant a long climb a rickety staircase, and good location meant that I was upstairs a block from the corner of Duval and Truman, over a non-stop rock band. That being said the rooms were indeed large, and the ceilings were high. Rent was reasonable, and the landlord hinted that, based on the fact that I could speak English and my shirt was buttoned, that I was a "desirable" tenant and the rent was negotiable.

Marking this as a possibility, I continued on my day's journey and looked at a total of a half dozen or so places. Mostly it went downhill from there as I could see the places in my price range were mostly just terrible. One was on the third story of a doctor's private residence and the ceiling was not an inch higher than six foot four, with one single window in the whole place. I banged my head on the doorway going in, almost lost three fingers in a ceiling fan while brushing my hair back, and got instantly claustrophobic. The next one sounded like a dream in the paper. '*Large one bedroom, private yard, extra storage room that could be made into another bedroom, ample parking, etc etc.*' The landlord almost fell over herself trying to rent it to me, but it was again, tiny little rooms, extremely low ceilings, no storage, window air conditioners. I felt like I was house hunting in Munchkin Land. The "yard" was a three foot wide stretch of concrete alongside the house." She said that everyone that had ever moved out did not want to because they loved it there so much, and that it was so much nicer than what they had come from.

I would guess they had been living under that bridge.

The next one I went to look at had a slight identity crisis. It might have been in the "Apartments, Unfurnished" category in the paper, but it had wheels underneath the skirting and would have been advertised as a "single wide" in most other papers. So much for that.

The third one was vertical living at its best. Three rooms, about eight feet by ten, with a staircase taking up a third of each room. Bottom floor was a tiny kitchen, and living room that would hold one chair. Above that a landing that would hold another chair and a bathroom that would make a cruise ship head look spacious. Above that a loft with a mattress on the floor. It was advertised as having a pool and Jacuzzi. The pool was four feet wide and seven feet long, and was shared by the tenant next door, two large women with tattoos, Birkenstocks, short hair and calves that would make an NFL player blush with envy.

Just a little too scary for me.

After a few weeks, disappointment turned to despair, and then to fear. Was I going to sentence my children to growing up on a dirty mattress on a tiny boat?

Then I thought about Bo's houseboat.

A Houseboat for my Doorstops

The Key West dream is to live on the water. Strangely enough, this place is surrounded by water, but there are only a handful of places in the entire city that are on open water, much less a view of the water. Most of the oceanfront is either public beach, or private hotel. You have to move up the Keys to get on the water, and to rent a place on deep water you have to pay a ton. At the same time, living in a houseboat can be rather exciting during hurricane season. Hurricane Georges nearly decimated Houseboat Row, a collection of very colorful homes near the airport, many of which ended up piled in a heap of rubble and ruin on the highway after that storm. But this place was furnished, and besides it was not in exposed ocean but a bay. Big storm comes, I grab my stuff and bug out. Little storm comes, well, material for a book someday.

Like many places I have lived, this one had its dog population to win over. Bo had two large, old, smelly, dusty, Rottweilers named Debby and Scooter, and a goofy young Dobie named Lucky. The Rots were true watchdogs and trusted nobody but Bo and his son Tack, and the existing tenants. For the first few days, it was kind of like trying to become a roommate with a couple of grizzly bears. I wasn't welcome and at times felt downright in danger of getting my ass chewed. I knew the way to their heart, and invested in case lots of beggin strips. I started by throwing snacks from the balcony to the dock, but in only a few days, all three dogs were knocking at my door as soon as I got home, mooching snacks and giving full indication they were willing to move in. I love dogs, but these both last had a bath in the mid 90's and reminded me of the smell of being downwind of a stockyard. I fed them from the door, and made good friends and from that point on I didn't have to worry about attacks or, for that matter, ever locking my front door. I had other pets too, hundreds, of mangrove and grey snapper, plus the occasional nurse shark and a stray barracuda, not to mention the occasional black angelfish and lots of sergeant majors, along with a few stray starfish and lots of horseshoe crabs. They lived underneath the houseboat or around the dock, and it didn't take long for them to gather under my patio door to accept a free handout of Friskies cat food. Some of the snapper were big enough to be considered keepers, and although I occasionally let the kids have the novel experience of catching fish from a living room, I never converted any to dinner. Brody got a big kick out of waiting till a big barracuda cruised close to the boat, and then throw a big handful of cat food on top of it. The snappers would ignore barracuda teeth and attack the food, freaking out the predator who thought he was being stalked by food, and he would split the neighborhood. I have no idea if Brody's repeat performances were with the same barracuda. They were smart critters, and I suspect it was a one-time event for each, but there was no shortage of these toothy creatures and he could have repeated the gag a hundred times and not run out of would be predators.

While the location was great, the digs lacked a little ambience. Stark-white walls and peel-and-stick tile floors does not describe a candidate for a Better Homes and Gardens story. I asked Bo if he minded if I did a little painting and he said "help yourself." As a bachelor, single, straight guy, I had no education, advice or inherent taste as to how to proceed, so I went to Ace Hardware, grabbed a few color chips that looked fairly decent and bought paint. Let's just say my paint job was just a tiny bit, ah, loudish. My gentle pastel yellow on the color chip ended up on the wall like a school bus. The living room did a bit better, two shades of blue that might, just might, have looked good in a bathroom (or a brothel). The few visitors I got needed Dramamine to stay more than twenty minutes.

But, hey, it's me.

From the inside, you would need a little chop in the bay to tell you were in something that was floating. After all, it was a big structure. Each of the four units was more or less identical – small living room, a kitchenette that would make the galley in a cabin cruiser look spacious, little bar top you ate from, decent bedroom with a small closet, and bath and toilet so narrow you had to walk in backwards if you wanted to sit. The place was too small for me and two teenage kids of different genders (and, it seemed, species), but it's the hand that God dealt me this time around, so I figured to make the best of it. The bedroom had two twin beds, one chest of drawers and a nightstand. Grace took the couch. At least there were hot showers, hot food, and TV and Internet access. (That's right, gotta get a laptop)

We had three neighbors; Robert Portier lived across the way, was the lead singer in my band. Robert was a ten generation conch like me and was a celebrated black prince of Bahama Village. He sang at two or three places a night, doing a sunset celebration at seven, Sloppy Joes at eight and Buzzards with the band from nine till two. Robert was good people. Downstairs directly below our apartment was Scarlet, who worked at Aqua in the drag queen show. At six five, three hundred pounds, Scarlet, whose real name is Kevin Montclaire, was once an All-American Defensive Tackle at Tulane University in Louisiana before "jumping the fence" and ending up a star at the show at Aqua. He/She did some Aretha

Franklin, Queen Latifa and Oprah in her fat phase, and could also roller skate. Add a pair of seven inch acrylic heels and you got one heck of a mountain of a neighbor. Scarlet didn't have to appease the Rots. One stern look and they hid under the car, ass-first. Actually Scarlet was an incredibly gentle person, a fantastic singer and Grace immediately latched on for some karaoke combos. Kevin/Scarlet's bedroom was a sight to behold. Not the forty Marabou boas draped all over the wall, but that both twin beds were arranged end-to end to accommodate the altitude. Scarlet never had visitors. I really wasn't sure what the gender preference was. I did hear someone call her a fag and a transvestite cross dresser, and he/she responded "I ain't none of those honey. I'm jus a big black man in a dress."

Across the hall downstairs was a young married couple, Jack and Carla. Jack was a really nice guy, working three jobs as a waiter for the lunch crowd at Mangos, bartender on the pier at Sunset, and running drinks outside at Buzzards till late night. Carla was easy on the eyes and hard on the ears. Possibly the most miserable woman that has ever balled for a beer, she didn't work, wore her hair in a towel or curlers 24-7 and was most the time dressed in a nearly sheer, spaghetti-strapped shift that started deep in cleavage, and ended about halfway between the knees and the playground. I'm pretty sure she wore less indoors, not to entice Jack, but to constantly remind him of what he was not getting. I think he thought of her the same way I read National Geographic – always looking at places that I will never get to visit. They say a man's home is his temple; well this one was Our Lady of the Perpetually Angry.

Compared to the rest of us misfits, they were damn near normal.

We were hardly out of our live aboard boat when it was re-occupied. Anyplace that had a roof of sorts and a place to cook and sleep wouldn't be abandoned long. I suspect Bo Morgan gave this couple the heads up that it was vacant. I didn't know them but saw only a day or two after we moved in that there were lights on out in the bay. The following morning, I could see movement on the boat, about two hundred fifty yards from the houseboat. Grabbing my Ricoh 7x35 binocs from the counter, I focused in on my old home. It was a young couple, a skinny, bearded guy with dreadlocks, wearing dirty shorts and not much else. His wife, or significant other, was totally naked in the warm morning sun, and appeared to be about full term pregnant. Nudity likely wasn't a lifestyle, but a practical response to ninety five degree days, ninety percent humidity and no washing facilities. She wasn't pretty, and I almost felt embarrassed watching her, but watching them set up house was fascinating. It scared me to think this was likely a step up the food chain for them. It looked like they didn't have a penny to their name. I didn't have much myself, but I resolved to help them in some way. The following morning, I hit the local K-Mart and blew $150 bucks on baby stuff. Blankets, diapers, toys, bottles, pacifiers, a baby bath tub, and other items. I came back to the house and knocked on Bo's door. "I think you know who these are for. Please don't let them know where it came from." Bo accepted the items without comment, just nodded and took them in. I never saw how the stuff got over there, but a week later, I saw them boating over to the boat, and she had a little bundle in a familiar green receiving blanket.

Bless their hearts.

Flashback – Near Boca Grande Key, June 1918

Stavos Miklos Sykas sat on a reinforced bench in the summer sun on the Greek sponge boat Mania, while two crew members wrestled the heavy brass alloy Schrader dive helmet into place, and then tightened the large wing nuts to make it waterproof. The headgear, rubberized suit and lead-weighted shoes weighed over 185 pounds, and it took a strong man like the burly Greek to be able to stand up unattended. The two helpers reached under his arms, and with a pat on the helmet, Sykas drew to his feet. Another sailor was already hand-pumping the air compressor, and Sykas gave the "ok" sign that he was getting breathable air. A large hook with a strong rope and the air hose was attached to the back of his suit and he turned around to back down the steps to the water. The overhead crane pulled the line tight, and Stavos stepped off the ladder. Straining under nearly four hundred pounds of weight, the crane lowered the diver some fifty feet to the bottom. In the wheelhouse, the captain kept a close eye on the horizon. Greek spongers were not welcome in the Keys, and there was some risk in harvesting prime sponges in this area. There had already been some skirmishes, and more than one Greek sponge boat had been burned or sunk by Key West Conchs. Local divers still relied on the traditional method that of using a long pole with hooks on the end to harvest sponges. Hard-Hat Greek divers could go deeper and gather many more sponges in a day than the locals. The animosity was real, and

81

so was the danger.

The crew lowered a weighted basket along with the diver and as soon as he landed on the bottom, he began pulling up the large commercial quality bath sponges from the bottom and dropping in the basket. As the basket filled, he tugged on the line, and it was hauled up, emptied and quickly returned to the bottom. Sykas worked as fast as possible, knowing his bottom time would be limited to about an hour before being hauled up to avoid the affects of "Caisson disease", now more commonly known as the bends. Divers and bridge workers, who spent hours working under pressurized air digging bridge footings underground, only knew that, after an extended period of time breathing pressurized air, that they would suffer excruciating pain in their joints after re-surfacing. It would be years later that it was discovered that nitrogen bubbles would diffuse into the bloodstream under pressure, and then turn back into bubbles when returning to normal atmosphere. Sykas only knew that he would be hauled back on the boat after about an hour and that he would let another diver take his place for an hour before he re-donned the gear and went back down.

Nearing the end of his dive, his sponge hook caught on something as he scooped up a sponge. He pulled, first gently, then much harder, and the hook suddenly came free, causing him to fall over backwards. Sitting on the bottom, he pulled the hook toward his faceplate and stared dumbly at a large very heavy necklace. The links were as big as pecans, and it looped over twenty inches in diameter. Sykas rubbed one of the links and, under the encrustation, the unmistakable shine of gold emerged. Yanking on the rope to help him get back to his feet, he got a three-tug return, advising they were going to pull him up. A little surprised as it hadn't been near an hour, he signaled back he was ready, and felt himself slowly lifting off the floor and pulled to the surface. His dive suit had a large pocket, and he slipped the chain in, not sure how he might keep this discovery to himself.

Sykas emerged to a flurry of activity. He was rather unceremoniously dumped on the deck while the crew was hoisting anchor and unfurling the sails. Pounding his fist on the deck for attention, they ignored him for the moment, and then pointed to the east, where the sails of three boats showed over the horizon. Key West spongers were approaching fast. The breeze caught Mania's sails and the sponger turned north through the pass between Boca Grande and the Marquesas. The tide was outgoing, and the big sailboat made slow progress as the lighter Key West sloops gained ground. At a hundred yards, the nearest boat fired a rifle: the puff of smoke was followed a moment later by the whizz of a bullet flying through the mainsail. The sound of the shot was seconds behind. The crew finally took a few moments to get Sykas out of his dive suit and he joined them behind the forward cabin of the Sponger. They had a single firearm on the boat, and knew they would have no chance in either outrunning the lighter boats or outfighting them. The Key Westers came to do battle and serve notice to other Greeks they were not welcome in these waters. Seeing no other option, the Greek boat, furled its sails and hoisted a white cloth in surrender. As the Key West boats approached, one exuberant waterman fired his pistol, hitting Sykas in the leg. The captain of the Key Sponger struck the shooter down with the back of his hand. "We want no bloodshed," he shouted. "I'll make sure this man is punished, but we're going to burn your boat." The Greeks, seeing no other alternative, stepped off the Greek boat at gunpoint, carrying the wounded diver with them. "My dive suit!" Sykas pleaded. "It's all I own. Can I take it with me?" The captain nodded, and the crew gathered up the heavy suit and loaded it on the schooner. With all off the ship, the conchs lit the wick on a bottle of kerosene and threw it on the Sponger, and backed off to watch the ship burn to the waterline.

Stavos Sykas' wound was not life threatening, and a doctor managed to remove the bullet and dress the wound. News of the "battle" was all over town, and the police put the Greeks in protective custody until they could be shipped out on a boat back north.

A week later, the Navy destroyer USS Lawrence took charge of the Greek Spongers and transported them back to

Tampa, where they made their way home to Tarpon Springs. Sykas recovered from his wound, and eventually managed to buy his own boat with the money he made from selling the gold chain he found. He also made a careful note on a chart where he found that chain. He knew there was likely more treasure near there, maybe even a complete wreck. His non-welcome status in the Keys, followed by World War two, and then old age, prevented him from ever returning to the site, but the chart and his journal were kept in his chest, and one day they would inspire his great grandson to return to that place to seek treasure.

Needle in a Haystack

Monday morning, the *Captain Morgan* cast off from the dock in front of the houseboat and came up to speed, moving west at eighteen knots towards Boca Grande. The *Morgan* was an old, big, deep hulled boat with decent speed. If you loaded it with plenty of provisions, you could make a pleasant home aboard for days at a time, and she was big enough that you could comfortably ride out all save a serious storm. Now that my kids were ashore on the houseboat, they would be fine for a few days, and Maggie would drop by occasionally (and unannounced) to make sure everyone played nice. Bouncing along behind the boat was Bo's Zodiac, which would come in handy anytime skinny water was around. On the way to the site, I chatted with Bo and his son about the fake gold bars, and puzzled over what they were, where they came from and how they got where they were found. Something was tickling the back of Bo's memory, and to be honest, a distant memory was rattling around in the cobwebs of my brain too. A little microfilm research in the Key West library might be in order when this treasure hunting thing was over. Either that or I needed to pay a visit to a hypnotist. Maybe a psychic?

Coming out of retirement wasn't new to Bo Morgan. He had done it before, and, if push came to shove, he was actually enjoying the chance to get behind the wheel of the *Captain Morgan* one more time, a boat he had enjoyed so many incredible experiences with. Along with finding treasure with Mel Fisher, there was the time it had been boarded – and impounded by Cuban rebels. Bo had ended up in a Cuban jail, interrogated by none other than Raul Castro and Che Guevara and almost ended up in front of a firing squad. He was sure that he would never see the boat again, and for that matter, thought the odds were good that he would never come home. Accused of being a spy and a smuggler (one of out of two wasn't bad), he suddenly was released in the middle of the night, thrown on his boat and told to never come back. It wasn't till the following day that he found out President John Kennedy had blockaded the island, flown over with spy planes and threatened to start World War Three. They just apparently decided to clean up all the loose ends at the same time, and it was a lucky break they didn't decide to hide Bo, the *Captain Morgan*, and the rest of the evidence in 900 feet of the Florida Straits. There were other stories, some public and denied, others private and unbelievable, but sufficient to say, Bo Morgan had enjoyed a life that was far from dull, and it appeared there was going to be one more chapter in the play.

Morgan throttled down the big boat as we approached the place where we found the Spanish cannon. Tack and I stepped down into the Zodiac, and Bo passed down a couple of long poles with flags attached, which had been quietly borrowed from the 7th and 8th green at the Key West Golf Club last night. We beached the Zodiac and I had little trouble finding the site this time. Jamming one flag right in the depression, Tack walked ashore about fifteen feet, and shoved the second flag in the sand, lining up with the depression as best as we could reckon. If Harry's hunch was right, the wreck was lying somewhere out "that way" in about thirty five to fifty five feet of water. Maybe two to three miles away. We shall see.

Re-boarding the *Morgan*, we began to plot a grid on the

marine chart. Assuming this wreck didn't break up, and scatter treasure over Hell and half of the Caribbean like the *Atocha* did, I think this wreck will be covering a relatively small spot, say about forty by ninety feet, with most of the treasure concentrated at the stern. That's 3600 square feet of target; say the size of a four bedroom house, lying on a three mile by three mile grid, totaling 251 *million* square feet of ocean bottom. A needle in a haystack would be considered child's play compared to this. This challenge, combined with the very real possibility that there would be virtually no visible surface evidence of the wreck after more than 150 years and the task becomes nearly inconceivable. It took Mel Fisher sixteen years to find the *Atocha,* and he had more boats, more people and better resources. Of course, the treasure he found was greater too. Finding this wreck could still make some people exceptionally rich.

So, how to find this needle? By towing an underwater magnetometer, which detects magnetic anomalies in the immediate area, and "mowing the lawn", dragging the device back and forth over an assigned grid. Using a GPS, the task was much easier than years ago, but it was still slow, boring work, and the false alarms would drive you nuts. Piled at the back of the *Captain Morgan* was a mound of used lobster buoy balls, each with a length of fishing line and a piece of cinderblock. Every time the Mag recorded a "hit" Bo would call out, and we would toss one of the balls overboard. Unfortunately, it would hit on every piece of sea junk, World War II practice bombs, shrimper junk and other flotsam that had been thrown in the ocean since man could float a boat, so false alarms were countless. With time and more importantly money, at a premium, we decided on a different tact, at least to start. We plotted a very narrow area to concentrate the search. Lining up the two flags, and starting at about twenty feet of depth, we began working the grid. We wanted to take a few weeks to do what might take ten years, and it's possible, even likely that we might never find our target.

From sunrise to sunset the boat worked the pattern, and, for the moment we tried ignoring the light "hits" and concentrated on the strongest signals. After three days, we had five areas that showed real promise, and it was time to get back in the water. I called the crew, and they came out to start working the spots, and we took the *Captain Morgan* back to Key West and the kids. I would come back for the weekend.

As expected, there was a lot more trash than treasure in that ocean. First find was a rusty bicycle, then an outboard motor that had likely ripped itself off a fishing boat. The next dive revealed two World War II 500 pound bombs lying partially covered on the bottom. You never know if you should avoid these or not. This entire area was used as a practice bombing range during the war, and actually up and through the seventies and you never knew if these were dummy practice rounds or a live shell that could go off with the lightest touch and blow you to Valhalla. The last site turned out to be only a mass of crab and lobster traps. These have a tendency to gather together during a hurricane and create a massive ball of useless wire. Mankind has used the ocean for a dump for a century. It made treasure hunting all that more complicated.

I had to take a little break from the action as I needed to get the kids registered in Key West High School. I had already got their transcripts sent to the school. It was no huge surprise that Grace was majoring in singing and in honor roll classes everywhere else. It was also no major surprise that Brody was majoring in auto shop with a minor in recess. Grace would no doubt graduate high school near the top of her class, and equally likely that Brody would hold down the other end of the bell curve. It wasn't that he was dumb. He was actually smart as heck but just didn't see any major need in school. He would probably figure it out some day but likely long after I succeeded in dragging him kicking and screaming through his senior year. At the open house night, we met teachers, instructors and coaches, and in fact, as we walked out of the school to get in the Bitch Box and drive home, the varsity football coach, Ralph Curry, followed us out. He introduced himself to me and made nice with Grace, then shook Brody's hand like a politician running for office, you know, those one hand on the shoulder kinds. I think he was just feeling for muscles as he tried to see if Brody's six foot, three inch, 260 pound frame was fit or flab. He headed my boy off before he could get in the car and asked if he had thought of playing ball. "I played freshman and junior varsity in Sandusky," Brody replied. Mostly rode the bench, so I didn't go out in my junior year." I watched, mildly amused, and kept my mouth shut as I knew at the beginning of his Junior Year, Brody was about five-five and weighed 200 pounds and was about as coordinated as a five-legged donkey.

"Well, son, are you in good health?" the coach asked.

"Not really, sir. All I eat is junk food, I don't exercise, and I'm non-violent. I don't think I've got what it takes to play football."

This was an outright lie. Well, the food part isn't. If it's not called a cheeseburger, or is breaded and fried, he doesn't eat it. He says green vegetables isn't food, it's what food eats. But as far as physical condition, he has over six hundred scuba dives in his log book, can free dive to seventy feet, and stay under for just a bit over two minutes, not to mention he's a second-degree black belt in Tai-Kwan-Do. I suspect he could handle a football game.

"Broderick, would you mind taking your sister for a five minute walk? I would like to chat with your dad." Brody put his hand in his pockets and strolled back toward the school entrance. Grace Alice got out of the car and went the other way.

Ah, sibling love.

"You know, Mr. Wahl, being a native Conch has its advantages. Our boosters would love to have a home-grown starting lineman with the potential your son has. He's got All-American written all over him. Let's just say that we have a special arrangement with the Nissan dealer. How would you like to be driving a nice new King Cab tomorrow and throw this piece of junk away?"

"Mr. Curry, I appreciate the offer. I'll ask my son if he wants to play ball, it's entirely up to him. Throwing a new truck at me isn't going to change his life much, and his heart is in the ocean, but you will have to ask him."

"I already have and he said no. This was my only other chance."

I thought the coach was going to cry.

The weekend came, and I farmed the kids out to Maggie again. This was gonna cost me dinner at A&B Lobster at the least and jewelry if it stretched out much longer. Bo and I stopped by Conch Marina to top off the *Captain* with gas before heading to the site. One of the crew was there in the Zodiac and jumping up and down when he saw us. "What's up?" I ask as I pulled up to the dock. "Anchor! We found the anchor to the treasure wreck just off Boca Grande!" "*The* anchor? You mean *an* anchor. And could you maybe yell the location a little louder? I don't think the crowd on the Sunset Pier two miles away quite heard you the first time. From now on, it's not Boca Grande. Just call the site Treasure Key." I looked over at Bo, who was casually sipping on bottled water and looking at best disinterested. He shrugged and quietly suggested maybe it was time for a look. We tied the Zodiac behind the *Morgan* and headed out to the site. The rest of the crew was equally animated and couldn't wait to help me into my dive gear. I tipped backwards over the side of the *La Brisa* and followed the line down 45 feet where the unmistakable bulk of an old anchor tip loomed in the afternoon light. Despite the sea life that had it covered, the sharp, arrow point shape looked to be correct for the period we were seeking. The size was maybe a little small for a ship of the line, but it was still worth checking out. It was most likely a Spanish anchor and hopefully from the ship we were seeking. The *Captain Morgan* didn't have any gear to haul this much weight up, so it was going to have to stay in place till the *La Brisa* came back to life and back on the site.

Aside from archeological value, ships anchors are some of the best possible direction finders in the ocean. Assuming the galleon was probably in distress due to a storm (since it sank, duh) and dropped that anchor in an effort to stay put, the anchor would have been directly upwind from where the ship may have eventually ended. The shaft of the anchor could be likely pointing right at the wreck. Since we had a possible line of sight down those two golf flags over the old cannon that might be also pointing at the wreck, we might just have that site triangulated to a few square miles. How darn lucky would that be?

But it looked like our calculations were going to have to be put on hold for a few days.

There was a storm a brewin.

Spam Insurance

From very early in my life, I've had a nose for weather. Along with loving rain, waterspouts, powerful thunderstorms and hurricanes, I've always had a strong interest for what weather was doing, or what it was going to do. My Grandpa, John Pinder Russell fed some of that Conch instinct into me, teaching me the way to read weather before there was a Weather Channel, NOAA, satellites and buxom blonde weathergirls on TV that were hired more for their ability to fill a sweater than find a low pressure center. I so fondly remember Saturday morning sailing trips in the little Key West built sloop *Johnny B*, while grandpa showed me the difference between fair weather clouds, icy cirrus clouds, towering Cumulus clouds and ominous Mammus clouds, (called so because of their shape that resembles a woman's breast). He would point out flat bottom clouds that frequently create waterspouts. He showed me how incredibly blue the sky was a day or so before a hurricane arrived, and how to track a hurricane without the use of a computer or weather channel by noting wind direction. "Hurricanes in the Northern Hemisphere rotate counter-clockwise. If it's approaching from the east and the wind is coming dead out of the north, then the storm is pointed more or less right at you. If the wind is from the east, it's below you, from the west it's above you. If you're soaking wet, swimming for your life, and your house is blown down, then it's pretty damn near." Grandpa also reminded me to respect storms. "My granddad died in a hurricane," He told me. "Took his boat out in the gulf like a fool on some wild assed mission at the end of the Civil War, and he was never seen again. All they ever found was the boat he stole from his Uncle Joe."

Part of weather sense is instinct, a "feel" for the weather, and sometimes that intuition can be more valuable than all the technology in the world. Combine that instinct with modern technology and you can sometimes outguess the so called experts. In the Keys, storms can come from almost any direction, dead out of the east, from the south over Cuba, or from the west when a storm comes through the Yucatan Channel and then hooks back to the right as they often do late in the season. No place in the United States, and for that matter, almost nowhere on the planet, is more susceptible or in danger due to tropical storms than the Florida Keys.

Anytime between June and the end of October is hurricane season, and when you lived in the Keys, you always stayed aware of the weather. When a storm formed out in the Atlantic, you pay attention when the storm is "below" you or in latitude under the 24 or so degrees that was home to Key West. Storms in the Atlantic usually curved north as they approached the mainland. When they drew abreast of you, you could ignore them; they were someone else's problem. Sometimes they didn't turn. Hurricane Georges in 1997 was one of them. It was the first storm to directly impact the Keys since Donna in 1960 the four-decade quiet spell had created a sense of false security. "Storms don't hit the Keys," was a commonly heard quote. "The reef protects you," was another. Apparently nobody read the history books as in years gone by, the middle and lower Keys had been hit time and time again with strong tropical systems. The 1935 Hurricane that hit Islamorada marked the lowest barometric pressure ever recorded, a record that still stands to this day. A total of 51 hurricanes have been over, or near Key West in the last 140 years. Every year there isn't one, its one year closer to when you will be hit.

Now, just two weeks after moving into our houseboat home and the same day we found the anchor, a tropical depression formed south of Puerto Rico. As anxious as we were to try out our hunch in the ocean, we needed to pull up and head home. Like I said, the *La Brisa* isn't very fast, and it would not be wise to hang around out here too long. We took careful GPS coordinates of the anchor, and the location and direction of the cannon and headed back to the harbor. It was good that we did as in three days the depression became Tropical Storm Elaine and quickly after that, Hurricane Elaine. NOAA and the weather channel predicted it to become a major hurricane, then "shoot the straights" between the Dominican Republic and Cuba, and move northwest into the Florida Straits. These storms are the most dangerous. They are close, and preparation time is limited, and when they get into the Gulf of Mexico, it's a certainty that it will hit *somebody somewhere*. As it was, The Keys, and especially Key West would likely get some impact.

While I had a good instinct for storms, I wasn't above using technology at hand. Getting Grace a laptop when we moved in to the houseboat gave me a new tool. Satellite views, NOAA live feed and radar gives the ability to help interpret the fluff that was being delved out by the current Tits-on a-Tray that was doing the six-o'clock weather on channel four. That intensely blue sky that my grandpa had shown me long ago was over Key West right now. The wind was a light breeze, but dead out of the south – the storm was below us and, it would be prudent to keep an eye.

I reached in my wallet for some cash. "Brody, take the Bitch Box and head down to the Publix for a few pre storm items and pre mad rush items. Won't hurt to have them around anyway."

"Ok dad. What do I get?"

"Pick up two cases of Zephyrhills water, some chips, a box of those coffee creamers that you don't have to refrigerate, canned Canadian bacon, some bread, peanut butter, some Top Ramen, canned chili and some soup, apples and a can of Spam."

"Spam? What in the world do we want with that?"

"It's my hurricane deterrent. Even God wouldn't make someone have to eat cold Spam. Keeps the storms away. Oh, and a dozen D and AA batteries, and drop by Home Depot for some plastic drop cloths, a large roll of duct tape, and a waterproof flashlight if they have one."

Brody drove off while I consulted with my landlord about storm prep. "The houseboat did fine in the last few storms," reported Bo. It just rises and falls with any surge, and as long as you pull away the gangplank to the entry, tie it away from the pilings and make sure nothing runs into it, you can weather a pretty good storm.

By Tuesday afternoon, the storm track had narrowed to a likely landfall right over Key West sometime Thursday morning. The county had already issued a mandatory tourist evacuation the day before and followed with a mandatory resident evacuation the following morning. Like all Keys hurricanes, these orders are met with mixed response. About half the people that left during the last storm vowed they would never leave again. The other half that stayed vowed they would never stay again. After Wilma, when much of the island ended up underwater, the leavers were a little more prevalent than the stayers, but it was still likely that Elaine would have the chance to threaten more than ten thousand souls.

I weighed several options and concerns. My biggest concern was Grace, a problem that was solved fifteen minutes later when Maggie came by to scoop everyone up and head north. I thought for a minute but between concern for my personal belongings and Brody's pleading to stay and experience his first hurricane helped me with the decision. I elected to send my daughter north, while the men would stay and, as they say, "hunker down." As Maggie drove out of sight, I knew we had committed to something, but I wasn't sure what.

Now that it was a real threat, it was time to pad our stockpile of storm supplies a little more. We climbed into the Thing and headed down to the Publix grocery store and walked into a scene from "Panic in the Year Zero." People were careening through the store with shopping carts, throwing anything that wasn't perishable or bolted to the floor, into their cart. All liquids, water, soda, juice, beer and wine, was long gone. Chips, canned food, bread, hard fruit, pasta, sauce, Mac and cheese, rice, all cleaned out. All that was left were frozen foods, deli and fresh meats. We drove by the other two stores, and they were much the same, and there wasn't a drop of ice anywhere on the island. I mumbled that hurricanes must have been invented by the grocery and liquor stores, and then made a decision, pulling the Bitch Box out onto US1 and headed up the Keys.

"Where we headed?"

"We need to expand our foraging horizons," I explained. "Marathon."

Marathon Key is about fifty miles from Key West, and, at the posted 45 miles per hour, a little over an hour away. By Wednesday afternoon, all the evacuates had long gone, and the road was devoid of both traffic and Monroe County Sheriffs, who were all gathered at the Cudjoe Substation to get their emergency program in order, which probably meant they would try and determine which Dunkin Donut store would stay open the longest. As I drove by the station, I counted four cars which meant we had clear sailing all the way to the Seven Mile Bridge. Not that I could trust my car much above forty-five miles per hour, but better time could definitely be made. As suspected, Marathon was in nowhere near as much panic as Key West. They expected no more than a glancing blow, and you could hardly see more than business as usual at the grocery store. We grabbed a cart and stocked up on the kind of essentials that you took so much for granted on normal days. Water was important, ice critical, and protein. You never think that carbs are a room temperature product while protein must be refrigerated mostly until you start thinking that you may be without electricity for a few weeks. I also splurged and bought a twelve pack of Icehouse beer and a dozen six-packs of IBC Root beer for my son, and back down the Keys we headed. If there were few cars heading north, the southbound lanes were nearly empty. As close as the storm was, less than ninety miles away, the day was still beautifully sunny and blue. As we passed through Big Pine, over the bridge to Ramrod Key, on impulse I slowed and wheeled into Boondocks. "Let's get a cooked meal. Might be a while before we see any restaurant food."

The parking lot at Boondocks, normally semi-full with both tourists and locals, had only a few vehicles in it, and looking at the collection of pickups, tattered convertibles, mopeds and bikes, it was evident they were mostly all locals. We hoisted up on barstools and, after ordering beverages, turned our attention to the Weather Channel. I sipped a draft and sat quietly amused as the locals boasted with loud bravado about experiencing dozens of hurricanes, and this one didn't scare them one bit. One dirt bag announced to the room that he planned to sit here all night and the next day drinking beer and having a "Hurrycane" party.

I sipped my beer and fingered my lucky pendant. I always thought of it as my personal hurricane luck charm. It looked like it might have lost some of its mojo.

"Dad, can I look at it for a second?" Brody asked. I pulled the chain over my neck and handed it to him. The four-Reale coin was grade one, meaning excellent condition and the hand stamped image was nearly perfectly centered, which was fairly rare. The bezel was eighteen carat gold, designed and custom made by my friend Cindy. Three dolphins and a mermaid surrounded the coin, and the mermaid held a tiny chip of emerald from the Atocha that had accidentally found its way into my dive glove one day. Dozens of people had tried to buy it from me, and a few stupid ones tried to take it away. Up till now, it was still in my possession, although Key West Pawn had occasionally "stored" it for me for a few months when I needed a quick thousand bucks.

"What do all these markings mean?" Brody asked. I used my best Discovery Channel voice and explained. "The Spanish Reale, or Cob, was hand struck in Mexico, Peru and Columbia, starting less than forty years after Columbus landed in the new world. The design changed a few times, mostly depending on who was currently in charge back home in Spain. For this coin, one side has a crowned multi-element shield representing the lands under Spanish control." I flipped the coin over. "The other side displays a cross with lions and castles in the four

95

quadrants, representing the two main principalities of Spain at the time, Castille and Leon. The cross had another use. These coins were called 'Pieces of Eight', or eight Reales. Back in the day, that was quite a bit of money for the common man so they would cut the coins into four pieces, using that cross as a guide. You could even cut it into eighths, which were called 'bits', so two of them was 'two bits'. Today, an American quarter is still called 'two bits' and the high-school cheer, 'two bits, four bits, six bits, a dollar' stems from Spanish Pieces of Eight."

"Wow dad, home schooling. Any more wisdom so I can ace my next history test?"

"Now that you mention it, yes. During the California Gold Rush, one of the quickest ways from the East Coast to the West was via ship to the Isthmus of Panama, then mule overland to the coast, and back on a ship to San Francisco. The Forty-Niners learned that if they changed their dollars at home into bags of dimes, those dimes would be treated as 'bits' in Latin America while a silver dollar was treated with the same value as Eight Reales, so that meant that eight dimes were equal to a dollar. Twenty percent more value."

I also explained how those guys that used to hack the coins into four pieces would often nick a tiny piece of silver off each one and keep it for extra profit. Their nickname is still in use today to describe someone who cheats. They were called "Chiselers." That's why the newer "Pillar Dollars" were so popular because they were milled around the edges and it became much harder for the chiselers to nick a piece off. It was too obvious.

"Enough edumacation dad. I'll get an A on the term paper now. What's going on with the storm?"

We turned back to the Weather Channel, and the current tits on sticks had just gone remote to Marathon Key. Although it was only twenty five miles away and forty five minutes since we left there, it was a much different place. The camera showed a sky black as night, and palm fronds, trash can lids, and everything not bolted down was flying past the screen. The reporter was leaning into a strong wind and trying to shout above the noise level. We looked at the TV, then outside of the open air tiki hut bar in puzzlement as it was still blue skies and light breezes. "Is this live or some other old storm they are showing on TV?" I stepped out under the thatched bar and looked to the East and saw a low, gray cloud in the distance. As if in fast-motion, the cloud grew larger, and in moments, enveloped the entire horizon. No more than a few minutes later, Ramrod Key changed from summer tranquility to Hurricane Elaine. Dense overcast zoomed over the island, and winds whipped the flag at tropical storm force. In my whole life, I had never seen a storm arrive in such abrupt fashion. I started to remark to the locals that it looked like the storm was here and the whole room of drunks that had been sucking beers down a few seconds before, were nowhere in sight. Beers were half consumed, cigarettes still lit, food left on the countertop. The bartender was even gone. I turned to Brody with a smile and said "guess we need to finish and pay up." We finished our burgers, and I tossed the rest of my beer down. I dug out a twenty and started to tuck it under the beer mug, and then realized all I would be doing was throwing money at Mother Nature, so I re-pocketed the money, and we left. I'll return next week and settle this tab.

If there happened to be a Boondocks left.

Climbing in the car, we were now confronted with a 27 mile trip to Key West in an open air car through steadily increasing strong winds, driving rain and flying debris. My weather mind started to kick in, and you could see the wind was just slightly west of due north, meaning the storm was at our back and likely taking dead aim on Key West. By the time we were halfway home, we drove back out of the storm and into blue skies again. Brody turned around in his seat and watched the storm cloud in awe. "Stop the car again dad! I want to go thru that again!" "Not in your life," I replied. "We need to get home, unload and button up."

97

Muther Nature's Blowjob

We drove into Key West and down Hilton Haven Drive to the houseboat. I was honking the horn before we pulled up, alerting Bo and Tack that the storm was hot on our heels. They had already double tied the boats, and the heavy metal gangplank that attached the houseboat to land had been replaced by a two by twelve. With Tack's help, we unloaded the VW, and then I told Brody to throw his bike in the Bitch Box and drive to the covered parking lot on Caroline Street and park on the third floor. Ten minutes after he drove away, the storm arrived. I was a little concerned, but not too much. After forty minutes, I got a little more worried, but there he came, on foot and soaking wet. "What happened?" I asked. "I got the car put away, and was halfway back when the storm hit. The first gust blew me off the bike and into the street. I jumped up and got out of the way, but the bike is now a hood ornament for a Budweiser Truck." Toweling his hair off, he turned to me "Okay Dad, I've had my hurricane, can we leave now?" That was with a grin.

The houseboat was still a boat, and the trick to getting a boat to survive a storm is to tie it secure, but not too tight. You have to be sure it's not grinding into immovable surfaces, and that water doesn't fill it up. Aside from the problem of the wind blowing water through windows and sliding doors, the houseboat was fairly tight. It was securely tied and cushioned with old tires. The other three tenants had fled the island, leaving their house keys with Bo, so we made sure nothing breakable was sitting on any shelves and with all other preparations made, turned on the TV and started dinner. I opened the laptop to check the National Hurricane Center, while Brody got some pork chops going in a skillet. "Wow dad, whitecaps in the frying pan!" Winds were only about forty knots, but the houseboat was already banging around quite a bit. Every time the boat slammed into the pilings, the whole structure shuddered, even through the circle of tires. I started to get a little concerned that the houseboat would not fare well with winds twice this strong.

Did we screw up?

As darkness approached, the view out of the sliding glass door became almost surreal, with the wind whipping the bay into foam, debris flying by, and at least three boats in the bay, including our old home, already broken loose and heading for unknown destinations. Just as Brody served dinner, there was a bright flash reflected in the back window and everything went dark. Blown transformer likely. "Well, that's that," I said. "No more power, no TV, no computer, no running water, no flush toilets. Time to go caveman." We turned on the battery powered storm lamp, and ate dinner in silence. Then I remembered the battery powered radio and tuned into US1 Radio, where the news crew was again providing non-stop news and information, like they do every time we have a storm. Operating on generator power, the radio station was the only link to reality for the "hunker downers." It was good to hear a voice, and good to know you weren't the only person in harm's way.

Sleep was impossible that night. The temperature was eighty five degrees and the humidity was one hundred percent, but you didn't dare crack a window as the wind was fast approaching hurricane strength. The houseboat was slamming into the wooden pilings every few seconds with a shuddering impact. We sat in the living room, helpless, half worried and half exhilarated with excitement. Then about three a.m. there was a loud crash downstairs, and we checked the unit below to find a tree branch had blown in from someplace up the street and taken a bathroom window out. Now exposed to the elements, the room was awash in blowing papers and driving rain. There was no way to secure the broken window and all I could do was close the shower curtain and the bathroom door and hope for the best. The night raged on. The radio said the eye should pass over Key West about nine a.m., and the storms winds were expected to peak at 105 knots.

In the gloomy dawn, the storm's full fury attacked the houseboat. We were now hanging on, literally, and despite both being experienced watermen, it was starting to wear us out. Those pork chops were sitting in my stomach like bricks, and we were exhausted from the constant banging and jostling all night. Winds outside were screaming, and the houseboat was starting to take some damage. Roof tarpaper was flying off, and another window blew, this time on the upstairs unit across the hall. You could also start to detect a slight list. This was not good. About three p.m., the wind started to die down, and in moments it became eerily calm. "Is it over, just like that?" asked Brody. "No. We're in the eye," Quickly, we ran down the stairs and jumped across to dry land. The yard was a mess. A big ficus tree across the street was down, laying over a carport and the hood of somebody's BMW. Bo poked his head out of his door. "Everyone okay?" He asked. "We're fine, but I think the houseboat has a leak." "Saw that. No huge worries," he replied. "Grab my generator and plug in the bilge pump. Worst case, it will just settle to the bottom of the bay. Maybe flood the bottom two floors a foot or so. Can you go in the downstairs unit and put things up for them? Better hurry, this eye won't be over us for more that fifteen minutes."

We each took a unit and did our best to put everything possible on countertops, dresser tops and shelves. Unit number one was already starting to get wet, and by the time I was done, I was wading in eight inches of water. I sat the generator in the stairwell, with the exhaust hopefully pointing towards outdoors and ran a cord to the pump in the hull of the barge. With luck, we could hold even with the leak.

As we started back up the stairs, the wind started to come up again, this time from the south.

The backside of a hurricane can be worse than the front side, but, being on the north end of the island, we would get a little break from the worst of the winds while it tore up South Roosevelt Drive. While the front of the storm caused a little storm surge, raising the water level about a foot, the backside was doing a much better job of pushing water around and out of the bay and in twenty minutes, the houseboat was sitting high and dry on the bottom. This was a good thing, as the bilge pump was going to be able to keep up, and we would stop banging all over the place. It was a huge difference from Wilma when a five foot storm surge darn near flooded the whole island.

After spending most of the day in a washing machine, this seemed almost like fun. Most of what was loose in the neighborhood had already blown away, and most of the flooding and damage was occurring somewhere else. As dusk approached, we both fell asleep, me on the couch and Brody in the chair, lulled by the slowly descending winds.

The sound, or actually, the lack of it, woke me up. The loudest thing I could hear was the chatter of the little Honda generator that covered the hum of the bilge pump. A full moon shown on the bay, and the boat rocked slightly, and, thankfully, normally. I flipped the radio back on, and Brody bounced out of the chair like a prizefighter at the bell, tripping over the coffee table and missed bailing over the balcony into the bay by dad catching the back of his belt as he flew by. "Whoa there, big guy, where you heading?" I asked. Brody came to his senses and looked outside. "Was that a really bad dream?" "Nope," I replied. "You just popped your hurricane cherry."

The power was still out, not just in the boat but probably in all of the Lower Keys. Thankfully the houseboat used propane for the stove, so I poured some bottled water in the kettle and made a cup of coffee in the plunge press. It might have been eighty degrees with a hundred percent humidity, but that coffee was the most delicious thing I have ever tasted in my life. Brody's inability to go more than eleven waking minutes without eating kicked in and he pulled out some bacon and eggs for a four a.m. breakfast call. I didn't know how much damage was done to the power grid, but it was very likely that our perishable food would not stay fresh till the juice came back on. We might as well eat it all now. There were some nice steaks in the freezer that would keep us nourished for the next few days at least. As long as you keep the freezer door closed, it will keep meat stiff for five or six days. You eat from it till things thaw and then have one gigantic barbecue and invite the neighbors.

Looking backward, I would say that the two weeks after Hurricane Elaine were worse than the two days of the storm. We ventured out after the storm and walked into town to get our car. It was a mess, but not a terrible one. Georges back in 1998 took out all the shallow rooted ficus trees, so it was mostly loose debris, lots of palm fronds, and everybody's aluminum storage shed that littered the neighborhood. We fired up the Bitch Box and motored down Duval Street to explore. About forty feet down the street a Monroe County Sherriff flagged us down. "Lock down curfew till Friday," he advised. "Okay, we will just drive home then," I responded. "The bridge at Garrison Bight isn't passable, so we have to go the long way." He motioned us on, and a hundred feet later, we got stopped again. "I know, I know, curfew," I preempted the conversation. "My dog ran a way, and we saw him run this way. Can we just go fetch him?" We bullshitted our way down Duval till we got to the end, and then used fifteen different stories to get us as far as the Casa Marina. Fortunately, I know half the Monroe County Sheriffs and Brody knows all the Fish and Wildlife guys that were out helping keep the town safe. I knew the Sheriffs for good reasons; Brody was in a little more of a grey area with the FWC guys. They never caught him with contraband, but were convinced that he fished, shot and hunted sea life by his own standards. That being said, they almost respected his skills. Either way, we had gotten close enough to the other side of the island that our excuse "we're going home", will work from here on. As it turned out, home was about the only place we could go from here as all the man-made beaches that surrounded the south side of Key West were now a couple of blocks inland, along with lots of flotsam, debris and at least one sixty five foot sailing yacht that was high and dry, two blocks up White Street. The south side of the rock got it worse than us for sure.

We headed over to the harbor to see how the boats were doing. *The La Brisa*, fondly nicknamed La Brick was bobbing happily at anchor, resting nicely on top of somebody's forty five foot Scarab go-fast boat. Lots of other boats were in various stages of sunk, but my crew knows how to tie off boats and all of our craft seemed to be just fine. As anxious as I was to get back out on the site, I knew it would be a while as some of the crew had families to take care of and houses to repair. For that matter, we had some work to do ourselves. We made our way back to the houseboat and got ready to survey the damage. The little generator was still running and keeping the leak at bay. We re-filled the generator and Brody, and I donned some dive gear to inspect the hull of the barge. The bay was murky with silt and mud, and we couldn't see a thing. I got out and climbed into the inside of the barge with a flashlight. This was not a place for the claustrophobic, and for that matter, the smell wasn't all that wonderful either. It didn't take long to find the issue; a whole seam on the side had taken a significant hit and was buckled. Water was dribbling out through a crack in the plywood and into the hull. This was going to need some major attention.

I walked over to Bo's place and described the issue. He offered a short term, and a long term solution. Digging in a box in the storage room he came up with three tubes of certified Gorilla Snot, guaranteed to be waterproof, bullet proof and leak proof. I thanked him and asked about the long term solution. "Something I did with a boat many years ago," replied Bo. We can have a fiberglass impregnated 'diaper" built for the boat."

"A diaper? Now that would be quite a changing job." Bo laughed and explained that it's a waterproof cover that goes under the entire houseboat and comes up past the waterline. "You just throw it in the water, drag it under the hull, snug it up and then start pumping out the ocean."

I gave Brody the honor of going back in the water, scraping the hull with a wire brush and then gooping the stuff all over the seam. One application and it was down to a trickle and by the third tube, the leak had stopped. Our little home was waterproofed again for the time being.

The next week was spent doing cleanup, replacing some windows and drying the place out. Power was still out in the Keys and we were down to eating canned beans, canned chili, canned tuna and canned soup. We had about ten days' worth of supplies, and I had already shared part of my stash with some of the locals that were far worse off than us. Still no power, no water, no flush toilets (don't even go there), and of course no A/C. That meant hot days followed by cold showers followed by a canned dinner and a night of sweating in a very warm bed.

Like I said at the beginning, I'm getting too old for this shit.

Back to Normal in an
Abnormal Place

There was one up side to the aftermath of a hurricane. Every night all the people in the neighborhood would pool their food and beverages and have a barbecue. Bo locked the dogs in the house, and we invited families on both sides of us to join us every evening. We sat around the grill, consumed beer and wine, ate steaks, pork chops and lobster tails and we pulled out acoustical guitars. The more we drank, the better we sounded. It was a great way to pass the night, but if the power didn't come on pretty soon, half of us would be committed to AA, and the other half to Jenny Craig.

As I mentioned, when a hurricane is coming you have a pre-hurricane party. When it's here, you have a hurricane party. So what do you do after it passes? Have a post-hurricane party! Sandra, one of the waitresses from Buzzards came by at about day seven and told me they were going to open Saturday night, and can I make it to play with the band? "Okay, I give up," I responded. "What do they plan to do? Sit in a circle jerk, suck on raw potatoes, shove kazoos up our ass and play fart songs?" "No, were gonna have power!" Sandra went on to explain that they had hauled in a big mother diesel generator, three hundred gallons of fuel, five hundred pounds of ice and a medium sized truckload of food and adult beverages from Miami. And get this: all free to locals. Nice guys.

I've been playing off and on at Buzzards since it opened six months ago. A gay couple, John and Ed, moved into town

105

with the concept of opening a restaurant. They wanted to name it the Hidden Pickle and have all the wait staff dress as drag queens and serve tables in roller skates. The concept was good, but the mission would be finding people coordinated enough to wear roller skates and still be willing to wear a ball gown. It became clear in a hurry that staffing would be as much of a challenge as it was for Hooters when they came into town in 1998 and couldn't find thirty five decent looking young women that would wear both a bra and pantyhose, had less than fourteen visible tattoos and more than eleven teeth. The only real taker was Scarlet, who fit all the requirements and could roller skate. But, alas, that was the only qualified applicant, so the dream faded as quickly as a cobalt blue size fifty-four silk dress in a morning sun window at Fast Buck Freddie's.

I met John and Ed one afternoon at A&B Lobster, where I was enjoying the local's appetizer specials and soaking up Mojitos. They were from Bermuda, where they had just sold a highly successful lumber business, kind of the Home Depot of Bermuda. Between selling that and their amazing house, that was located on the top of the highest point on Bermuda, they had a buttload of cash burning a hole in their pockets, or in this case their European shoulder bags. We chatted, and they lamented on their restaurant concept that they couldn't get off the ground, and suddenly the Mojitos took control of my mouth. "Guys, I have an idea for a restaurant that's a guaranteed winner, and I'll give the concept to you for nothing, except for maybe an occasional steak dinner."

I proceeded to tell them about my idea of a restaurant/bar named Buzzards, sort of a road kill café concept, where the menu and drinks were named after disgusting dead creatures. The keystone of the restaurant was a special made cooktop that had grill irons in the shape of tire tracks that would lay the pattern on all of their grilled steaks, chicken and seafood. They flipped out over the idea, bought a bar on Duval Street and opened up six weeks later. The theme was perfect, and the place became popular with tourists and locals. The idea was taken a step beyond as they bought a couple of animated parrots from Disney and had a taxidermist in Alaska convert them to stuffed buzzards, and placed them over the entryway. The staff took turns at a microphone from the second floor, and the animated birds chatted with the guests all day and night while they made off-color comments to everyone. It was a great hit, and quickly became a "must do" addition to the Duval Crawl.

I ended up doing more than eating there. I hooked up with my old band, the "Conch-outs", and we became the house band for Buzzards, and I played bass guitar when work didn't get in the way. Tips were pretty good, beer was free, and the scenery was never dull. The Conch-Outs were a four piece classic rock and blues band, consisting entirely of Key West natives, both black and white, and, we didn't sound half bad, especially after I had consumed four or five beers. The wreck had kept me away for the last month or so, but I was looking forward to some hot tunes, cold beer, and, get this.... friggin AIR CONDITIONING!

I didn't need to be asked twice.

Brody and I headed over early Saturday, partially to help set up and also to feel cool air for the first time in a week. We were still bachelors as Maggie and Grace continued to hang up the Keys with friends. I probably wouldn't see them until her house had power and her hotel opened back up. I was good with playing caveman with my son for another week.

I had completely forgotten that my bass was stored in a closet at Buzzards, but when I dug in the closet there it was, high, dry and ready to roll. Even though I had bottomed out a couple of times, my guitar was something that I never considered selling, even during the tough days. It was a 1973 Gibson Eb3 Ripper, one of the longest, heaviest and sweetest sounding musical instruments ever made. Thirty six inches of ebony fret board, two Super Humbucker pickups and a blonde wood finish that made it clear it wasn't one of your run-of-the-house-Fender Bassman. I went to work trying to get it tuned after forty days in humid weather, but it didn't take long till it acted like it would hold a tune.

What a crazy night. Give an island person free beer, free food and free music and they will get just as stupid as possible in a matter of a few hours. Just about the whole wreck crew showed up, and they did a terrific job killing brain cells, and most of the hospitality industry inhabited the rest of the room. Even Mick Murphy, local writer and part-time crime solver was camped in a corner, sitting with a beautiful Asian lady, nursing what was most certainly a Jameson's on the rocks and looking among other things, short. I saw Tack playing den mother and motioned him over to make sure nobody was blabbing about the wreck. I was especially concerned with Doobie, who spent half his paycheck on weed and the other half on Columbian marching powder. He was sitting with a couple of hygienically challenged Key West lowlifes that I know. I was concerned that his mouth appeared to be several chapters ahead of his brain. Robert was belting out his best Barry White impression so I could play without paying too much attention. I had only played those songs with Robert like six million times – I watched Doobie in some sort of animated conversation and the two dirt bags were listening carefully. They were half assed divers and had a fast boat – *The Nose Knows*– likely purchased with some of Doobie's money, as they were suspected of being one of the main local suppliers of cocaine. One was a conch and probably related to both sides of my clan as our family tree tends to not have too many branches over the last 150 years, with Russells, Currys, Alburys, Sawyers, Pinders and a few others popping up everywhere on a genealogy chart. You could sell "Happy Birthday Uncle Daddy" cards down here at the Walgreens. I gave Tack a raised eyebrow and motioned toward the table. He slid over and joined the party, and suddenly everyone got a little less animated. When a break came I sat my Gibson on the stand and joined the little party. "Well, if it isn't Itchy and Scab! You know, you guys sound like a diagnosis at a VD Clinic. What brings you to this fine establishment on a Saturday evening? No room under the White Street Pier?"

"Hey man, we're just enjoying the tunes and the free beer. It's a free world and, for that matter, a free ocean." Scab took a big pull from his longneck Bud, stared at me, and showed me three of his five lower teeth.

"This is true. Free for all of us, but between the two of us, there's only one with a permit to salvage a wreck out thataway." I motioned to the West with my thumb. "May I suggest you forget any parts of this little event on the outside chance you want to start freelancing? I don't want to see either of you or that butt-ugly boat anywhere past the kiddie pool on Trumbo."

"Yeah, and like who's gonna stop me?" Itchy replied, brilliantly.

I stood up. Tack stood up, and I heard about thirty chairs scrape the floor behind me. I was fairly sure the odds were in our favor, but this had the possibility of becoming a donnybrook that would make the six o'clock news. I turn around to see where the crowd was gonna line up, but when I turned back, Itchy and Scab were nowhere to be seen.

Disaster averted, we went back to music.

Something afoul was afoot.

The band played loud and hard all night long and I don't remember when I last had that many offers of casual nookie in one night. Between my son and a sense of guilt that Maggie was playing den mother to my daughter, I didn't accept any propositions, but it was not for lack of opportunity, and all that grain beverage bravery made it very, very tempting.

We got back to the houseboat at sunrise. I'm really glad my son is a good designated driver.

Eight days later the lights came on, the toilets flushed, Grace was on her way home and life started to return to normal. At least as normal as my life can get. There were a few less ficus trees on Simonton Street, a few less aluminum storage sheds in back yards, and almost no houseboats remaining on Houseboat Row. One was resting nicely on the bottom of the bay with only the top half sticking out of the water. Some joker had hand-painted a big sign and nailed it to the side. "For Sale – Luxury Home – Sunken Living Room – Make Offer." The big trash pile out on Sugarloaf that had marked the dumping grounds for Hurricane George's dirty work was growing again, and would eventually be trucked off the Keys, one semi at a time. Everybody had at least one "I

Survived Hurricane Elaine" tee shirt, and the Citizen had gone back to reporting petty crime and incompetent politics on the front page.

Maggie dropped by with Gracie in tow. I took her suitcase and put it on the bed, and started telling her about the storm and the cleanup, the houseboat leak and playing at Buzzards. I noticed that she was just standing in the middle of the living room with her arms folded. "What's up, baby?" I asked. "I'm done with this," she replied. "I called Aunt Laura Jane and Uncle Nick in Sandusky, and they said I can come back up there and go to school this year. All of this is about you, chasing treasure, playing music and drinking. I see you maybe twice a week and then you come in and go to bed. You can't keep a promise, and never listen to what's important to me. I've had it. Book me on a flight tomorrow and you won't have to worry about me anymore."

It wasn't a request- it was a statement. She stood in front of me and stared at me. Several responses came to mind, but none were correct. She was right. This was not the place for her, and it was likely that I was going to be working the wreck for days at a time. Brody was more or less a grownup and didn't need daddy time. Grace needed *ME*, but without me, she needed a stable and loving home. Aunt Laura and Uncle Nick would look after her. They didn't care for me or my lifestyle, but I know how they loved her. I merely nodded, fighting back tears and told her to get her things together. The following morning, I put her on a Cape Air flight to Fort Myers, and from there on Delta to Cleveland. Hopefully, we could figure out this father/daughter thing better in the future.

Sometimes you can't be the perfect person for someone. I know she hated me for divorcing her mother, and it didn't genuinely matter whose decision it was. She hated me more because her mother died, than she actually hated me.

I also know that I can only be who I am. So I try to be the best person I know how to be.

Losers Weepers

It was time to round up the gang and get back to this shipwreck thing. As the power on the houseboat came on and the air conditioning started cooling the room, I kicked my lead doorstop out of the way and closed the door. I closed my eyes for a second and wondered what it would have been like to grab the brass ring. There was still something about that lead bar that was tickling the back of my neck. I felt that I had seen it someplace before in my past.

You never know as they say.

Anyway, Monday morning Bo, Tack and I jumped into the *Captain Morgan* and cruised over to the harbor. The team had already cleared *La Brisa* off that go-fast Scarab boat, and they were loading it with provisions. Everyone reported to work except Doobie. I noticed with no small concern when I glanced over toward the Galleon Marina that *The Nose Knows* was not at her berth.

Loaded down, the *La Brisa* can just about outrun a glacier, so we took the *Captain Morgan* ahead to the site. I was anxious to see what we had, and wondered if the Hurricane added or took away from the overburden, and if our anchor was actually pointing at the main part of the wreck.

As we rounded the tip of Boca Grande, my fears turned out to be founded as you could see a boat extremely close to the site. I picked up the glasses, and the green and white form of *The Nose Knows* was easy to recognize. It used to be a pretty boat, and one of the fastest fishing/dive boats in the Keys, but the druggies scabbed a cabin on the boat a few years ago and turned it just butt ugly. I motioned to Bo to slide the *Morgan* around so we could approach from the bow of *The Nose Knows*, and maybe not get their attention till we were close. As it turned out, we could have brought the Marine Band with us, and it wouldn't have made any difference: Doobie was standing at the back of the boat, smoking a huge blunt and rocking out to his Ipod, oblivious to the world. There was a compressor sitting on the deck and two air lines snaked over the side. The boys were on the bottom with Hookahs. Doobie never knew we were there until Bo's boat bumped into the side of *The Nose*. Doobie just about jumped out of his skin as I stepped over the side into his boat. "Hey Doobie, what's up?" I asked. He really didn't have much of a chance for a snappy response. He was definitely caught, figuratively, with his dick in his hands. "Hey Man, don't get upset. They just paid me to show them the wreck so they could look around. No harm in that."

"Nope, no harm at all. So, if I pull this little ol line up there won't be anything in the basket but empty conch shells?" I asked. "How many days have you guys been out here?" "Just a couple of times," Doobie responded. "Like I said, we ain't taken nothing. Just looking."

"How long they been down?" I asked.

"Nearly two hours. They are about ready to come back up now."

Hmm. Two hours. A hundred twenty minutes. At fifty feet, after about seventy minutes they would have to stop to decompress on the way back up to avoid getting the bends. Perfect. "Bo!" I called out. "Any cherry bombs?" Bo nodded with a smile, reached in a box and produced four nice round balls with fuses. Cherry bombs are waterproof, and if you drop them in the water, they can seriously mess with a diver's ears. I motioned and he lit a couple, dropping them over the side. "Man, that's not cool, we're not doing anything wrong," Doobie said.

"You're poaching on a wreck site that I have a license to salvage, for one thing. For another, you're really starting to piss me off. I'm sure about now those two dickheads are genuinely unhappy and know they can't surface, or they will get the bends.

112

Here's the deal," I went on. "For one thing I'm not going to call the cops. What I *am* going to do is radio into town in a moment, so my people can call the college and have them warm up the hyperbaric chamber. They are about to receive a couple of guests. Your piece of shit boat is ugly but fast. If you crank up and drive like hell, you just might get them there in time to prevent them from becoming permanent cripples and drinking beer from a straw out of the cup holder on their electric wheelchairs for the next twenty years.

"What are you talking about?" asked Doobie. "They are probably up at thirty feet doing a 'decom'. "Yes, they probably are," I replied. "Up till just about *NOW*." I reached over and picked up a large crescent wrench, and knocked the top off the spark plug on the compressor motor, then pulled my dive knife out and cut both air hoses in two. "Doobie, you need to get that anchor up right now, just as soon as you pull these turds out of the water. I suggest you get a move-on."

Bo eased the *Captain Morgan* back up to the side of *The Nose Knows,* and I stepped over the rail back on board, just as two heads popped up to the surface, choking, gagging and screaming, probably both from ear pain and a growing pain in their joints as nitrogen bubbles started collecting. They were almost already incapacitated, and it's lucky Doobie was a pretty husky guy as he had to haul them on board almost by himself after they abandoned most of their gear over the side. I yelled to Doobie to just throw the rope that probably had a collection basket on it over the side, and watched him just cut the anchor line off and spool up the twin diesels for the ride back to town. As promised, I radioed our office and told them to put the word out to the college that they had guests en-route. If Doobie had half a brain, which was probably a stretch for him, he would be scooting directly to Florida Keys College. Those guys were going to be in a world of hurt in the next 45 minutes.

"Well, I think that went rather well," remarked Bo. "I doubt they got too much treasure, and we just gained two hookah masks, flippers and a nice anchor to boot. From now on you need to be parked over this wreck twenty four - seven for the duration."

Amen brother. I also knew this dance wasn't over. Itchy had conch roots and no doubt when he gets better he will be on the phone to cousin-uncle-daddy to tell them what a terrible person I am, and provide GPS coordinates for our wreck. This will likely get uglier before it gets prettier, and being on the right side of the law won't necessarily be to my advantage. It will be a lot simpler to play the edge for a while.

With our visitors out of the way, we used the GPS to find our anchor again, plotted the location on our charts and the exact direction the shaft of the anchor was laying. The eye and ring, long ago corroded away, the part that the wooden stock used to be attached two, should, be pointed in the general direction of where our wreck will lie. The theory is that, in a storm, the ship will drop her anchor, and then the winds will push the ship away from the anchor. If the anchor holds, it's pointing at the ship, and even if the anchor line breaks, the ship will continue running downwind so the anchor is a excellent permanent pointer, providing the shop eventually sank.

No telling if it was fifty feet, fifty yards or five miles in that direction, but it was a starting point. Using my portable marine GPS and noting the angle, I jumped in the little boat to mark the direction from where we had pulled the cannon out from the shore. Thankfully I had hammered in those golf flags deep, and they were still in place after the storm.

We drew the angles from the shore on the chart, and they crossed exactly where one of our "hits" was. "Forget it," I told Bo. "I dove that mark myself, and it was three five hundred pound World War Two practice bombs sitting on a coral head. I don't think the Spaniards dropped that many bombs in 1733."

"Well", Bo said, "maybe time for a second peek. Take the portable metal detector with you. By the way, you might notice that it's within a few feet of where your buddies were just diving."

Normal procedure would call for us to notify the Navy so they could look at what we found to either detonate them or declare them duds or practice rounds. If we did that every time we found ordinance, we would never get anything done. Most of the bombs were practice rounds and anyway, they are so rusted out it's likely none of them could ever blow up on you.

The keyword in that sentence is "likely."

Oh well, who said this job was safe and easy?

We parked over the spot and dropped anchor. I pulled on my gear and dropped in. It was slack tide, so no current and visibility was excellent. I could see those three bombs lying there before I was halfway down. It would be impossible that these were dropped as they wouldn't be lying in such a nice row, probably fell off a ship in a crate and just stayed in place as the crate rotted around it. That really didn't confirm if they were alive or dead. As I got down to them it was obvious it didn't matter; they were just rusted shells. I moved down and to the left of the shells and reached back for my little portable metal detector. I had an earpiece already in place, and when I turned on the detector, it came on screaming at me. Great. Malfunction junction, all I need today. I picked up the detector to see what was loose or broken, and it shut up. Back to the surface of the reef and it went bonkers again. Up – quiet. Down – scream. I moved a few feet to the left and tried it again. Same results. I didn't have anything to dig or hack with but my dive knife, so I pulled it out of my leg sheath and hacked a little at the rock pile with the titanium blade.

It responded with the distinctive clink of metal to metal contact.

Oh my.

I backed off a few yards to let my heart settle, and size up the lay of the land. There was a lot of topographic action in the area, but not that much different than anywhere else on the reef. The detector was definitely saying that *something* was down there. Based on my recent luck, I was almost afraid to look harder and find somebody's 57 Chevy buried in the sand. Then I spied the basket the two slime brothers had used. I paddled over to it for a look. There were a couple of picks, a hammer and chisel, and a black lump. I picked up the lump and flipped it over and the unmistakable shape of coins covered the bottom.

We had found the ship.

Trying not to hyperventilate, I swam back to the surface. Spitting out the mouthpiece, I gave a little whistle. Bo peered over the side, and I pitched the lump up to him. "Looks like we be the luckiest sonsofbitches on planet earth," I told him. Pulling off my gear, I climbed up the ladder and took a look at the prize in the sunlight. Silver turns black with corrosion in sea water – it will take a while before we know what we have, but that won't stop us from going to work. Once we get some coins cleaned up, we can date them and get an idea what we have. And how much.

An hour later the *La Brisa* lumbered up, and we slid the *Captain Morgan* off the anchorage so the salvage boat could make home. She would likely not move again for a while unless we needed serious repairs. With the diesels shut down, the crew fired up a 12kw generator and started bringing the boat to life. I brought the lump of silver over to the *La Brisa* so the crew could pass it around. "I think we're on the main part of the wreck guys. We can officially arrest the wreck, and I'll contact the state and claim salvage. The State of Florida will send someone out here, hopefully sooner than later." At this point, we only needed a small crew to guard the wreck so we could take the rest of the crew back to town. In the meantime, I told the gang to get the lift set up and rigged for about fifty-five feet of water, and wait for the go-ahead. They could use metal detectors and start staking out the operation, but had to wait to pull treasure. "Don't forget to watch your time on the bottom. Let's call it forty-five minute turns and two hour rests. I'm going to radio the government so they can get someone out on the boat ASAP. Bo and I are going to take this piece into town and see what we have. Have fun!"

The crew cheered and got to work. They, like I, had expected to take weeks or months finding this wreck. Triangulating the canon site and the anchor made our work a breeze. Harry's hunch paid off nicely. Maybe in millions.

Harry Sykas has a small operation in Tarpon Springs, but we thought for this first true find we would consult with the real pros in Key West, Treasure Salvors, Inc., AKA Mel Fisher's company. They have recovered more treasure than just about all the other salvage operations combined, and their process for turning black lumps of concretion into identifiable silver coins is state of the art. There's a combination of suspicion and comradely between salvage operations down here, who fiercely protect their sites and treasure, but lend a hand at a moment's notice if you are in need and are more than willing to help us figure out what we had. Having worked for them occasionally in the past, I knew my way through the back door of the operation on Whitehead Street. I knew the process and handed over my lump with confidence. I'm sure you have seen many a treasure movie where divers scoop up handfuls of bright silver coins, but in truth, after four hundred years, you almost can't recognize silver. To the untrained eye, this lump looked like a big black rock. When I handed it over to Danny Thompson, he recognized what it was immediately.

"Found something on your site?" Danny asked. The Coconut Telegraph kept the industry in the know. Fisher's people knew we had a license to work an area off Boca Grande, and likely didn't give it much hope of being productive. Hopefully they were wrong.

"Yep, looks like we might have something. This is our first pull from the site. We want to see if we can get some dates off the coins so we can figure out what it is."

"We can do that for you. I should have an answer probably by the middle of next week. I'll call Bo's cell when I know something. I'll keep half of what's in this concretion as a fee."

Yikes, twenty five percent to the fine state of Florida, half to these guys. By the time I send the balance to Harry, I'll have to include a check to just break even on it. Oh well, the price of high living, as they say.

What the coins and all other silver coins, bars and metal objects go through is a fairly involved process, converting crusted, corroded lumps of metal into recognizable shiny treasure. The first step of the actual conservation process is to remove some of the hard concretion encasing the coin, and then a mixture of muriatic acid and water is used to soften and deteriorate the encrustation for just a few minutes. Only a section of the metal must be accessible to attach an alligator clip. The coin is then attached to a wire. The coins are placed into the tank, beginning the electrolytic cleaning process. The electrolysis tank consists of soda ash and water, with a stainless steel plate (anode) and a low voltage current. During the process of electrolysis hydrogen bubbles are released and the chlorides are expelled from the metal. The average amount of time required for a silver coin is three to four days. The coins are removed from electrolysis and rinsed thoroughly in fresh water, and then back in a weak nitric acid solution, which helps bleach the coins. The coins are rinsed and brushed with baking soda and water. Finally, the coins are placed in a jewelry tumbler with stainless steel shot and burnishing compound. Rinsed again, the coins are dried and are ready for inspection.

A few days later, Bo tapped on my door and told me that Danny wanted us to come to the office. We jumped in the Thing and headed over. Finally, we would know what we had.

"Fifty six coins. They have dates that are between 1727 and 1732," reported Danny. "About a third of them are Pillar Dollars, and this is almost for sure part of the 1733 fleet. How in Hell did you find this off Boca Grande?" he asked. All those ships went aground between Key Largo and Marathon or thereabouts."

"Not a clue. Yet," I told him. "We had found a couple of other items that hinted it was from the 1733 wreck. It might be quite a bit of treasure, but doesn't appear to be a big galleon, nor does it look like a big debris field. Don't you love a mystery?"

We gathered up our coins and left. I had to hand these over to the state so they could get their piece of the action and would return to Fishers with their portion after that. We thanked Danny and went outside to call Harry, and give him the good news. Yes, he had his wreck, no we didn't know how valuable, yes it was 1733 treasure, no we didn't know how valuable. Sheesh. I also took a moment to call the college and inquire about pond-scum friends. They had been transferred to Fisherman's Hospital after decompressing. I called Fisherman's and found they whisked off to Jackson Memorial in Miami as soon as they showed they were unable to pay. They were banged up, but it was nothing they wouldn't recover from, four perfectly perforated ear-drums and mild symptoms due to the bends. I'm sure they would be back on the rock annoying me in the very near future. I had already heard around town that Doobie was knocking down beers at the Green Parrot the other day telling everyone I was a dead man. No question I would be dealing with this eventually down the road.

Back on the site the crew had done a good job of working the wreck area. Whatever ship it was, it appears it didn't sink in pieces. Metal detectors were pinging on an area only about seventy by forty feet, with little blips here and there outside that perimeter, and the debris field we had been having spotty success with over the past months. It was obvious there was a lot of non-ferrous metal under the sand, with some concretion sticking above the surface of the bottom. When staked out, it resembled a fairly small ship, or a part of a bigger one. The guys were already finding coins and other artifacts, and were anxious to get to serious digging.

It was nearly two weeks later that the Florida State Archeologist graced us with his presence. It was darn near painless. He rode out to the wreck, poked and prodded in a few places, gathered up my bag of coins and gave us license to salvage, advising that they got the pick of the litter, twenty five percent of the value and call them if anything that looks like a historical type artifact shows. He also offered that he didn't have a clue what 1733 wreck coins were doing on Boca Grande and would welcome any revelations.

In the meantime, Harry was sending down another half derelict boat for us to use as a second dive platform. I put word out in town that we were hiring, and spent another week interviewing the shallow end of the gene pool. I didn't know if I needed a shuttle van or a prison bus. Harry flew down in time to be in Key West when his second boat arrived, an old fishing boat named the *Lady Mania III*. The only real advantage was a large winch on the rear deck that will come in handy if we have to haul up anything of size but by and large it was a pitiful POS that should have been put out to pasture long ago and turned into an artificial reef. Harry did bring me a gold corporate AMEX card and a cell phone. I was officially in charge of the operation, and also got a little bump in pay, plus a promise of decent payout if we scored a big treasure.

Such a big heart that Greek pirate asshole dipshit slimeball dickwad cheapskate.

Yeah, Bric, hold it back.

Like all absentee owners, Harry wanted to go down and look at his prize. The water was warm enough to cook shrimp in, but that didn't stop him from struggling into a three mil arctic dry suit, complete with hoodie, booties and gloves. He said he didn't want to get bit or stung. We had repaired the hookah setup that we acquired off Itchy and Scab, and showed him how to use it and threw him over the side. Tack played nursemaid to sort of keep him from drowning. There was nothing to see, so we salted the site with a few pieces of eight and some other artifacts so he could feel important.

It went pretty well till he "discovered" the Kennedy Half Dollar. He got pissed and wanted to come out of the water, but we couldn't figure out how to get his fat ass up the ladder.

"Bric," Tack suggested, "let's just tow him over to the beach and haul him on shore. Greenpeace will come by in a day or so and rescue him."

It was tempting, but we did finally manage to get him back in the boat, with two guys hauling on his arms and another shoving his fat ass up the ladder.

After we got the boss out of our hair we set up a schedule. Each boat would spend ten days over the wreck, four days in port, and four days overlapping. This was a much happier arrangement than the original deal that had the La Brisa parked over the wreck forever. With poachers already underfoot we would have to babysit this thing for the duration. But before we got up to speed, there was a little interlude approaching.

It was Fantasy Fest Week.

Come as You Aren't

Here's the "Official" history of Fantasy Fest

The first Fantasy Fest was held in 1979 when two local businessmen, Tony Falcone and the late Bill Conkle, organized a party to stimulate business. The event has escalated to a ten

121

day celebration that includes balls, a parade, costume competitions, AIDS fundraisers, body painting, drag queen contests, costume parties, lots of drinking, as well as pet and neighborhood parades for the whole family. Fantasy Fest has grown to rival New Orleans' Mardi Gras as an event drawing out-of-towners.

If truth be known, had it not been for two Spanish galleons sinking off the Florida Keys almost 400 years ago, nubile young women would not be permitted to frolic down Duval Street dressed only in high heels and body paint during the last weekend of October.

Mel Fisher loved parties. In the early days, long before the main pile of treasure from the Atocha was found, they started having Halloween parties on the ship that had been converted from a Swedish lumber ship into a treasure museum galleon by Treasure Salvors Executive Vice President Captain Robert Moran in the 1960. The parties were complete with a band, and they were wildly popular. (The galleon was parked in front of where the Galleon Resort is located today), it was a BYOB party, but it seemed like half the town would show up. It got so popular that they had to limit the number of people on board the ship because all that weight was causing it sink to the point that the pumps couldn't keep up. Everybody just congregated in the parking lot next to the ship if they couldn't get aboard. The Galleon Halloween Party became so popular that after the galleon sank at the dock, some of the local businessmen continued the tradition.

That's what turned into Fantasy Fest.

For the uneducated, Fantasy Fest is a week-long celebration in October that consists of parties, pageants, parades and plenty of nakedness. I think of it as a cross between Mardi-Gras, a group sex skin flick and the bar scene in Star Wars. This island of perennial permissiveness always plays the edge a little, but during Fantasy Fest week it falls way off the edge, over the brink, and down into the chasm of drunken, erotic, partially clothed debauchery. If God ever gets mad again and decides to smite someplace, it's likely that everybody on that one-mile stretch of Duval Street will be transformed into Pillars of Salt during the Fantasy Fest Parade.

It didn't start that way. After the Mel Fisher Halloween parties turned into something more, it was just a party and a parade, but people just kept pushing the envelope when it came to attire and conduct. The city pushed back occasionally, "officially" trying to temper the enthusiasm, and even at one point arresting women that didn't fit the decency rules. One year the police walked around with scarves in their pockets and handed them to women with bare breasts. Lots of signs and notices proclaimed that "Body Paint is Not Clothing," a statement that has as much effect as someone trying to sweep sand off the beach and back into the ocean with a broom. In recent years, the officials have more or less given up. Notably it's a double standard. You can see lots of women with nothing on but paint, or at most, a tiny G-string, but if a guy walks around in public waving his willie in the moonlight, likely he will win a short vacation in the hoosegow.

Call me a voyeur, call me a pig, but I like Fantasy Fest, at least parts of it. I have no patience for people that think they can come down here and be jerks for four days. I know there are swinger groups, BDSM groups, and probably every level of pervert on the planet mixed among the fifty thousand or so people in town for the weekend. To each his, or her, own. I have no interest in that kind of play but when it comes to casually worshiping the female human form, count me in. And I'm not talking about only those size six, perfectly tanned, perky titted eighteen year old model types. You see as many sixty year old grandmas with saggy boobs, cellulite asses and big tummies, wearing nothing but body paint. They aren't here for me, they are here for themselves and I admire them for being comfortable in their own skin.

My weekend at Fantasy Fest was work combined with play. The band could work as much as we wanted to all week, and if I didn't mind playing bass till my fingers were bloody, I could knock down a cool two grand in four days. I was picky and played about half as much as was offered, and opted to play mostly at Buzzards, where the bandstand had an optimum view of Duval Street and all the fun and games. It must be like what the house band at Hedonism II gets to experience every

123

night. The crowd didn't really care what we played, as long as it was loud and we riffed for hours at a time, doing some version of Free Bird or Light my Fire. My fingers were on autopilot, and my eyes were popping out of my head. Thursday night was the toga party at Sloppy's so the bar was quiet early. We parked the equipment and just kicked back for a while. I was enjoying a beer on a sidewalk table when this vision of beauty strolled into the bar wearing airbrushed tiger-stripes, a fake tail, whiskers, little ears, six inch heels and not a stitch more. Of all the people in the bar, she strolled up and sat at my table. We chatted and made small talk about the weather, the people and the parties. I put a lot of effort into looking at her eyes, but couldn't help but do the occasional nipple-check.

I would have given a week's pay for my Costas that were sitting on the kitchen counter at home.

After twenty minutes, I was about ready to dive across the table and jump her bones when, thankfully, the band started climbing up on the stage. I stood up and thanked her for the chat and bade her good bye. She smiled and stood up too and answered. "And Bricklin Wahl, if you EVER tell anyone that you saw me like this, I will hunt you down and kill you." And she strode out of the bar.

To this day, I haven't a clue whom I was talking to.

We played Thursday till two and Friday from about noon to three a.m. Saturday the band moved to Smokin Tuna, and I switched to 4 Orange Vodka and cranberry juice for my drink. Not smart when I was trying to coherently play rock and roll music. By Saturday; I was weary of the playlist. Every other tourist requested Margaritaville, and that was my song to sing. I told the crowd it was gonna take an Alexander Hamilton or larger to get my throat moving. It's not that I don't like Buffett. Heck, back in my early days I probably jammed with him a few times, filling in for other players too drunk, too stoned or too much in lust to show up. Buffett had a little vacation home across the street from Bo's place on Hilton Haven Drive after he moved up to the mainland I had a nodding acquaintance with Jimmy when I occasionally bumped into him while he was walking his dog. I guess a lot of us local Key West musicians resent that he made it to the show and we didn't, but you can't take away what he's accomplished, and heaven knows since he got big, my half-assed decent voice has kept ten-spots in the tip jar for the last 25 years.

Then somebody in the crowd called out for my song 'Part-time'. It has been ages since I sang that song. It got on the charts twenty years ago in a few markets. I heard I was huge in Corpus Christi and Bozeman Montana. I really didn't get a chance to say no as the band kicked into gear with the opening bars. It almost sounded good again when the refrain came around.

"I love you even though it's only part-time. I couldn't live without you, I know I'd lose my my-iiiiind... Please say you'll never leave me, and say you'll settle down, stop your honky tonkin, stay at home don't run around....."

Don't quit the day job, Bric.

The street fair on Saturday drew a enormous crowd and people started drinking for effect by ten a.m. Brody came by for a while and sucked up all the root beer in the bar, and then left to walk home about dark before the parade began, which was scheduled to start at seven. As the parade started, we stopped playing and went out the side door at Smokin Tuna to watch the show. Compared to the spectators, the parade is almost tame. It was like being at a reverse zoo. Parade people in G-strings and bikinis, and the crowd wearing body paint, beads, high heels and not much more. It was one wild freaking night for sure. I had always wanted to create a Key West Bag Lady Precision Shopping Cart Drill Team for the parade, but never could get enough people to commit to being sober on Fantasy Fest Saturday night, and couldn't convince the true bag ladies that it would be fun to do.

After the parade, the bar instantly jammed up to the walls with visible human flesh. We played our hearts out and rocked till after three, when Key West's finest showed up and busted a crowd in the alley for having public daisy chain sex, much to the enjoyment of the people in the bar. We took it as a good cue and locked the gear up in the music room and bolted for the door. I got a ride into town that morning, but the chance of finding an available cab at this time of day was slim or none. It was a half hour walk to the houseboat, so I headed up Eaton out of downtown. It was like walking out of Disneyworld through a side door, turning around and seeing plywood nailed on a wooden frame. Behind me was all the lights, noise and music, and in front a steadily quieting walk. First there were some party goers in various stages of disrobement, then some girl puking in the gutter with a friend holding her hair, two gentlemen in a driveway practicing the fine art of sodomy, and then a loud argument between a couple. I could only hear the words from her "Well what did you expect me to do? It was just sticking out there for everyone to grab!" By the time I neared Simonton Street, I had pretty well cleared the crazy zone. I was crossing the street next to the old Methodist Church that my family attended when I was a boy when I heard a commotion behind me. I turned and there was a pretty good version of the Captain Morgan's Pirate smiling and waving his cutlass. I vaguely recall seeing this guy hanging around Buzzards most of the evening. "Nice outfit," I said. "I didn't know you were allowed to even bring fake cutlasses to the party." "Well, if you need to know, it's not fake," he responded, and lunged at me. Twenty years ago, or five 4-Oranges Vodka/Cran's earlier, or a combination thereof, and I might have avoided the thrust and provided a broken arm and a trip to the hospital for the assailant. As it was, I spun to the left and instead of one through the heart, I felt the blade go through my arm and into my side, right between ribs. I went down to one knee, and he pulled the sword out, and got ready to finish the job. With one arm back and ready to strike the blow, I reached up with the good arm and grabbed him by the nuts as hard as I could. I actually managed to levitate him about six inches off the ground by the plumbs. He dropped the cutlass, screamed like a girl and tried to grow longer legs.

Why do I always feel like a Charles Schultz hero in a Hunter S. Thompson novel? That was all I had in me and I fell back while the house lights dimmed.

Pardon Me Saint Peter, But These Wings are Only Loaners

An eternity later I woke up. I've been in that place before and knew that I was waking up from anesthetic. You don't sleep when you get put under. You shut down. No dreams, no sense of anything, and you don't know if it's been two hours, two weeks or you have been in frozen preservation next to Sly

Stallone in the year 2525. I was on my back and looking up at a hospital ceiling. Afraid to try and move, I just let my eyes search what I could see from this position. Ah, I.V. drip above me, monitor to my left, window to the right with the blinds closed. Now time to take stock of me. I wiggled toes. Good. They worked. Fingers? They wiggled, but the left arm was wrapped up. That made sense. I turned my head left and right and felt the pick line in my carotid. I could also feel the catheter in my dick and the aforementioned drip in the right arm. My throat felt like I had given a blowjob to a live porcupine with an armadillo chaser.

But hey, at least I woke up.

Apparently, something I was plugged into had alerted the duty nurse that I was stirring, and I could hear her coming down the hall. Due to self-induced trauma as a result of foolish hobbies in my younger years, plus a chronic kidney stone issue that popped up about every ten years, I knew what the inside of a hospital felt like. There are exactly two kinds of nurses. Glenda the Good Witch and Nurse Ratchet. No grey area here from my experience. I was already wondering what the Department of Practical Jokes had dealt me. "Well, Mr. Wahl, it looks like we're awake." (Ah, the Glenda type). I tried to respond with something snappy and cynical, but all that came out was a croak. I pointed at my mouth and gave the universal sign for "I'm fucking thirsty," by holding a fake cup. If I was not done with surgery, I know she would smile and politely provide a cup of ice chips, but she reached for the container beside my bed and poured me a cup of water, then helped me take a few sips. For all I know, it could have been dipped out of a gutter behind the wino's hangout at Smathers Beach, but that was the best tasting liquid I had ever had in my life. One more sip and I was again prepared to attempt to speak human. "Where? What?" was all I could come up with. "You're in the Key West hospital. You've had surgery to stitch up your arm, and another to repair a collapsed lung, perforated diaphragm, and a little nick on the kidney. Doc says you are going to be just fine. I think when you are up to it; Monroe County Sheriffs want to chat with you."

Yeah, I bet.

"There are also a few people that are ready to take on our entire security force if we don't let them in to see you. Let's get a few things done, and they can come in for a few minutes."

A half hour later, Bo, Tack and Maggie came in the room. Maggie had tears, Bo shook my hand solemnly, and Tack had a cold Mountain Dew under his jacket that he sneaked into my water pitcher. "Where's Brody?" I asked. "Haven't seen him since Saturday morning," replied Bo. "We thought he might be down here. I don't know where he is." I pushed the attendant call button. "I need to speak to the cops now," I told the nurse. "My son is missing." "Oh, Mr. Wahl, I didn't tell you that part. When the Sheriffs told me they wanted to talk to you, they also said they had your son. That's all they told me."

Bo and Tack headed home, and Maggie stayed with me till the Deputy Sherriff John Russell arrived. It was my time to cry when Brody walked in with them. The bear hug from that lummox hurt in more places that I cared to note, but it was worth it, and I didn't let him know that the pain almost made me faint, and I was glad that pain tears look just like happy tears. "Well," John said, "it appears we have several things to discuss Bric. I'm sure you want to know how cousin Broderick ended up as our guest. Brody, you want to tell your dad what happened? He's really not in trouble Bric, but three kids are in the hospital and two more are in custody."

"It's no big deal dad," Brody said in his typical "aw shucks" attitude. "I left Duval Street about six and was walking down Eaton. Daryl Roberts and some of his buddies were sitting on the corner of Simonton and Eaton." (Wow, I thought, same place I got whacked). "Wait a minute, Daryl Roberts, Itchy Roberts' kid? This is all starting to make sense. Okay, go on."

"So," Brody continued. "They all stood up and started in with the 'Brody the Toadie' stuff, which I don't terribly mind. After all, I'm big. Who cares? Daryl starts in on how you tried to kill his old man. I told him that if you wanted Itchy dead, that he would be dead and that his dad was messing around someplace he didn't belong. So Daryl said they were going to kick my ass. I told them I don't fight. They called me a candy ass, and I told them again that I don't fight. That's when Tony Franzone took a swing at me with an aluminum baseball bat."

John Russell took over from there. "We have witnesses. Brody took the bat away from Tony and took out his kneecap. Another kid pulled a knife and Brody broke his wrist with the bat. Then he dropped the bat and your chubby son kicked Daryl squarely in the chin flat footed. If he had been wearing real shoes instead of Crocs, Daryl would have more than a broken jaw right now. As it is, he will be taking nourishment through a straw for the next month or so. You had some formal training cousin?"

I answered for him. "If you ever drop by my houseboat, you can see two black belts in frames on the wall. One has two stripes, and one has three. Brody is a second degree black belt in Tai-Kwan-Do. His sister is a third degree. Their mom put them in martial arts when they were young, not to teach them how to fight, but how to have self-discipline and self-respect. The kids are not permitted to fight. He wasn't kidding those guys. If I ever caught either one of them using what they learned in martial arts to bully people, then all the belts in the world wouldn't save their ass from dad. My biggest fear when they moved back was that they would piss each other off, which I'm sure, would have ended in a trip to the ER. So you said five kids. What happened to the other two?"

"They ran. But somebody had already called the cops and they grabbed those two kids before they put the cuffs on me," Brody replied. "I didn't do anything wrong so I just cooperated. I knew they would figure out what happened."

"That's right, we got matching stories from witnesses, but he told us you were working all night, and we didn't just want to drop him off at his house, so we gave him a private cell and dinner to make sure he didn't mess up any more bad people. Then I heard your name pop up on a 911 call, and the paramedics responding and figured I would deliver him to you this morning when I came to hear your story. My, my, it's been an enthralling night with the Wahl family. It appears both of these incidents happened on the very same corner, and I'm guessing they are related. Care to share? Any description of the guy that stabbed you?"

"Sure. Just go down to Conch Liquors and buy a bottle of

spiced rum. His picture's on the label. Couldn't have been more than five thousand buccaneers in costume on Duval last night. That should just about narrow it down."

John looked weary and took a deep breath. "Bric, we have all the smartasses we need in jail this morning. It's been a very long night, and I haven't been to bed since Friday. Let's get just a teensy bit serious. What's this about your trying to kill Daryl's dad?"

"Look, here's the deal. I have a permit to salvage a wreck west of here. It's a Spanish galleon, probably sunk around 1733 and might have quite a bit of treasure on it. Itchy Roberts and his thugs got wind of it from one of my former employees and went poaching. We caught them over the site and in their haste to depart, they messed up their eardrums and got out of the water without stopping for a decompression cycle and got the bends. I even called the college personally and had them get the hyperbaric chamber ready."

"So as payment for your kindness someone ran you through with a rusty cutlass? Well as they say, no good deed goes unpunished. Bric, I'll give you the benefit of the doubt on this, but I smell a rat, and it's likely these rats aren't done. In the future, leave the law to us, and you concentrate on raping the ocean of its treasure. Now, I know the guy that stabbed you was in costume, but do you have any clues or descriptions that might help?"

"Well, now that you ask, I would think this dude has a very sore set of balls, so look for a guy that's talking in a soprano and definitely not riding a bicycle. He also might answer to the name of Itchy."

After the cops finished taking the report, I kicked Brody out so I could get a nap. Just talking wore me out. I had just dimmed the lights when there was a knock on the open door.

Karen

"So, I hear you brought your dick to a sword fight."

"Yeah, something like that. Come in and have a seat." I pushed the up button on the bed controls and got myself as upright as pain would tolerate. Karen had some flowers in one hand and two cold long necks nestled in her purse. "Thought you might need some nerve medicine."

"Thanks but with all the pain meds in me, I would be doing laps on the roof if I had a beer. You go ahead, and I'll live my beer buzz vicariously through you."

"Don't mind if I do," and she unscrewed the first beer and emptied about half of it in the first pull. "I saw Maggie on the way in," Karen said. "Didn't leave too much cat fur on the floor. I don't think she likes me checking in on her property."

"Maggie's a great friend, but she ain't peed on this tree yet. Besides, I thought you wrote me out of your will and crossed me off the Christmas card list."

"Nah, just gave you a little space so I could think. Now I've thunk. You're still a pretty decent guy, even if you don't know how to treat a girl, and when I heard some jerk rammed a toadsticker in your side, I thought I better come check up on you."

"So the word's out?" I asked.

"Front page of the Citizen," She answered. "Brody got better coverage because they had witnesses. Says he did a good Chuck Norris imitation, took down the pack and got arrested. It just says you were found lying in the street in a pool of blood from an unknown attacker. Any juicy tidbits to add?"

"That's pretty much it. Well, maybe a little more. It was deliberate. Someone tried to send me to the Promised Land I think." And I told her the Reader's Digest version of recent developments.

"Itchy. That jerk and his pack of hoods need to be kicked off this rock. They give petty crime a bad name. I've got half a mind to head over to the Hogfish and nail his balls to a barstool."

"Karen, he's bad company. Give him a wide berth and I would suggest you don't even mention that we are friends. He's looking for people to hurt."

"We're friends? Aww," And she got up and kissed me again on my bald spot. This time it sent a warm glow through my body. "Look," she said "I gotta get going. You take care of yourself and let me know when you are back up to speed. I'll take you on an afternoon sailboat ride. Can I bring you anything?"

"Sure." I picked up one of the magazines sitting on my tray. It was a 1992 Sports Illustrated. "Drop by the house and pick me up a book. Ah, make it 'A Salty Piece of Land' by Jimmy Buffett. Reading it for the fourth time will be better than this fugitive from a time capsule." Even though Buffett's fiction is somewhat autobiographical, I always felt there was a little Frank Bama in me, or a little of me in him. Reading his books make me feel a little more like 'me'. Then I thought about something she said one afternoon at the Fishwagon. "Hey, by that way, what about that 'real live man' that you have in your life?"

"Honestly, Bric. A guy in Key West that cooks, cleans house and comes home every night? All those guys already have boyfriends. I'll pick it up your book this afternoon and drop it by later." And with that, she walked out of the room and back into my life.

I wish I could figure out the female species.

They let me out of the butcher shop four days later, with explicit orders to not dive for at least six weeks in fear that I might blow out the patch in my lung. I had plenty of knuckle draggers out there for the heavy work anyway, and was happy to set up shop in a warehouse on Stock Island where we could start cleaning, cataloging and researching the artifacts from the wreck. Tack Morgan took over on the wreck. This wasn't his first rodeo and he did a great job keeping the guys organized, working and honest. Using the lift, they spent almost a month just clearing off the overburden and exposing as much of the wreck as possible. With some digging, it was apparent that there was a fair amount of ship's timbers still intact, and enough pieces of porcelain, bottles, cups and other items to seem to confirm this ship was probably abandoned in a hurry. Not to mention a lot of silver. Over eight hundred coins in the first two weeks, plus fifty silver bars, one decent gold bar and a few small gold chains. We were really hoping for more gold but as of yet, very little had turned up. The silver coins would continue to help date the wreck, but the silver bars might be cross referenced to ships manifests and let us know what we were possibly diving on.

Personally, nobody else had tried to kill me in the last few weeks, but I still avoided dark places and stopped walking around town. Even when I got healthy enough to join the band on weekends, I either drove or had Brody pick me up at night. For Brody, he had become a bit of a celebrity at school, which he didn't welcome. Fights breed fights, and he had to turn his back on more than one bully that wanted to have a go at him. They were lucky he was a confirmed non-combatant. While I was buried in this wreck project, Brody was spending a lot of his time on, or in the ocean. We never had to buy seafood, and enjoyed lobster, snapper, grouper, hogfish, and the occasional cobia for dinner as many times a week as we wanted. He wasn't beyond lifting the occasional out of season lobster, and ran a constant cat & mouse game with Fish and Wildlife officers. To create variety, he would occasionally cruise over to Stock Island and trade fresh hogfish for a bucket of Key West pink shrimp or even some jumbo stone crab claws.

Every four or five days, Tack showed up at the warehouse with several plastic tubs full of encrusted lumps in varying sizes. Each item would go through the cleaning, and de-crusting process, then photographed, cataloged and off to the state so they could get their pick of the litter, then the balance to Tarpon Springs and Harry's grubby paws. Anything truly interesting, I held back and locked them in a spacious storage safe we had trucked in. At this point we had to hire 24 hour rent-a-cops to guard the building as there was just too much neat stuff hanging around. I enlisted some of the Mel Fisher people to help me determine what we were digging up. I took close-focus pictures of the better marked silver ingots and emailed the files to their people. The response came back totally confusing. One bar was definitely on the shipping manifest from *Capitana El Ruby* one of the principal ships from the 1733 fleet that had sunk between Marathon and Key Largo.

Huh?

Then it all came clear. This was a salvage ship that had harvested the *Captitana* wreck after the 1733 hurricane, and then had its own bad luck and sunk too. There could be some huge treasure and at least a good chance of some gold, along with a lot of silver. I radioed Tack with the news, and then called Harry to tell him what we were over. Oh, yeah, I had to tell that archeologist puke too, so all the mystery was out.

We did more research and came up with four possible Spanish salvage ships that had been assigned to recover treasure from the 1733 wrecks that disappeared – the *El Alacran*, *El Arco*, *Merced* and *La Mesa*. The *Merced* had reportedly been captured by an English Privateer in 1734 and re-flagged, but that's where the story stopped. It's unlikely we would ever know, but we did know that there was a lot of treasure on the Capitana, and at this point, that's all that mattered.

I eventually felt good enough to go back in the water and work the site, but I still left most of the grunt work to the team. As we continued removing overburden and treasure from the wreck, lots of interesting items surfaced. Personal stuff, china, bottles, pieces of guns, knives cookware, and, as we got deeper into the wreck, silver. Lots of it. Whole lumps of silver coins, that had probably been in chests that had long ago rotted away, were just huge, rectangular lumps of encrusted, black material. Silver bars, weighing upwards of ninety pounds were lined up in the hold like cordwood. It looked like all of the ballast had been removed from the bottom of this Spanish ship and replaced with silver bars. There was no evidence the ship was in terrible disarray, as if it had been wrecked and destroyed, and actually it appeared the ship had been abandoned almost intact. Cups, saucers and plates still in stacks, large black clumps of what appeared to be weapons, sabers, knives, muskets and pistols. We also found eight more light cannons. Not big ship of the line guns and no valuable brass cannons, but eight and ten pounders. It appears this salvage ship was just assigned to bring home gold and silver. The big guns would be the responsibility of ships larger and heavier. There were also several sets of shackles built to detain prisoners or slaves. It was a common practice to use slaves or Indians to dive the wrecks, using them up by making them dive repeatedly without rest, often strapping weights on them to get them to the bottom quickly and not hauling them back up till they had treasure in hand. It wasn't a career job with long-term security.

Under the state's watchful eye we cleaned, photographed, categorized, valued and tagged every item that was brought in. We ended up with over 300 silver bars – all from the *Capitana* and about 25,000 silver "cobs" mostly eight Reales, or "Pieces of Eight" and some four and even two Reale coins, plus a single gold bar that weighed nearly five pounds. Many of the coins were milled "Pillar Dollars", from Mexico City that had just started being minted the year before the 1733 wreck. They were immensely popular around the world and even accepted as legal currency in America up until 1857. Total value of the treasure, some twenty million bucks, plus another three million in non-treasure artifacts. Uncle Sugar gets twenty five percent off the top, so we ended up netting a little less than fifteen million. Decent, but not the biggest treasure. And strangely, only one solitary gold bar. Whatever had happened to the gold?

Oh well, no time to anguish over what wasn't there. Our little wreck was one of the most significant finds, aside from the big Mel Fisher wrecks that had been discovered in Florida in many years and the only actual Spanish salvage vessel that had ever been found and recovered.

The inbound flow of treasure from the ship had slowed to a trickle, and I had set aside some time for a very special few days with my son.

Lobster Mobsters

Once a year, the state of Florida celebrates a kind of holiday. It's sort of a cross between water polo and the running of the bulls in Spain. Annually, people dust off dive gear that hasn't been touched, cleaned, washed or tested for exactly 363 days, buy a lobster stamp, drink themselves half blind and then wander bleary eyed into the Atlantic Ocean, Gulf of Mexico, Florida Bay, or other various bodies of water in search of the elusive lobster, or Florida Crayfish. Unlike their distant, better armored Maine cousins, Florida Spiny Lobsters don't sport monster claws, and all edible meat is relegated to the tail. Regardless of that shortcoming, that tail is several forkfuls of butter soaked, lip smacking, ORGASMIC flavor, especially if you cook them right. And, they are frigging free! All you have to do is buy a fishing license for fifteen bucks, then buy $250 to $3000 worth of dive equipment, climb in your $30,000 family truckster, towing a $60,000 boat, burn $3.75 per gallon gas and stay in a $200 hotel room for three nights so you can have a chance, no guarantees, to gather six, yep, six of them prickly little guys per day, with a twelve bug possession limit. Go over that limit and you can be subject to a $5000 fine and up to sixty days as a guest in the Monroe County pokey. Yep, free, lobsters, just sitting on the bottom of the ocean for the taking.

And they make fun of me for sucking silver coins of the bottom of the ocean for a living.

Of course we live here and have a friend with a boat. Much cheaper investment and we make the odds better too.

It can't get any better than this.

I'm a diver, but I don't partake in this annual madness, although I'm surely guilty by association. Brody has had his face in the water since he was three, and when he was old enough he became SCUBA certified. A few years later, he got sufficiently experienced to inherit a probationary spot on Rumpy's boat, *Wave Whacker*. Rumpy has a system where he manages to fill his freezer with lobster tails without putting as much as a toe in the water by enticing a group of "Lobster Mobsters" into fishing off his boat, paying for gas and giving him half the take.

I sincerely believe John Rumpendorfer may be the smartest person on planet earth.

For example, last year, Brody was ecstatic that he brought home three, count them THREE lobsters in the two day mini season, diving off a boat in Deerfield Beach while staying with friends on vacation from Ohio. He called Rumpy to advise him that he got on the scoreboard, and Rumpy, rather embarrassingly admitted he had brought back a limit for all six divers before breakfast. My son made a firm decision that the following year he would resolve to join that larcenous mob.

I was okay with that.

Then suddenly Brody became a permanent resident of Key

138

West and the opportunity to become an official Lobster Mobster became his obsession. The *Whacker* had been booked by the same six people for a long time and getting a spot on that boat was like trying to inherit seats on the floor level of a Lakers game. I merely asked for him to be put on the waiting list and, with three weeks to go, Rumpy said one guy could not come, and there was indeed a place open on the boat, and that Brody would get a probationary chance at pulling his weight. Brody would pay for part of the gas and collect crustaceans. I envisioned tying a tether to him for two days and sending him down to the bottom to collect bugs, bringing them dutifully back to me like some sort of human cormorant, the way Japanese fishermen used to catch fish.

The day before mini-season started, we motored up to Rumpy's place on Big Coppitt Key, pulling into the yard about four p.m. His car was there, but no boat. I figured he was either out getting some gas, scouting locations or fishing. They all showed up ("They", meaning Rumpy and the Mobsters) after an hour or so. After introductions, we were informed that the pickings looked slim. Instead of a sea of bugs swarming over his special "spot" there were just a few here and there. Lobsters can be hard to find. Water temperature, currents, pollution, and, despite my firm conviction that lobsters can't read, a lot of stock is taken in some esoteric almanac prediction of a big hurricane season. Any of these indicators can send these relatives of the roach scurrying to deeper water and different places. Being eternal optimists, we resolved to make the best of the day, and headed back into town for the evening.

Dinner was first on the menu, and I could think of no place better than the Hogfish Bar. Noted as more or less a locals place, primarily because people that don't live here can't find it half the time. Hogfish is open air, hot, sleazy and normally peopled by the shallow end of the gene pool. It's also the favorite hangout of my current pain in the ass, Itchy Roberts. Not like I'm afraid of him and maybe up to three of his friends, but I really don't want to involve my son in this deal more than he has already been. It's a lot more fun being a teenager for sure. Itchy's kid took a shot at Brody, got his lumps and two weeks later at school they actually made peace. On the other hand, my issue with Itchy isn't going away, and I'm afraid that dickhead will escalate the issue till someone ends up in the morgue.

Fortunately, Itchy, Scab and the rest of the bottom feeders were someplace else tonight, so we had the opportunity to dine in comfort. I had a blackened hogfish sandwich (duh) and Brody had a cheeseburger (duh again). Dinner over, my son asked if we could crawl Duval for a while. I agreed, and we parked near Schooner Wharf and walked over. My old friend Mike Mcloud was playing to my delight. He recognized me when I walked in, we shook hands and I dropped a ten-spot in the tip jar and asked him to play the Key West National anthem for my son. He would have probably rather have done a do-it-yourself root canal, but he conceded.

"Key West Florida's my home, and I know I'll never roam, where the ladies are pretty and drinking's considered a sport. I'd rather be here, drinking a beer, than freezing my ass in the North."

We bid goodbye to Mike and wandered over to Sloppy Joes. Pete and Wayne, the recognized shock duo of Key West were on summer tour in Ohio, but Barry Cuda and the Sharks were filling in, and we were again greeted warmly. One beer and out, and we headed back to the houseboat.

Wednesday morning came early 4:50 a.m. We dressed, found a local health food store, easily recognized by the golden arches, procured nourishment, and proceeded to Big Coppitt. The gang showed up about the same time we did, and all we had to do was bang on the sliding glass door for a few minutes (Déjà vu all over again) to get the skipper to fill in the team. Everyone jumped to the task, and the boat left at 6:30 a.m. in search of lobster.

As mentioned before, lobster mini season isn't just a date you go look for lobsters; it's an event. On any given weekend in the Keys you can occasionally find a place with a half dozen boats in sight fishing, or, on the sandbar by Holiday Isle you might see 100 boats parked with their drivers peering through a drunken fog at women, equally drunk and well charged with alcohol laden bravery, showing body parts that they wouldn't dream of exhibiting anyplace else. Well, on this day, as we headed out to our "secret" spot, there were more boats than the Christmas Boat Parade on the water, perhaps over 500, certainly, more than 300. Most were in a line over fairly shallow water with some good hidey places for lobsters. No doubt the legal ones were hauled into boats within minutes of sunrise, and all the rest of the "shorts" were going to be worn out from the top down as they were repeatedly caught, measured and thrown back in the water. No doubt some of these undersized bugs got more airtime than a 747 that day. For a lobster, it was a good day to be less than 3½ inches from the top of the head to the end of the carapace.

Rumpy, not known for running with the pack had a spot that was in sight of this horde, but more than a mile from most of them. As mentioned before, the outlook for a good lobster hunt was not encouraging, but the area we were headed was definitely a road less traveled, partially because it was just about on the outside edge of what an experienced snorkeler would want to undertake, averaging between 12 and 15 feet deep. Anybody can go 15 feet underwater, but try to go down there, find pair of antennae sticking out of a hole, then, using a "tickle stick" and a net, coax the reluctant crustacean out of the hole and into the net so you can bring it back to the boat. That takes some skill and experience. Most of these guys had a minute or more of "downtime", and that was the secret weapon. We could put five people in the water in depth that was out of the reach of most people without scuba gear. The lobsters might not be plentiful, but what was there would be ours.

One other trick was to throw a few ski ropes over the back of the boat and tow the gang around at slow speeds. While it was trolling for lobsters in Florida Bay, it would have been trolling for Bull Sharks had we been in the Gulf. Either way it looked like we were doing a re-make of "Weekend at Bernies", with two or three guys at a time being dragged all over the ocean. Visibility was at best poor, and the gang was not looking for lobsters, just a hint of promising habitat. Spotting something, they would let go, and you would see flippers point up and then slide out of sight toward the bottom. Sounds like a crazy plan, and had all 500 boats been doing the same thing it would have looked like a Guinness record attempt at synchronized swimming and would probably made Worlds Wackiest Videos.

But it was just us in this place. Despite predictions of doom, the lobsters started showing up in the boat at a steady pace. And, being in somewhat untouched territory, these were mostly "horses", hefty sized lobsters and almost all males (females with eggs have to be gently replaced in their spot unharmed). The system was a good one. Each diver would catch his lobster in the net, and then head up to the surface and hand it up to the boat, net and all, while we threw an empty net down. Any lobsters that looked questionable were re-measured for legality, and then duly dumped into the bait tank, which was doubling for a live well on this journey. Six lobsters per person, five guys in the water plus two on board with licenses meant our legal take was forty two. Now you would think that two grown men could count to forty two without much effort, but between steering the boat, watching for our wayward sheep as they scattered hither and yon, measuring and taking pictures. Rumpy and I spent the next three hours arguing over the count.

This ain't freaking rocket science. It's third grade math.

Oh, I forgot to mention Scooter Steve. The de-facto leader of the Lobster Mobsters. Steve plays way off the board. He looks like a poster child for steroid use and must start the day with six cups of coffee and four Red Bulls. Just a little amped up, Steve is. He has an electric scooter, lungs that rival any respectable Sperm whale, (probably sperm that would rival any Sperm Whale), and a hunter instinct to go with it. When we got to our spot, as soon as the boat came off plane, Steve went over the side with his devices and sped out of sight. About a third of our time was spent looking for Scooter Steve, sometimes with little success. He would return to the boat only for an occasional drink of water and to empty his lobster bag.

I won't say that he caught more than everyone else together, but I won't say he didn't either.

142

Well, bad counting or not, we arrived at a limit after about three hours. Hauling aboard the hunters, it was back to the house for cleaning and bagging. These guys were as efficient at processing lobsters as they were catching. They were pulled from the live well, and each was quickly dispatched by "wringing" the act of holding the body in one hand, the tail in the other and doing a vigorous twist. Tail in hand, the hapless other half of the creature was tossed unceremoniously into the canal, where it was targeted by any number of scavengers. One year Rumpy said the lobster bodies attracted a number of large tarpon, a few big Atlantic Barracuda and more than one large nurse shark. Today it was a few happy jacks, and local snappers that were taking advantage of the windfall.

So, you ask, why would this huge investment be made each year for two daily limits of forty two lobsters, half of which go to the boat owner?

Ah, well, mmmm. I won't say we cheated. Whatever you do, don't make multiple trips in one day, bagging limits, returning to the dock, cleaning, bagging and freezing your catch before turning around and doing it again till dark.

That's a no-no.

Wednesday, day two, was a mirror of the first day. Blue skies, warm seas, and steady, if not spectacular hunting. It took a fair piece of the day to fill the freezer, and you could tell by the middle of the afternoon that the grueling work was getting everyone fairly tired. I had to work the next day, so there was no chance to kick back, have a beverage and tell lies. We loaded the ice chest with our share of the booty, threw our gear in the back of the Bitch Box and headed back down A1A. Tired, happy, happy, happy.

Brody's invitation to join this adventure was described as "probationary." These guys knew that this level of effort was not something everyone could hold up to, but he did a admirable job and held up his end of the bargain, and was warmly invited to return next year if there was a spot on the boat. For me, yes, I'll go back in a support role if possible, but my boy is 18 now and may be on his own by next year, although dad might still be necessary to be around to make his PBJ's in the morning before he kills lobsters.

Don't want to do the work, but I love the results!

Slumlord

After all the divvying up was done on the wreck, I got a bonus check from Sykas. Seventy grand. I thought that was a little thin compared to what we brought in, but I also understand you can't convert treasure like that into liquid currency overnight. Harry promised more later along with some vague mumbling about a long term position with the company. I guess Practical Pig would have banked that money, but I'm still the grasshopper – live for today and not tomorrow. My gut feeling was that I needed security for now, for me, for my kids. If I was going to invest, it should be in some sort of permanent housing.

Hmmmm. Time to pay a visit to Bo.

I walked next door, stepped over the two sleeping killer watch dogs and knocked on Bo's door. He opened the door, and I barely avoided getting knocked into the bay by Lucky, who treats everyone like she hasn't seen them in a year. After he found the main part of the wreck, Harry paid Bo off, and I hadn't seen too much of him beyond the occasional hello wave over the last six months. The *Captain Morgan* was back in more or less permanent berth, and Bo had exchanged the captain's chair on the boat with the captain's couch in the living room, with a much fatter wallet. We sat, exchanged pleasantries and he poured a cup of coffee. "What event honors me with your presence?" That's Bo. Cut to the chase.

"Well, I finally got a little check from the fat bastard," I said. I'm thinking it's time to put a root or two down. You ever thought about selling the houseboat?"

Bo never answers anything in a hurry, even if he knows the answer. He took a long sip of coffee and turned inward for a moment.

"Seventy, no, Sixty grand to you. That's cash."

"You been looking in my wallet?" I asked. "Cash is the only thing I can bring. My credit's so bad I'm surprised my cash doesn't bounce. I'm assuming there's no wiggle room on that number?"

"It sounds like I just wiggled down ten grand for you. Thanks to you, I've enjoyed some decent cash flow over the past year. It's the least I can do. Anyway, you now have an instant positive income. All the units are occupied. The couple downstairs are a little behind, but not bad. Oh, don't forget, there's also a couple of hundred a month for dockage, and since there's only one meter running onto the compound, I'll pay a fourth and you get the rest."

"Well, I kind of planned on kicking the Ice Queen out of the lower unit and moving Robert down there anyway, then taking the whole upstairs as a two bedroom unit. Makes it a little more livable for the kids and I don't have to worry about the chance of homicide if Grace gets mad at her brother. Grace's not back yet, but I know she will be soon. In the meantime, Brody can enjoy his own personal man-cave."

"That can happen," Bo replied. "I've got a friend with a small mother-in-law efficiency unit underneath their stilt home in New Town. We can slide the odd couple over there at lower rent, and everyone will be happy."

"So," I said. "Done deal?"

"Done deal." Bo extended his hand, and he walked away whistling Jimmy Buffett quietly under his breath. *'Yes I am a pirate, two hundred years to late'*

By the time I got Jack and Carla moved out, paying for the move, Robert moved downstairs ($50 per month rent reduction as he preferred the view from above), new paint and furniture for the second upstairs unit, I had converted my briefly inflated bank account into a strong four-figure checkbook. I loved having my own place, but didn't like being this close to the belt. One major "OOPS!" and I would be flat broke again, just like playing Risk or Monopoly. At least most of the furnishings for Brody's unit were fairly inexpensive, all courtesy of the Internet. Did you know you could buy Camo Lazy Boy chairs? Computer table? Lamps? Rugs? Sheets, bedspreads, pillowcases, towels and a bean bag chair?

Much to my surprise, most of everything I bought arrived as a kit. Buying furniture that's labeled "some assembly required" is the real "in" thing these days. I guess it's a sign of growing affluence. When I was young, I would pull my truck up behind one of those expensive furniture stores and load up a couple of the boxes, which would BE my furniture. Someday I'll plan to make purchases inside of one of those fancy stores. In the meantime, my upscale furniture store is the World Wide Web and the stuff you get online often requires "some assembly." Being the thrifty person I am (labeled by some as cheapskate), and being fairly handy with tools, I figured if anyone could assemble one of these composition board miracles, I could.

The first thing that arrived was a ceiling fan, to replace the existing one that you could hear run from downstairs. It sounded sort of like rocks under a lawnmower, and had enough dust on the blades it looked like it had sawed through a bear. Any dimwit could see that there was "some assembly required" as the box with the new fan was exactly one fan blade long and six fan blades deep. I've done these before and, other than some mild juggling and careful attention that all power is turned off to that room, they are not too hard to put together. Because it was a largish fan, and had a light kit hanging from it, I mounted it flush to the ceiling instead of hanging from a mount. For one thing the ceilings on the houseboat were fairly low, and you could risk losing fingers if you did much more than brush your hair back. (Scarlet had to completely avoid this part of the living room during visits). This has the added benefit of not having to worry as much about balance. I've seen a wobbly ceiling fan take out 20 square feet of acoustic ceiling tiles followed by ten square feet of carpet when left on high and unattended. Assembly was pretty straight forward, but the wiring instructions were in black and white, and the wires were in living color. I had the bonus of two switches on the wall – one for the fan and one for the lights. Without a test kit, the only way to make sure which was which was to give myself a tiny tingle YEEEEOOOWWW! Okay. That's the light side. Let's just assume the other is for the fan.

There was supposed to be this little hook that you could suspend the fan from when doing the lighting, but it wasn't in the box. I will maintain that the only way one person can hang a ceiling fan unassisted is to either be born with three arms or have a promising career in the adult movie industry. Being the beneficiary of neither, I secured Bo's assistance, which both provided assistance and offered the use of his volt meter, which I told him I would graciously accept after I got back the feeling in my right hand, and where the Hell were you thirty minutes ago? Finally, with him holding up the assembly and me attaching wires together, the fan came on with a satisfying quiet *whoosh*. Other than the mistake I made by putting four 75 watt bulbs in the light fixture, which gave the living room the gentle warm glow of a hospital operating room, my first assembly job was complete. (Memo to get some forty watt fluorescents next time I'm at the store)

You would not think a cast-iron double sized sleigh bed would come in a box that was four inches high, twelve inches wide and six feet long. Fortunately, it came with instructions. Unfortunately, it also came with about two hundred hex head screws and a little Allen wrench about three inches long. Fortunately, I had a second Allen wrench. Unfortunately it too, was about three inches long. Fortunately, it came with instructions. Unfortunately, the instructions were a sixth generation mimeograph of a hand drawing with instructions straight from a Pakistani-English literal translation book, filled with incomplete sentences like "Please to install sub-post forward C towards then upper end of lower sub-section B but not forcefully." I was really hoping to field-test this bed later that afternoon, but at this rate my kid would be sleeping on an air mattress until after Christmas.

Actually it got done in about three hours. Once created, mattress installed and bedding added, it looked really nice, and I was almost surprised that there were no extra parts in the box. That brings to mind something I did many years ago. My wife's cousin, her husband and their four heathen kids moved in with us one August "for a few weeks" till they could get back on their feet. They were still there at Christmas, and I was beginning to feel like *I* was *cramping* their style. I get home from work, and the deadbeat dad had four boxes in the living room with brand new bicycles for the kids. They couldn't give me a dime to help with expenses, or spend on house hunting for that matter, but they could buy four bikes for those urchins. Anyway, after they went to bed, I went out to the garage, and dug a bunch of washers, screws, bolts and other weird, non-matching hardware out of a can, put them in little plastic bags and sealed them with a soldering iron. Then I dropped two or three of them in each of the carrying handle holes of the bike boxes. The next night was Christmas Eve, and deadbeat dad was up till sunup trying to use up all the parts in each box. They still didn't move out for two more months, but I enjoyed it sooo much more.

Anyway, once the bed was built I moved on to the computer table. This was more parts but better instructions, and apparently designed by someone that had at least a fair grasp of the English language. The initial challenge was that, although several parts were clearly marked "Front" and "Back", both ends appeared exactly the same, and you would not know which was wrong until you had screwed a half dozen other things to it, thereby requiring the disassembly of those parts so you could start over. It was kind of like double solitaire with three cards missing. After a dozen panic attacks when I could not find anything that looked like "End Unit F" or a "Modesty panel", four hours later, I was out of parts, and sitting at a computer table, remembering how to put keyboard cable "A" into CPU "B" (sheesh).

Where's my monkey? Where's the football?

That left me with the big guy. An entertainment center that came in two boxes that was slightly larger than a coffin and slightly lighter than my Volkswagen Thing. I cut open the first box and parts fell out of it for fifteen minutes. The instructions were thicker than a Key West phone book, and they did not look all that user friendly. Of note, there was also a 1-800 number you could call if you needed assistance. I didn't even get the second box opened up before I called them for moral support. What I got was an operator that asked for my zip code. I gave it to her, and she gave me a list of companies that will come out to your house and assemble these behemoths for you, at a nominal charge. The nearest one is in Miami, and they charge forty-eight cents a mile, plus labor. It kind of concerns me that they don't actually have someone to help you assemble, but just assume you need someone to come do it for you. So much for saving money by buying kit furniture. Well, two out of three wasn't bad. So a few days later this guy shows up to "expertly assemble" my entertainment unit. At first glance, he did not look like the sharpest crayon in the knife drawer, and in fact, I think he probably couldn't pour piss out of a boot if the instructions were printed on the sole, but four hours later, and only one broken part, I had my entertainment unit sitting proudly in the living room. Now the main reason I wanted this big unit was so I could put Brody's stereo inside and hook it up to my cable box and be able to play music through the stereo speakers. Much to my displeasure, the stereo must have been dropped during shipping from Ohio and doesn't work. Now I can't afford a new stereo, but I really want my music. A few days ago, I saw this ad on the Internet for a build it yourself CD/Stereo for about half the cost of a regular system.

Says on the information "Some assembly required."

It took a week of work, but eventually the apartment was furnished, and actually didn't look that terrible, provided you were a registered member of the NRA.

All Brody wore 24-7 was camouflage clothes so when he walked into his living room he more or less vanished into the scenery. Should some unsuspecting eight-point buck happen to wander into Key West from Wyoming, break into the compound, get past the dogs and come up the stairs and into Brody's house, he will be totally unaware that anyone actually lives there.

Unless the deer has a sense of smell.

One week later Grace called and announced I was no longer a subject of lifetime banishment. All was forgotten, all was forgiven, and she was coming home.

She texted her brother five minutes later and told him to get his shit and lazy ass out of her half of the apartment.

It wasn't that long ago that this little girl was a bundle of lap-daddy love with a wet kiss on one end and a wet diaper on the other. I miss my baby.

It was less work getting Brody uprooted than I thought. He knew I would clean for both of us, and he likes company. His only request was that we flip decorations, which I grudgingly agreed too. Now MY house looks like the showroom floor at Bass Pro Shops. Sometimes I throw in a CD with sounds of the jungle just to make the package complete.

I truly fear that something wild lives in a corner of the living room, but I can't see it.

Grace arrived the following Saturday and, per her original request, we went puppy shopping on the way home from the airport. I was thinking like maybe a Chihuahua or even a little pug, surely nothing bigger than a Jack Russell, (distant relative you know), so when she chose sometime small and compact, I was even convinced to let her get two. Ah, daddy has a soft heart, I know, so we sprung for two, count em, two, puppies.

FRIGGIN ROTTWEILER PUPPIES

The pet store had a photo of the mom and dad. It looked like they could both eat hay and tow a Budweiser Wagon. I'm sure they will grow up and want to sleep with the only person that feeds them. Me. Oh well, that's more security for the three lead bars I have keeping my doors open.

We named them Daisy and Duke.

Changes in Latitudes
(Or, Hang on…It's Gonna Be a Bumpy Ride)

I had some sort of fantasy that life was beginning to calm down. Itchy had spent the last half year as a guest of the Monroe County Correctional System due to a burglary in Marathon that led to fenced items at a Key West pawn shop with a very clear surveillance camera. I wasn't being asked to work the dive-site too much – Tack was running that part of the show, and my work at the warehouse was starting to taper down too as we finished cataloging the backlog of items. The haul from the wreck had slowed down quite a bit as all the obvious treasure had been pulled and the team was down to the hull timbers. It was clear the wreck had not come apart in pieces, but more or less sank intact. There was even a suspiciously ragged and charred hole in the hull timbers that hinted the boat may have been scuttled. That would actually jive with the cannon on shore pointing toward the wreck. My guess is that the salvage boat had been damaged and disabled, and had been intentionally sunk to hide the treasure, with plans to return later to recover it. It made no sense at all that there was almost no gold found, unless more than one ship was salvaging the galleon, or the treasure was still someplace around here. I shared that with Tack, and he put a crew on the beach at Boca Grande near where we found the cannon with some strong metal detectors. They did a quick and dirty search and did come up with a few period artifacts, part of a sword, the metal from a flintlock pistol, and three pieces of eight, but no gold.

Perhaps we shall never know.

Just when you think things had settled down to a low roar, the Fairy Godmother Department of Practical Jokes decided to deal from the bottom of the deck. Minding my own business on a Tuesday afternoon, my cell phone rang. I didn't need to check the caller ID as I had loaded Harry's ringtone as the Darth Vader theme from Star Wars. Just so fitting.

"Your dime," I answered.

"Bric, Hey, glad you answered. Ah. We have a little situation-slash-opportunity that I want to talk to you about. Can you jump on the next plane to Tampa? I'll pick you up. Put the plane ticket on the company card."

"Whatever you say, boss. Any hints why I'm punching holes in the clouds on a Tuesday?"

"Better you come, better you come" he answered. He sounded out of breath and like he really didn't have the balls to come out and say what was on his mind.

"Okay," I said. I flipped the laptop open and started checking for flights. "Looking online right now. Comair to Lauderdale and Delta connecting to Tampa. Looks like I can be there about five-thirty."

"Great. Call me from Fort Lauderdale. I'll be waiting outside of baggage claim in Tampa, and we can talk on the way back up to Tarpon Springs."

For some reason, what little hair I had on the back of my head was standing up. I didn't for a second think this trip was going to be something for my benefit, so he was flying me up there to put the full-court-press.

There are very few things on planet earth that I truly dislike (besides Itchy) but one of them is flying. In the old days it was a snap. Jump on a commuter, gun down two rum-cokes, down the jetway and off to your destination. Now it was more like checking into a maximum security prison. You learned to leave anything that looks like metal at home and wear slip-on shoes which is no biggie for me as I own a total of three pairs of shoes; Sperry Topsiders, a pair of Reef sandals and my dive-booties. Key West International is secure but never crowded and when you get to Fort Lauderdale you're inside security so with luck, the only true interaction with the TSA people (Which stands for Thousands Standing Around) will be on the way home from Tampa.

Wish I could take a bus.

The rum-drinks were still on my in-flight menu. I really couldn't stand to face a one-hour drive in the same car as Harry totally sober. After a rough landing that felt about two levels under a CNN Breaking News Bulletin, I stepped out of baggage claim into the normal August afternoon Tampa thunderstorm. 100% humidity, dark as night and raining like Hell. Harry's black Expedition was dripping out in front, and I climbed into the leviathan. I have no idea why people, especially Harry, drive a pig like this. Four miles per gallon, long as a locomotive and the capacity to carry twice as many friends as Harry actually has. Harry was alone in the driver's seat, bathed in sweat despite having icicles hanging off the A/C vents. Harry Sykas had to weigh four hundred pounds and looked like he's never picked up anything heavier than a fork full of saganaki. I sincerely doubt he's ever had a date with anyone he didn't buy in an adult book store and inflate first. He jammed a cigar the size of a summer sausage into his mouth and reached for his lighter till I glared him down. He pocketed the stogie, and we headed west on Hillsboro Avenue to catch highway nineteen to Tarpon Springs. Now I was glad I was in an Expedition. I would have been happier in a Sherman Tank. Harry drove about eight inches in front of his bumper and progress was accomplished in a combination of pedal-to-the-floorboard and panic stops. Sheesh. I've been in a Fiat 500 taxicab in Bogota and been less scared.

Where did he learn to drive? Bumper cars?

After ten minutes of terrifying silence, Harry blurted out his entire problem/proposal/solution in one non-punctuated paragraph, in his squeaky, whiny, smarmy voice. "My family wants me to move the whole Key West operation to Tarpon Springs except of course for the dive operation, so we're gonna close all the properties up and move them here." I felt my heart sink. Jobs are just impossible to find right now, and it sounded like I was getting the axe, but it didn't really make sense that he flew me to Tampa to fire me.

"So I guess I can still work the wreck for a while?" I asked, rather weakly.

"No. That's why I asked you up here. I'm going to consolidate the treasure operation with my salvage and underwater construction operation. You have experience in all three, and I'm offering you a job to manage the whole ocean operation. That's the wreck project plus our underwater construction program in the Gulf. You worked hard for me for several years now and you're honest. (I inwardly cringed) But here's the deal. The family is going on vacation back to Greece in a month and a half. I need you here and on the job by the fifteenth of next month."

Well, good news, bad news. That's five weeks away. I've got a house I just bought, minimal cash, two kids, one about to start tenth grade, and two Rottweiler puppies. Okay, that's terrible news. My head was spinning. "Harry, that's a lot in a hurry. I can live with leaving Key West, but security for my family is really important.

"That's the good part," Harry answered. "I'll give your son a job. He can either come up here or stay in Key West and work on the wreck site, and I'll put all of you on the company insurance."

Insurance was a big deal, and that carrot made it much more attractive.

"When do I need to tell you? Do you have any way to help with relocation?"

"Honestly, I need you to tell me by tomorrow. We have this trip planned, and I want it all in place before we go. I'll throw in a couple of grand to get you up here, but that's it. This is a business, and I'm giving you a business offer. I'm not taking you to raise."

Ah, the real Harry resurfaces. Prick. Dickwad.

"Turn this half-track around, Harry. I gotta get back to Key West right now and have a family meeting."

"But were having dinner with the family tonight. It's all set!"

I've had dinner with Harry's family before. It brought to mind a really bad Chevy Chase/Dan Ackroid movie. The only way you could tell the men from the women is that the women wore dresses. They all had moustaches. I counted to five and told him the only way I was going to be able to meet his timetable was for him to honor mine. He reluctantly turned around and deposited me in the front of the Delta terminal at Tampa International. I barely made the last flight south and was home by ten pm. The flight gave me time to think, but I had absolutely no idea how to resolve the problem. Unemployment in the middle of a recession loomed. Key West had suffered more than most. This island is a tourist juggernaut. It thrives on mega prices, high hotel rates and an exponentially rising economy. It was also a house of cards and the dip in the economy really made the place suffer. The thought of being out of work scared me. We would be through that meager savings in weeks. Then we would be eating the fish in the bay, and after that probably the Rottweilers.

I really had to take this job.

I kept the news to myself till the next morning, and then called a family confab. Bo and Tack were enough family to be included. I briefed them on the deal, and then, using a tactic I had learned long ago the hard way, shut up. Brody was the first to talk. "Dad, I'm cool with it. I'll work on the wreck. Shane works for Tack, and he has a two bedroom apartment and his roommate just moved away. I was already thinking about moving out when Grace moved back. I'm good."

Grace spoke next. "Yeah, let's go. I can get in a good music school in Tampa. I'll be driving next year and can commute or something. Anyway, it's closer to places that offer things I want to do."

Well, that gave me a green light to move, but what to do with my home, what I do for transportation, where will I live when I get there. Way too complicated. I vocalized that and Bo offered a solution.

"Why don't you take your house with you?"

"Excuse me?"

"Take it with you. I brought both houseboats here from Key Largo. It was an adventure, but towing across Florida Bay into the Gulf of Mexico shouldn't be that hard. You just have to try and go when the weather's nice. Right now is a good time. It's a quiet fall, no storms in the area, and a big high pressure dome over the area. Could be pretty smooth sailing, so to speak."

I asked Bo about the hull damage that we had repaired. "I've already ordered and paid for that diaper. Throw some extra patch on the spot, and I'll either ship or bring the diaper to you when it gets in. It should be okay for this trip. Just don't run into anything."

Moving the houseboat to Tarpon Springs had never occurred to me, and seemed overwhelming. I had nothing to tow it with, and if I was going to do that, I needed to be on the way in the next few days. Not sure if there was enough time to plan this thing. First off, I called Harry and asked what he thought about the idea. He was actually cool with it, and offered a free berth at the salvage yard, complete with power and he thought easy access to sewer. There were some other live aboard "real" boats there, and it shouldn't be that big of a deal. With that problem solved, I had to figure out how to get it there. I asked Bo if he would consider using the Captain Morgan. "She's down for repairs for the next two weeks, Bo responded. "We worked her pretty hard finding the wreck, and I'm sending her over to Stock Island tomorrow for a good going over. Sorry."

I called some of the local companies, like Sea-Tow, and they wanted like fifteen grand for the privilege. That was a no-go. My only other resource was Rumpy. I called him up and made the only offer that would bring him out of the man-cave.

"Rump, I got an eight a.m. tee time tomorrow at the Key West Golf Club. Wanna play?"

"What do you want?" was his first question.

"Hey, just a social round of golf. Need to clear my head a bit and I can't think of anyone I would rather play with but you."

"Okay Pal, bring your wallet. I'll mop the floor with ya."

Why They Call it Golf
(all the other four letter words were taken)

Rumpy plays golf about four times a year, always on somebody else's nickel. They drag him into local tournaments as a senior ringer, and he usually shoots in the 80's, despite equipment that probably belongs in the Smithsonian. He's just one of those naturals that you simply hate to get beat by.

Even though it was an 8:00 a.m. tee time, it was already eighty five degrees and one hundred percent humidity. I really didn't need to book a tee time on a Wednesday morning. Nobody else was dumb enough to show up in this weather. Summer temperatures in the Keys range up to about ninety, and when you factor in humidity in the high sixties or low seventies, the comfort zone outdoors is something between "unbearable" and "life threatening." Put it this way, for me, frequently observed as a person that tends to perspire in such circumstances, every day is a wet tee shirt contest.

The Key West Golf Club is actually not located on Key West, but on Stock Island, which is the next key up from Key West. Stock Island got its name back in the old days when it was used to run cattle to feed the locals. Today it's home for much of the lower Keys fishing fleet, half the homeless people south of Coconut Grove, and the Key West Golf Club. The golf course, which was originally a nine-hole course built before the turn of the century, encompasses over 200 acres of native foliage and wildlife and is surrounded by a fairly new country club community. Designed by golf legend Rees Jones, this 18 hole, 6500 yard course could probably rely on the fact that it is the only game in town. Thankfully, the course is interesting, inviting, and challenging, without tempting the novice to throw his clubs, golf cart, and partner into the nearest mangrove swamp. Interesting elevation changes, dog-legs around the swamp, well placed sand traps, and consistent greens give you ample opportunity to enjoy the day.

I met Rumpy at the pro shop and was sorely tempted to pretend I didn't know him. He strode into the shop with an ancient leather golf bag on his shoulder, wearing Columbia Outfitters cargo shorts and a worn fisherman's shirt with the dried blood of some long-forgotten Mahi-Mahi sprayed across the chest. A pair of Sperry Topsiders adorned his sockless feet. The long-billed fishing cap sat above a pair of mirror Costa sunglasses. "What?" He asked after I stared at him for two minutes. I motioned him to head directly out to the cart while I paid the green's fees. We climbed on a cart and headed for hole number one. The first impression of the course is that it is very green, exceptionally well tended, and forgivingly wide. While the fairways are wide, when you venture out of bounds, you don't really have to worry much about where to find your ball. It's brand new and in your bag. Most of the course is lined with natural mangrove swamp, dense as a Mississippi school boy and water-filled. It might be assumed that creatures of some type may inhabit these areas, and it would be foolish to go there.

The front nine has one par five and two par threes, with the rest fours. (The same ratio on the back nine)   Like most Florida courses, the word "water" comes into play frequently.   The signature hole is the infamous par three "Mangrove Hole" that was likely designed and funded by Titleist. It consists of a driving area, and a green with a couple of sand traps. Between the two is a field of tangled tropical mangroves, an area that will someday become solid white with golf balls. If you stand on your tippy-toes you can just see the flag.

Rumpy has played this course a number of times, and gave sage advice as to how Tiger might play this or that hole, not that it had a heck of a lot to do with how *WE* played it. Rumpy had a pretty good day, not counting the occasional mulligan and boomerangs that happened. He finished under ninety, and I didn't. Enough said.

We spent a leisurely afternoon on the links, enjoying great golf, spectacular scenery, and the mini-nature tour that the golf course provides you. We identified at least a dozen different types of birds, including a flock of white ibis, a couple of different types of herons, cranes, egrets and ducks.   A couple of the water hazards house what I thought were monster catfish, but I found out later were tarpon. Tarpon, normally an open ocean fish these guys apparently utilize the underground ducts that connect the water hazard to the ocean to swim in and take advantage of local fish, turtles and small children. We frequently saw rabbits nibbling the grass, and a family of raccoons inhabits a small group of trees near one tee and delight in raiding lunch boxes while unsuspecting golfers hack away.   I also happened to come across a little Lovebird, someone's pet that had apparently flown the coop, so to speak. It was sitting on the middle of the fairway on number fifteen, looking all in the world like an animated yellow tennis ball, and rather forlorn. I walked up to it, and it jumped on my finger. I sat it on my shoulder and played the last three holes with him perched there. He nibbled my ear a little, so I named him Iron Mike. I felt like a bloomin' pirate. After we finished our round, I brought him into the clubhouse and a kindly lady offered to take him. She departed bird in hand, for the Winn-Dixie, either for a box of bird seed, or some Shake-N-Bake.

Having been successful in letting Rumpy beat my ass soundly, I bought him a few rum-drinks at the bar, and started edging up on the sensitive question. He beat me to it.

"So, tell your godfather what everyone else seems to know" he asked.

"I want to see if you would like to make a quick two-grand with the *Whacker.*"

"Doing what?"

"Ah, need to get my little houseboat moved."

"Well, for one thing it ain't little. How far? Around the corner into the 'Row?"

"Maybe a little farther," I softly replied.

"Okay, done with twenty questions. Spill it."

I went on to relate the dilemma and the solution. Rumpy first gave a flat "NO!" but when I sweetened the pot to $3,500, two grand now, and the balance when I had it, plus gas, he perked up a bit. After some more discussion, he said he would come by Saturday morning to conduct a feasibility study. Best I have it unhooked and ready to roll by then.

"Oh, by the way, that's six skins I won. Sixty bucks and I'll assume you have the bar tab?"

"Yeah, sure, want me to sharpen your golf spikes in the process? Oh yeah, that's right, you don't have any spikes."

I headed home to make a list. I had to buy a little generator, find a way to store a lot of gasoline. Buy a port-a-potty from the outdoor shop in Marathon...

Oh shit, I have tenants!

I waited till Robert Portier got home and gave him the news. We had been friends for longer than I can remember, but this strained that friendship pretty well to the edge. He calmed down enough to be just pissed off at me, and headed back into town to look for some family. It would be an inconvenience but not likely a life experience for him. Scarlet, on the other hand, shocked me to death.

"You know," Scarlet said after listening to my story. "A

change of scenery might jus be what the doctor ordered. Mind if I tag along?"

I really couldn't think of a legitimate reason to say no. It would for sure keep Gracie company, and I would have positive income when I got there. I reached out to shake hands and was rewarded with a rib cracking hug.

Before I dove into this project, I had one little piece of unfinished business to take care of. I went down to the marine store and picked up 250 feet of very small, but very strong line, and then stopped by to say hi to some old Navy buddies out at the base on the way home to borrow a few items. Out in Bo's tool shed I found a couple of pieces of angle-iron and drilled a couple of holes, then ground all the edges to razor sharp. Late Sunday night, I quietly shook Brody out of bed and told him to pull his wet suit on. "Wanna play Navy Seal?" I asked with a smile. He grinned ear to ear, put his two-mil shorty suit on and followed me down the steps. The Zodiac was already loaded, and we motored away from the dock, first to the north, then west around to the breakwater behind the Key West harbor. We threw the anchor, and I helped Brody into a re-breather kit. After a few brief instructions, I put my gear on, and we slipped over the side. Without a light and from memory, Brody followed me around the breakwater and right toward the Galleon Marina. The re-breather gear meant no bubbles and the black wet suits made us moderately invisible. Brody got jazzed that he could sneak up on sleeping Tarpon unnoticed. And it was all I could do to keep him from trying to wrestle one. I counted six boats from the left and quietly surfaced to make sure we had the right boat. "This is it," I whispered to Brody, and we slipped back under water. Using the dive light, I pulled the two lines and weights out of the dive bag and tied each to one of the drive shafts of the *"Nose Knows."* Trailing the lines out in front of the boat so the prop wouldn't interfere with our fun, we dropped the weights in the mud and paddled back to the Zodiac for the trip back.

It was time Itchy learned that paybacks, are indeed, a bitch.

Motor Boatin'

We spent the next several days getting the houseboat disconnected, unhooked and untied. We left the power, water and sewer line on till the last possible minute until Rumpy showed up Saturday morning in the *Whacker*. He didn't waste any time with the current scuttlebutt.

"Hey did you hear what happened to your favorite boat?" he asked. "No," I answered. "And for that matter, which boat is my favorite?" "The *Nose Knows*," Rumpy replied. Seems his props got tangled in some thinline and pulled up some metal that more or less chopped the hull about in half. Sunk like a rock three hundred feet from the Galleon Marina."

"Do tell?" I answered, carefully. "Well you know this boat business. Accidents can just happen about anytime."

"Yeah," Rumpy answered. "Just a damn heck of a co-inkydink that two of those lines jumped up at once and tied themselves to the shafts. That ought to make Ripley's or something."

"Well either way, not my problema. Let's turn this barn into a

162

boat" was my response.

After flushing all the toilets a dozen times, we unhooked the sewer line, capped off both ends, and then disconnected everything. The houseboat was officially a boat now. Bo had experience in towing this boat down to Key West twenty five years earlier, and showed us the best way to get hooked up, rigging stout tow ropes so the boat would be towed sort of catty-cornered, hopefully to reduce drag. We hooked the ropes to the back of the *Whacker* and Rumpy slowly throttled up the twin Yamahas easing the houseboat out of the mooring, squeezing between the *Captain Morgan* and the next door neighbor's houseboat, and out into the bay. So far, so good. Once we were clear in the bay, I motioned to him to see what kind of speed he could reach, and everything went wrong. At about one-third throttle, the *Whacker* almost stood on its tail. Rumpy chopped the throttles. Too much horsepower and too little mass. Then a minuscule one-knot wind came up, and the houseboat took off for Marathon, with Rumpy a helpless passenger on a tether. He took the throttles back to about half power and was able to stop the runaway. He looked up and shook his head.

We were dead before we started.

We towed the boat back to the end of the dock and tied it off for the moment. Dejected, I was at a loss.

But Bo wasn't.

"If you take those motors off the *Whacker*, and bolt them on the back of the houseboat, I think you can make headway," Bo offered.

"Drive the houseboat? Mr. Morgan, I think you have been in the sun too long."

Bo went on to explain that it was a matter of mass, not horsepower that was creating the issue. The houseboat was a legal "boat" and as long as I sailed with the appropriate safety equipment, fire extinguisher, life jackets, horn, etc that it could be treated it as such. All we needed to do was fabricate a decent transom off one end of the boat, and link steering and throttle, along with some gauges to a place in the front. Load enough gas, and go.

"This thing is going to be like backing up a loose-hitch manure spreader in anything more than a four-knot wind," Bo said. "But I think you can make decent headway and get there."

Rumpy was still sitting in the boat, smoking a cigarette and soaking up his second nerve medicine beverage, trying to calm down after seeing the late morning sun out of his front windshield. I didn't want to approach him with this new fantasy until I could make some sense out of it myself. First I took pencil to paper and calculated how much gasoline I would need. Those twins at medium cruise speed would eat about fourteen gallons per hour. Miles to Tarpon Springs by boat – two fifty. Cruise speed? That's a guess, but I'm thinking four knots would be about right, maybe more, maybe less. No sense bucking a headwind. If it blows, you anchor. Yikes. Needed a good anchor rope for sure, and a spare hook. Okay. That's 820 gallons or so of fuel. Figure twenty two of those nice forty gallon blue plastic containers that you can find about anywhere around Stock Island by the docs. At six pounds per gallon, you have FIVE THOUSAND extra pounds to haul. Wow. This never occurred to me. That will take up a pretty good part of my lower floor and make this boat a lot heavier than I even thought about. One thing for sure, wouldn't be any smoking anywhere and cooking would be far from downstairs.

I then proposed "Plan B." I would rent his Yammies and then ship them back to him when I got there. His first emphatic "NO" was softened when he realized it would be a quick thirty-five hundred with no effort. We could tie Rumpy's boat up at Bo's, and he would even re-install them upon return. Next day we voyaged out to the dead boat bone yard on Stock Island and found enough cable, steering pulleys, a couple of decent marine batteries, and several truckloads of forty-gallon blue plastic barrels that would serve as our fuel tanks. Pulling the houseboat back to his original berth, we started fabricating a decent transom to hang the outboards on, and cleared out most of the furniture from the downstairs units. Scarlet was left with her double twin beds, which had been moved to the living room, and what was in the closets. It would be a full time job keeping the fuel balanced and pumped into the main tank to power the motors.

Don't nobody light a match.

It took us a week of nearly round-the clock work to get things hooked up and functional. We finally gave up on a remote throttle and just hooked up a somewhat normal setup, ripping the center console out of a wrecked 26 foot Conch Fisherman, and bolting it on the back porch between the motors. Somebody would have to drive, and somebody else would have to watch gauges and work the throttles. When we were done, we had a vessel with the agility of a floating K-Mart, cross section of the Mount Rushmore Monument, and seaworthy as the Eiffel tower, not to mention throttle response and steerablity something akin to a note in a bottle.

You play with the cards you're dealt.

I made a call to the marina and a few days later a truck showed up at the gate with a load of gas. I didn't have a clue how he was going to back out of this little street, but that wasn't my problem. We looked at several options and finally decided to beef up the ramp and fill the tanks street side, then dolly them one by one into the houseboat. Looked like a great job for my son, who could just about carry them under his arm. Each barrel weighed about two hundred fifty pounds full, and the dolly wheels dug into the dirt when loaded. It took strength to drag them up the gangplank, but after three hours, we had five in each of the downstairs living rooms and six in each bedroom. We put down heavy plastic and tarps so hopefully the place wouldn't smell like gas forever. We still had to turn it back into a house, after all.

Finally, we put a red and green light on the port and starboard vent pipes on the roof and bolted a powerful flood light on the balcony rail. A canned air-horn was duct-taped next to the light.

Legally we were a boat. Legitimately we were a prayer in the water. Hopefully we weren't a six o'clock news lead story. I really wanted to take it out for a test-run, but that would have made too much sense. Best to just fire up and set sail, and then adjust as we got moving.

I never said I was smart.

After ten crazy days we were as ready as we were going to be. We had gone through the checklist six times and ready or not, it was time to leave. I thought about motoring outside of the local islands to be clear of the shallows and then anchoring for the night, but the weather and the tides made it sensible to stage the boat in the bay tomorrow afternoon, and leave at the crack of dawn on the day after tomorrow. My Marine Garmin would give me the path, but it needed to be a comfortable high-tide to clear the last channel, and that would happen at six a.m. We decided on a "last supper in Key West" party. We have a small portable gas grill on the boat, but I'm not too comfortable yet about lighting an open flame upstairs with 850 gallons of high test leaking downstairs.

"Okay guys dinner time! Your call," I told the kids. "Anyplace with a cheeseburger" from Brody. "Steak and shrimp!" was Gracie's vote. That sounded like Outback to me. I called Karen for a sort-of last supper, and she met us in Sears town where we both parked in the Publix parking lot. Normally the kids are a running gun-battle when we go anyplace together, but tonight they were civil, even cordial while we ate. I passed on a cold beer and opted for mango iced tea. So did Karen in a rather unexpected gesture of support. She was pleasant and chatty with the kids but quiet, and we both knew that whatever relationship what was about to re-kindle was going to be nipped in the bud tomorrow morning. Neither of us were idealists or stupid enough to think any kind of a long distance relationship made sense. It was good-bye, adios, aloha before we ever got a chance to get the fire started again. We both read into each other's eyes, and clicked our glass to silently toast love that would never be.

Tomorrow was going to be the start of a extremely stressful week. Or two. Or three. We strolled out into the dark, and the kids climbed in the old Bitch Box for the last ride back. Bo agreed to let me store it at his place and then maybe find someone that wanted to buy it. The little VW had no chance of making it to Tarpon Springs, and I won't need a car much when we get there, at least not immediately. Karen and I sort of awkwardly stood around for a minute before I stepped up to her, grabbed her around the waist and tipped her over in one of those "World War Two Is Over" kisses. Her eyes got big, then they got soft, and she kissed back as hard as she possibly knew how. We untangled, smiled at each other and she turned away to her car without another word.

I jumped in the VW and stuck a guitar pick where the key was broken off and cranked. It didn't start immediately, which is no huge surprise. I cranked it again ad instead of starting, I heard a quiet "Whumpf!" from the back. I turned around and saw smoke and then flames. "Get out!" I yelled. Brody bailed over one side and Grace the other, and we ran out into the parking lot. Contrary to TV movies, cars don't explode, but given the proper fuel, they can burn nicely. The engine compartment was fully involved in seconds, way too fast for a "normal" fire as the fuel tank is at the front. It only took thirty seconds for the flames to reach the gas tank, and by the time the Key West fire department arrived, it was a cherry red ball of smoke and cinders.

"Well, looks like we need a ride home," I said sort of anticlimactically.

The fire department pulled the engine compartment hood up to douse the flames, and we looked inside. Despite the heat, you could see where the fuel line had been cut in two, and there was plastic residue on the top of the engine compartment. It would appear that someone had opened it up, cut the fuel line, pulled a spark plug wire off, and then loaded the back of the engine compartment with gasoline-filled balloons.

I would guess that Itchy was back on the scoreboard.

Karen dropped us off back at the compound. I was over this. Despite the darkness, I borrowed Tack's Zodiac and headed out without telling Brody where I was going. Normally you would crawl through this skinny water, even in the daytime, but I could do it with my eyes closed and ramped up the outboard to full speed as I pulled away from the dock. I sped around Dredger's Key through the pass by Oceanside Marina, and into the Stock Island Marina, tying up at the Hogfish Bar and Grill. Talk about walking into the lion's den, or should I say jackal's lair. As normal, Itchy and a bunch of his hygienically challenged thugs were sucking down beer, harassing the tourists and obviously celebrating about something. You usually have to visit a laundromat after midnight to find a group of people like this. Funny, I had gone to school with most of these guys and was probably related to a third of them. The Conch family tree looks more like a flagpole. I strode up to the bar and plopped down on a stool next to Itchy. I could swear there was a faint order of gasoline around him. The waitress automatically reached for the coldest longneck Budweiser in the cooler when she saw me. "Make it two," I told Barb. Barbara had been there for years. Her skin was tanned to leather, and the tribal tattoo on her lower back, which used to be an oval, had sagged down to a happy face smile. I figured the lung cancer would kill her well before the melanoma, but it would be a close race. Barb dropped the two beers on the bar, and I slid one over to Itchy, who, at that point was putting a lot of effort into not acknowledging my presence.

"Here you go, Itchy, this Bud's for you. Probably need something to put the fire out, so to speak." Ignoring the beer, Itchy turned around and stared at me.

"Whadaya mean by that?" (Catchy comeback)

"Look, Itchy, call it a peace offering. You poached on my wreck, and I sent you to the hospital. You skewered an arm and a lung, and I then made sure you could probably never be capable of fathering children for the rest of your life, an act for which I will likely receive a Lifetime Achievement Award from Key West Planned Parenthood. I hear somebody sunk your boat. Probably some irate customer that you sold Sweet 'N Low to and called it crank. Now you torched my car. We're even. Look, I'm leaving this rock tomorrow for a while, maybe forever, so it doesn't honestly mean a rat's ass, but I just thought a neighborly cold beer was appropriate. Drink it or don't. I really, really don't give a flying fuck."

I tossed down the rest of my beer, threw a five on the counter, stepped off the bar and headed back to the boat.

"I'm not afraid of you, Bric! You're just too chicken shit to finish what you started."

I spun in mid-step and walked back to the bar and jerked Itchy out of his flip flops and off the barstool by the front of his ketchup-stained tee shirt with my one good arm. I held him up about an inch from my nose with his toes just touching the ground. I glanced to see if the crowd was going to come to his aid, but they all froze. As for Itchy, he turned white.

He could have really used a couple of tic-tacs.

"Yeah, asshole, I got that. You ain't afraid of me, and I ain't afraid of you. Smart people call that a draw. I just call it life, but let me tell you this. My kids were in that car when it became a crispy critter. You want to come after me, give it your best shot, but from this moment on I make you personally responsible for the well-being of my children. If something happens to them, it's your fault. If it's an accident, it's your fault. For that matter, if one of them comes down with a case of athlete's foot, it's your fault. If ANYTHING happens to my children, I promise you will end up as crab shit at the bottom of Florida Bay. Get that?" It was a rhetorical question and didn't require an answer.

I always loved that scene from the Godfather.

With that, I threw him on the floor, turned and headed for the boat without seeing if he hit the ground. Nobody said a word. Nobody followed.

No Southern Cross to Steer By

The next morning, borrowing Bo's truck, since I was suddenly afoot, we made our last Publix run, stocking up on as much ice as we could pack, water, drinks, canned food, chips, dip, chewy bars and anything else that looked palatable and not spoilable. Then we dropped by the Pet Store and picked up a couple of nifty doggie floater vests so the puppies would float if they jumped (or I threw) them off the boat. I was planning on getting there in five days but had enough staples for two weeks. You just never knew.

Early in the afternoon, we said our good byes to Bo, Tack, Rumpy and Karen, boarded the houseboat, and cast off. The actual departure was almost anticlimactic after ten days of mad rush. The family had talked at length about naming the houseboat, but we really didn't want to give it a name and a personality. Anyway I hated to waste a good bottle of champagne on the "bow" and at this point I was afraid if I hit it with a glass bottle, the whole thing would tip over and sink.

The Key West Citizen was there to cover the event and planned to do a feature story for the following issue. I would have rather exited town quietly, and with luck, I would be far enough out to sea that nobody would come hunting by the time the paper hit tomorrow morning. I fired up the Yammies and slipped it into gear. It was truly weird to be holding a steering wheel that was bolted to my balcony rail. In a dead afternoon calm, we crept away from shore and threaded the house between The Captain Morgan and the houseboat next door. There was twenty feet to spare on either side, but it felt like I was driving a semi through a phone booth. We cleared the narrow spot, and the houseboat slowly eased out into the bay. The tide was inbound, and the leisurely three knot current turned us properly northwest and away from the dock. Loaded like it was, we were running deeper than I wanted and only about two feet between the waterline and the sliding doors on the first floor. I watched over the edge of the balcony, and it didn't look like water was building up too much of a wave. Watching the Marine Garmin GPS, we were in deep enough water and fairly well in the middle of the channel. The first trick was going to be to break away from the current that was going straight under the bridge at Fleming Key. I edged the houseboat as far to the right as I could without getting into skinny water. Control was more or less an imagined thing. I cranked the wheel, and at first nothing happened, then the whole houseboat did a lazy susan in the channel, narrowly avoiding some idiot that thought just because he was in a sailboat that he had right-of-way. With me at the wheel, Grace at the front door and Scarlet half way down the stairs to relay orders, I yelled to chop the motors and waited till we were almost pointing back in the same general direction, then yelled "Full Speed", counter-steering first left, then right then left. I felt like I was playing a bad case of "telephone" from third grade. We were going down a two hundred fifty foot wide channel like a drunken Indian and almost hitting both banks in the process, and I don't think we could turn this thing inside of a forty acre cow pasture. I called for quarter throttle, and then cranked the wheel a nano-turn to the right. Thirty seconds later the boat slowly inched in that direction. Holding it steady, she broke the current and cleared the corner. With Fleming Key now to my left, I had a good windbreak, and a couple of miles to breathe before the next adventure, the boat channel around the tip of the key. I had taken this corner a thousand times and felt you could drive a supertanker through it. Right now in my mind, I felt that I was about to thread a needle. I edged over to the right to be clear of traffic and called for all stop, and then to prepare to throw anchor. The current still had us moving, but slow. I saw rocky bottom and yelled "Throw!" We were only in about twenty feet of water, and I felt the house jerk, drag for a few feet, then hold.

First step accomplished.

By now the Key West reporter boat, along with Bo and the gang in the Zodiac, had been joined by a medium flotilla. It wasn't every day that somebody strapped a couple of outboards on an apartment building and left town.

My hands were cramped, my hat was soaked with sweat, and my knees were wobbling. I looked at my watch and we had been a boat for exactly eighteen minutes. This was going to be the longest week of my life. Or two. Or three. The trick at this point will be to wait till almost slack high-tide, then shoot the corner over the top of Fleming Key, through the shallows, and then we were in Key West roads and a clear shot north to the mainland. With luck we can do it in an hour, then clear the channel and anchor again till the next tide turn. Once out in the Gulf it won't be so complicated, but I couldn't turn this thing in a forty acre cow pasture and shooting the channel was going to be fifty percent skill, fifty percent luck and ninety percent balls.

Looking at my watch, the tide was nearly at peak, so we fired up again, and inched back out in the channel. I was starting to get the hang of things and found I had more control with throttles than with the steering wheel, especially when tight maneuvering. If I had throttles up in the wheel house it would have been twice as easy. As it was, I bungeed the wheel to center it on the balcony, ran downstairs and opened the sliding glass door on Scarlet's unit. Now I had a line of sight with Brody, and after explaining some hand signals, we made the sharp turn around Fleming Key, down the gap and out into the channel with nary a problem. Clearing through the Northwest Passage, I closed the door, went back up stairs, and resumed the helm. Signaling for 2400 RPM, we slowly adjusted the throttles till we were more or less moving in the right direction. It almost looked like we knew what we were doing.

Next stop, Tarpon Springs.

If the Gulf had been glassy calm, and if the moon stopped making the tides go in and out, this might have been a fairly uneventful voyage. And if a frog had wings, he wouldn't get his butt muddy when he missed the lily pad. As it was, we were incredibly lucky in some ways, since it was the middle of Hurricane Season and, with the benefit of a strong El Nino, the storm tracks kept the mid and late-summer storms curving well east of the Florida Peninsula. That doesn't mean you can't run afoul of some nasty afternoon thunderstorms, and with this motorized pig, it wasn't like you could just power up and run around them. Maybe we could outrun an approaching glacier and thunder boomers go mucho quicker than that. Right now we were running about twenty eight inches of freeboard – the distance from a calm waterline to where the ocean would flood under the sliding glass doors. Despite some artful sandbagging, the occasional wave would lap over. It gave Scarlet something to do, mopping up the floors, and a reason to cuss me out when I made it happen.

"What do I look like down here, Susie Fucking Homemaker?" Roared Scarlet. "One more big wave and I'm coming up these stairs and rammin dis mop up your white ass. Then you can mop tha floor while I chase you round da mo'fuggin livin room."

I had to chuckle. Scarlet has an MBA in literature from Tulane and can talk college educated white-boy English better than I can. She just likes to ramp it up when it fits. I knew it was just noise, and anyway, it wasn't like I was doing it on purpose.

We settled down to just a little more than three knots. Funny, we were making speed at about the same rate a Spanish Galleon averaged in the old days. It all depended on the tides and tides in the Gulf of Mexico are like no others in the world. In the "normal" world, tides cycled every eleven hours or so. You would have two high and two low tides every day on average, and the amount of tide was gradual and could be predicted years in advance. The Gulf of Mexico was a big round dead-end, and the tide might get half way in before the outgoing tide met it. Some days you got one tide, some days you hardly got any, and at other times when all the powers lined up just right, you got one ripping current coming or going. The Marine GPS was a wonderful thing. It would measure your forward speed, drift, current, distance to destination, and estimated date and/or time of arrival at your current speed. Right now it said we would dock in Tarpon Springs in about eighty hours. That's three and a half days. I'm thinking we would be lucky to get there in a week, and could take two.

The other good part was that in Brody, I had an assistant with me that was a seasoned skipper well beyond his years. I could nap during the day while he tried to keep the boat pointed more or less where the GPS said to go, and he learned after a while that the bobble to the right would cancel out the bobble to the left, and you actually only did a tiny change in the steering about once every half hour. By dark we had made about thirty miles, and we huddled to decide if we should motor on at night or anchor. We opted to anchor out over the West Florida Shelf for the night. In a full moon we might have motored on, but it made sense to get some rest. We opened some canned tuna, mixed in a few packets of mayo and ate it with some chips and soda. With the boat rocking gently I fell into exhausted sleep.

But when it comes to Mother Ocean, you either have bad luck or no luck.

Day two was thankfully uneventful, but slow progress as we fought the tide during much of the daylight hours. A school of bottlenose dolphin found us and took advantage of the mobile grocery store we were driving as small fish took sanctuary under the shade of the houseboat. There were other predators enjoying the portable reef too, and we saw several large barracuda, and at least one big bull shark in the area. I cautioned Grace to keep the puppies on a leash, as they would be just about bite-sized morsels for that bull. I didn't need to caution Brody – he had no fear, but a very healthy respect of sharks. I had brought along a towable float that we had envisioned using as a leisurely way to cool off in the afternoon but after that big bull shark cruised by we realized he would not know the difference between recreation and trolling for man eaters, so we left it in the closet.

A late afternoon thunderstorm cooled the air, and, even though the water got a little rough, the big heavy houseboat didn't actually do that bad in chop. As we anchored again at dusk, we calculated fuel consumption after seventy miles. At three knots speed we burned about twelve and a half gallons per hour and at four knots about fifteen. At that rate, it would be tight, but we would get to Tarpon Springs on fumes. Just too many stress things happening on this trip. A little good luck would be wonderful.

The nights were almost magical. We played US1 radio for a while after dark, and then shut everything down to go to sleep. There were more stars in the sky that could be imagined, and I leaned against the front balcony for an hour just to look. Remembering my early days, I drew a line from the point of the big dipper until I picked up a blurry ball. Our nearest galactic neighbor, the Andromeda Galaxy, invisible with binoculars in a light polluted sky, was clearly visible in the night sky. The light I was looking at started from that galaxy 2.9 million years ago, and that was the close galaxy. The Milky Way looked like a big white band of clouds. I wondered what thoughts were in the minds of the sailors in that sunken salvage ship 250 years ago, when skies looked like this every night.

With everything shut down, it was so quiet it was eerie. Water lapping against the houseboat, and you could even hear dolphin in the area surfacing and blowing, and even the occasional vocalism from them. Occasionally the automatic bilge pump would rattle for a few seconds as it pumped out leakage from the hull. You could get used to this.

It was just starting to get light, and I was starting to think about getting everyone up and going when I noticed an unfamiliar noise, or rather a familiar noise that was doing an unfamiliar thing. The bilge pump wasn't chattering for a few seconds, but running full blast. I looked over the side, and water was shooting out of the drain in a steady stream. I whistled Brody awake and headed down the stairs. Pulling up the trap door, I shined a flashlight inside, and there was about four inches of water in it. "We've got a leak!" I told Brody. I took the waterproof flashlight and climbed down inside. My first place to look was our patch job, and sure enough, the seam was leaking a steady stream of ocean. At this pace the pump could probably keep up but likely it would get worse. We needed to make repairs quick. We had packed a case of that waterproof gunk and I got it out of the closet.

"I'll go over the side dad. I did it before," Brody told me. I nodded okay, and told Scarlet and Grace to take the front and back upstairs balconies to keep an eye out for predators. "Nothing in sight, dad," Gracie called out. "Nothin on this side either, boss." Scarlet called from the other end.

"No dolphin?" I asked. I would have rather seen dolphin in the area, they tended to keep the sharks a little more timid.

"Nothing!" was the dual response from both ends.

"What do you think, son? Your call."

"Good to go, Dad. Just have the girls keep their eyes open." With that he put three tubes of caulking in his catch bag, slipped on his mask, put the snorkel in his teeth and tipped off the side of the boat. I watched over the rail as he started the patch job. After two tubes he signaled that it looked like he had sealed the opening. He reached for the third tube and then suddenly stuck his head above water.

"Dad, friggin big Cobia under the boat! Throw me my spear gun!"

"Probably not a good idea, Brody," I called back.

"C'mon! Dad, fresh fish for dinner! Pitch me the gun!"

Reluctantly I went to his closet for his spear gun, cocked it and handed it down to him. He disappeared for about half a minute and came back up with about a thirty pound Cobia at the end of his tethered spear. Grinning a big smile, he pulled in the line, and clipped the gun and the loop on the end of the spear to his belt, then reached in the catch bag for the last tube of calking.

"Five more minutes!" he yelled, and then dipped back down in the water before I could yell to him to throw me the gun and the fish.

The Bull Shark must have come from directly under the boat because the girls never saw it or gave warning. I saw Brody's head jerk under the water, and then in horror could see his body being shaken violently as the ten-foot shark spun, and then vanish back under the boat. I started heading over the rail to jump in the water when he surfaced. Throwing me his fins, he more or less levitated onto the back of the boat.

"Well scratch one Cobia and a three hundred dollar spear gun."

I was having a heart attack. "Are you okay?"

"Yep. He came up and grabbed the fish, and then started spinning. I went for a ride till the belt loop broke. He got his fish with my spear and gun attached, and swam off. I'm half tempted to go see if the gun is down there."

"Yeah, well you keep your ass right on this boat," I replied. "We can get more spear guns, but there's only one of you."

"I suppose you're right. But I hate losing that gun. That's twice this year. Shall we pull up the anchor and get moving?" And with that he started walking up the stairs toward his bedroom.

"Where are you going?" I asked.

"To change my shorts."

Two more days went by fairly uneventfully. We stayed close enough to shore to keep away from any large ship, and far enough out to not freak out the Sunday pleasure boaters, but as we passed North of Sanibel, another flotilla came out through the pass by Cabbage Key, ironically also called Boca Grande. The local news had been covering our voyage, and maybe a hundred boats came out past all the Tarpon fishermen to look at the funny boat. We made the six o'clock news, and then apparently it got strung on CNN, so the whole goddam world got six minutes of entertainment and apparently we got our six minutes of fame. They tried to get us to stop for an interview, and we politely declined. Scarlet was crushed at the opportunity, and narrowly missed the photo op as she emerged from the top balcony in an electric blue micro mini skirt, wide fishnet stockings, and a lemon cashmere sweater. The thighs at the top of that Miniskirt were larger around than my waist, and no doubt would have expanded our news TV coverage to the Playboy Channel with honorable mention on Girls Gone Wild. Eventually the flotilla just lost interest, and we motored on by ourselves.

The next, and actually, the last, real gauntlet we had to cross before getting to Tarpon Springs was the ship channel out of Tampa Bay. Big boats, big wakes, and a tidal flow out of Tampa Bay that could wash us halfway to Cancun. As we cleared the north part of Siesta Key, I called the harbormaster in Tampa to see what the best way was to cross the shipping traffic. He asked what kind of boat we were, and my smart ass mouth told him it was a four bedroom apartment. He told me he didn't have time for crank calls, and I suggested he catch the six o'clock news, and left him my number. Apparently he did catch the news and his response was to sic a Coast Guard Cutter out to us from Sarasota to give us an official inspection. Thanks to Bo, we were well prepared and showed our registration, vests, radio, fire extinguisher, horn and lighting. They grudgingly admitted we were legal, so I called Tampa back and asked for guidance or advice. They wanted me to come by the inlet in the middle of the night, but it would be big outgoing tide and I really didn't want to drive this barge in the dark. We argued back and forth and I finally decided to shut down and drop anchor a few miles off Holmes Beach south of Tampa so we could figure out how to get past this last obstacle. I was genuinely concerned that the wake from a big tanker or container ship would swamp us or worse yet, tweak the barge and open that leak up again. The current I could deal with, big ships, no.

Finally, after three days, the tides, weather and ship activity appeared to be lining up right. We would weigh anchor at o-dark thirty and try to get by the channel by 7:30 in the morning. It will be slack low tide, so if we get delayed, we will get pushed away and not sucked into Tampa Bay. When we got things going it was still pitch black and I had to rely on the GPS to tell me I wasn't driving down Hillsboro Boulevard. We punched up the power till we were maxing at a blinding four knots.

The top of the Sunshine Skyway started catching the first rays of dawn as we cleared the south tip of the inlet. So far so good. As we came into the ship channel, Brody saw it first.

"Dad! Ship!"

I peered in the dark to my right and could make out the lights of a big container ship, fully loaded and hell-bent for leather under the Skyway. "Take the wheel!" I gave the helm over to Brody – I grabbed the binoculars, sat them on the rail and sighted in on the ship. It's fairly easy, providing both objects are not changing speeds. If I'm looking at the ship and it's moving to the left out of my field of view, it's slower than us... moving to the right, it's faster. Sitting still - Collision Course. This boat was frozen in the eyepiece, and through the binocs it looked like it was about two hundred feet away. I pulled the glasses down and could tell it was still a good distance, but it would be near soon enough. I had a couple of options. Turn the boat around, which I hated to do. Slow down and let it pass in front of us, thereby facing a bow wave that could be six feet high, or try to squeak by in front.

"Brody, give her all she's got!" And I sent him down to peg the throttles. I could hear the outboards bang up to about 5500 RPM, and felt the neck-snapping acceleration go from four to four and a half knots. If we had put a power trim on the motors we might have squeaked a little more out, but they were bolted hard and fast and what was a comfortable ride at three was becoming a porpoise run at four and a half. Brody came back up the stairs, and I grabbed the field glasses, and drew down on the ship again. Thirty seconds went by and then the approaching ship moved a fraction of an inch backwards on the lens. I looked up again and calculated what that half knot increase would do over the next twenty minutes. It was gonna be close. Really close. I tried to hail the container ship and ask if they could coast for a few minutes but the captain – Brazilian if I caught the accent correctly – rather curtly reminded me of maritime law and advised it was my job to avoid him. I told him I was driving a condo and had little maneuvering ability. To show his sympathy, he merely sounded his horn three times.

I sighted again. Maybe, just maybe he would miss us by three hundred feet. With a half mile to go, it looked all in the world like we were going to become a figurehead on the *Marva Brazilique*. Then I noticed that the container ship was slightly altering course to the south. It was big and loaded, but the bend was making a difference. We were going to clear the big ship.

With death out of the way, survival became an issue. "Brody! Grab Gracie and Scarlett and make sure things are out of high places. Pots, pans dishes, glasses, top shelves on closets. You've got about three minutes! MOVE!"

While I piloted the boat up the coast by my ass cheeks, I could hear the gang doing the best they could to eliminate flying objects. We cleared the big ship by a hair, and it looked like a large city passing behind us. The whole Brazilian crew was hanging on the rail cheering our safety. Then Scarlet came up to my "bridge" and the cheers turned to catcalls and whistles at this bigger than life woman. Looking to see the kids were someplace else, she turned around, lifted her skirt and mooned the ship, much too enthusiastic response by the crew. Then the panties came down, the obvious and rather massive extra equipment came into view.

It was like someone just cut the sound off.

We were still running at full speed, and I was watching the bow wave chase, and slowly catch us. It was like a turtle race, and we were the slowest turtle. It took nearly ten minutes to reach the houseboat, and by then the wave had dissipated some. Thank God for that. The first sensation was that I was surfing with a Wal-Mart for a board as the back of the boat slowly rose up, and we slid down the face of the wave. Then the boat got to the bottom of the curl and the motors came out of the water for a second, making them scream. The front of the boat submarined down to about a foot high up on the forward sliding glass doors, and the top of the boat shook violently, throwing everyone to the floor except me, and I missed being first catapulted, then run over and ground into sausage by about four inches.

And then it was calm.

I hollered to throttle down to cruising speed, and after making sure everyone was okay, called for a damage inspection. Other than a few bruises, and two puppies that were trying to crawl inside Gracie's shirt, we were okay.

I think we were gonna make it.

By early afternoon, Anclote Key came into view. This low island is a barrier in front of the channel that goes into Tarpon Springs. It was too late to try and get home tonight, so I eased the houseboat under the bottom of the island and dropped anchor for one last night. We threw the puppies into the Zodiac and Brody, Grace and I headed over to the beach for a chance to get sand in our toes and feel dry land. Daisy and Duke were beyond happy to be able to run around, and Grace actually broke her poker face and smiled for a moment. We walked over to the gulf side of the island and watched the sun go down. "Nice, but it will never match a Key West sunset," Brody mumbled, arms folded.

I really couldn't disagree with him.

No Tarpon, No Springs Attached

As much as we wanted to, we couldn't just get up, pull anchor and motor the house into the inlet. The river wasn't very wide, wasn't very deep and while we were driving up it, boat traffic would be majorly disrupted. I called Harry at the office and he called the Coast Guard, who called the Sheriff, and the Harbormaster. High tide was at two, so I wanted to be in the inlet by about noon to both take advantage of the depth and to not have to navigate against a current. It's one thing pointing this boat at 250 miles of open gulf, an altogether different circumstance trying to actually steer this barge between shorelines and hard bottoms. I suppose we could have gotten Harry to get us a tow, but ego got in front of my brains, and I decided to go ahead and take her in under our own power.

One thing for sure, everyone in town would know we had arrived.

About eleven a.m. we got the go-ahead to start moving. Brody pulled the anchor and we fired up and headed for the Anclote River. It's a typical East Coast Tidal river, where everything is either four inches *above* sea level or four inches *below* sea level. There are lots of boats with more draft than us that came through here, but not too many that were as wide as the houseboat. Between having a big broadside that would react to a feather light breeze, throttle response that required two people to even function, and steering response something in line with a supertanker, this would test all of my skipper skills and then some. We eased into the inlet, and I had to bump the throttles up to just make headway. We had been careful to not push the motors too hard, (after all they weren't mine), but this was the home stretch with the destination in sight, so I leaned on them a bit more for the last push. The channel started right, then another little right, then a big left and a right around a point; I'd sucked about half the barstool vinyl I was using for a captains seat up my ass by the third turn, but we were getting close – you could see the city of Tarpon Springs around the last turn, and we had less than a half mile to go to get to our berth. One wide area to drive through and we were there. I throttled back and drifted for a moment so I could breathe and get ready for the home stretch. Then I jumped completely out of my shoes when a loud boat horn blasted from my bedroom patio door. "What the Fuck?" I yelled and ran to the back of the house. You could have blown me over with a feather as there was Bo, Tack and the *Captain Morgan* sliding up to the back of the houseboat. "They got the tune-up done, so I thought I would bring you your diaper" called Bo. "When you get the boat in the berth, we can slide it on, and that leak will not be a worry anymore." I waved thanks to Bo and asked if he would like to give us a tow once we got into the harbor. He agreed, and I went back to the "wheelhouse", and gave Brody the word to idle out. Easing out into the harbor, the river current was coming from the left and a breeze from the south and my control was just about one tick above zero. We waddled across the harbor with all the zip of a dump truck full of wet newsprint pulling away from an uphill stoplight.

Two hundred feet to go.

No way to tell it was there, we were just wider than anything else that had come this way recently, and the right side of the boat ran up onto an old submerged concrete piling. I yelled to cut the power, but the damage was done. We hit the piling with a lurch and stopped. The outboards went quiet, and we hung there in momentary silence, not knowing if we were floating or sinking. Then the current took over and we spun around the piling, and you could hear the crunch of wood ripping down the side of the boat. It was a fatal wound, temporarily plugged by a concrete post. "Get ready to abandon ship!" I yelled. I grabbed one of the puppies and pitched it to Tack. The second one was airborne before the first one landed in his arms and he snatched the little Rot out of the air like Lynn Swann going deep. Brody bailed over the back while Grace stood in the middle of the living room, texting to her cousin in Ohio on her I phone. The whole scenario was starting to play out like a bad Bruce Willis movie. I ran around the room trying to look busy and wondering what was going to happen next when I picked the distinctive aroma of seven ounces of Vanilla Fields Perfume followed by the thunder of at least three hippos and an elephant. Blasting through the door came Scarlet.

For the event, Scarlet chose a brilliant sheer yellow silk multi-layered scarf dress, with an electric blue lame top, accented by full ruffles, long sleeves and lighted cufflinks. Pink and orange feather boas wrapped the neck. Eight-inch hooped ear-rings adorned the ears and a fire-engine red wig, piled nearly twenty inches above the head topped off the upper part of the ensemble. Red fishnet stockings and eight inch, clear acrylic platform heels completed the attire.

"Jeeze Scarlet, you look like a parade float from Mars, and you know, you could have used the doorknob."

"I was dressed in sweats till I felt the boat starting to sink. I can't be part of a ship sinking in sweats."

"It's not a ship, it's a houseboat, and it's not Oscar night. You put that outfit together in twenty five seconds?" I asked.

"A lady has to be prepared."

"Okay, whatever. Hey pull Grace Alice out of her fog and drag her ass down the stairs and get in Bo's boat. I don't know how long this thing is going to float upright."

The second I finished the sentence, the living room took a fun-house tilt and the three of us found ourselves standing on the wall, with every pot, pan dish, fillet knife and fork raining down on us. I didn't give Grace any more chances. I unceremoniously grabbed her by the belt and threw her out of the patio door into the river.

Scarlet followed on his/her own, doing a Greg Louganis half-turn, spin flip, ending with a feet-in landing that almost drained the bay. I followed a second after, with the stove and refrigerator flying past me, missing by about six inches. Brody and the puppies were all aboard the *Morgan* as he moved around to where we were swimming. They pulled Grace and Scarlet up, and I climbed up the ladder behind them. I would probably need ten years of therapy after looking up Scarlet's skirt.

"Well, that's that!" I summarized. The houseboat was halfway on its side, and, for the moment, stuck on the bottom. "Tack, take the wheel!" yelled Bo. Tack scampered up the ladder as Bo came down the other side. Grabbing a mask and fins from the dive gear box, he trotted to the side of the Captain Morgan, slipped on the fins and dove into the wreck before we could say anything.

I was too stunned to stop Bo from diving into the shattered houseboat, and too exhausted to actually try to. Bo was no spring chicken, nearly seventy years old, but you couldn't really stop him from doing anything if you tried. For the life of me, I didn't know why he jumped so quickly. Then he surfaced and took a few big breaths. "Bo!" I yelled, "Stop and let me go get whatever you are looking for, or send Brody or Tack!" He glanced up at me, winked and dropped back out of sight. Thirty seconds later he surfaced again and yelled "Rope! Throw me a line!" I looked in a storage hatch and found a coil of that little quarter-inch nylon line that you can tow a truck with and threw it to him. Down he went again. "Tack, throw a mask on and make sure he's not killing himself." Tack had a mask on in a second and dropped over the side. Twenty five seconds, Thirty seconds. I started looking for a third mask when Tack and Bo both came to the surface, Bo holding the coil of line, "Here!" He yelled, "Tie this to something and pull me up!" I wrapped the line around a cleat, and stepped down the ladder to help Bo get out the water. He was too tired to climb out by himself and his clothes were soaked and adding weight. "Get the O2!" I shouted to Gracie. She went into the cabin and came out with the medical oxygen bottle. Bo took a couple of snorts and his color came back. Tack had levitated out of the water and was starting to pull on the line. You could see whatever it was, it was heavy and the tiny line cut into his hands. Then he reached down and pulled aboard his prize: My lead ingot doorstop. "Sheesh guys, there was a half-gallon of Appleton Estate Jamaican rum in the cupboard. If you're going to risk your life, go get something we can use."

Bo put the oxygen down for a second. "Tack, in my cabin below is a sea-chest. There's a satchel sitting inside. Bring it up. Careful, it's a little heavy."

Tack went below and came up a few seconds later with the bag.

"Open it up and look inside." He unzipped the bag and reached in. His eyes grew wide as he pulled out a perfect clone to my doorstop.

"Where did you get that?" Brody and I asked at the same time. "Brody, of all the people in the world, you should know," Bo answered. You've been stubbing your toe on this one at your grandpa's house since you were a baby. "THAT'S IT!" I exclaimed. I knew I had seen one of these someplace before. That bar was a doorstop down in the old man's carriage barn at Wendy's family house.

"Here's the interesting part," Bo said. He turned the lead bar over and it was hollow. The back had been chiseled off and the bar was just a shell. Well, that certainly wasn't like our bars, they were heavy as heck, and couldn't be hollow.

"Tack, get in the tool box and bring me my Makita and a quarter inch drill bit," ordered Bo.

Tack got the drill and handed it to him.

"Playing a hunch," said Bo, as he flipped the bar upside down and started drilling into the ingot. I stepped closer, puzzled. "Bo, we have been down this road before you know, and, like all the valuable stuff was scrapped off." "Bear with me a second," he responded. As he drilled into the soft lead, the fillings first came out of the hole a dull color lead as expected, then suddenly turned bright gold. "There!" he announced. "I thought so. Your fake gold bar is also a fake lead bar."

"What do you mean?" I really couldn't say more than that. "That lead ingot had been my official doorstop for the last two months, most of the time holding a door open and the rest of the time sitting in a house that was unsecured, if you didn't count your Rottweilers."

And it had gold in it?

"Bo, what hunch and how did you know?"

"It's really why I chased you to Tarpon Springs. Along with the diaper, I wanted to see if my research was true," Bo replied. "Ever since the day you showed me your doorstop, something had stuck in the back of my head. You said yourself that it was eating on you. Anyway, I looked at old newspaper articles around the end of the Civil War and couldn't find a clue, and then there was a short article about Broderick's great great, great grandfather, finding some Spanish gold bars that had been supposedly recovered in the water off Key West. There wasn't much more on them, other than he presented them to the customs house and claimed them as salvage. They were described as being 'square in shape, each about thirty pounds in weight, with no markings. Well, that doesn't describe any Spanish treasure that I had ever seen, anyway, I went over to the Sawyer house and paid a social call on grandma Nellie B. She's all alone now, rattling around in that firetrap, which is soon either going to fall down around her, or burn to the ground with her in it. By the way," Bo went on, "She was not aware her favorite grandkids had floated away. Perhaps you might write a letter or two. "Anyway", Bo continued. "Over coffee and last year's Oreos, I asked Nellie if she knew anything about this story. She didn't have much to offer except that the old man was a conniving thief, family to a long line of conniving thieves and she had no idea why she married into the family."

It was sort of weird to be getting a lesson in Key West history while my house, complete with a Sunken Living Room, (along with sunken kitchen, bath and closet) sat on the bay bottom, and we were starting to draw attention from various members of the local authorities. Bo was hell-bent to finish the story. I nodded for him to continue.

"So Nellie gets out the old family journal from 1860 to 1870 to see if there was anything. Thankfully the old man had pretty good handwriting, if poor spelling. We started in April of 1865, and I thumbed through the pages. There was a note about taking five thousand in cash from the bank, and two days later, the notes *"Three goald bars. Twntfive thsnd proffit. Good return on my investment."* A week later, just two words. *"The Scoundrel!"* I looked directly from there to the journal that matched the dates of the newspaper article and the only entry that may have been interesting was the words. *"Rich again. I am sure he did not know."*

"I asked Nellie if she remembered anything else about some large oval gold bars with a big "CSA" emblem, and she said no, but that did describe something in the barn, but she doubted it was gold. We went out behind the house and into the old carriage barn, and there sitting by the door, was a perfect match to your lead bars, right down to a few flecks of gold plating around the letters. I picked it up and it wasn't very heavy and when I turned it over, I knew why. It was hollow."

Bo continued that Nellie let him borrow the lead bar for a few days, and no, she had never seen more than one.

"I'm guessing that your bars were part of this story," Bo explained. "Someone saw them being put in the barn, and sneaked to steal some of the "gold" bars then hid them where he thought nobody would find them, under your Spanish cannon out on Boca Grande."

"Okay, that explains about half of it," I replied. "But why was the gold put into the lead bars, and how did gold bars get plated with lead?"

"Hard to say," said Bo. Broderick Sawyer had a nephew, his brother's son that was a Confederate Lieutenant, and worked close to Jefferson Davis. There are tons of legends about how the Confederacy sneaked away with millions in gold and silver from the banks in Richmond. My guess is that Albert Sawyer was part of that effort and maybe made away with part of the gold, then plated these lead bars and tried to scam his uncle. By the way, do you know where your other two bars are?"

"Sure," I told him. "Right about now they're sitting in nine feet of water, keeping my bedroom closet from floating to the surface. We can strap a tank on and go get them, along with that bottle of Appleton." Brody grabbed a mesh catch bag, the loose line and slipped back underwater. Of course he didn't put on scuba gear.

I'm gonna check him again for gill slits behind his ears like Kevin Costner had in Waterworld.

After what seemed like a week, but more like ninety seconds, Brody's head showed back on the surface. He calmly took in a breath, and handed me the line, and slipped back under. This time I had to wind the line around a deck cleat to haul up nearly a hundred pounds of dead weight, but after a minute or so, the mesh bag came aboard with the other two ingots. I really wanted to grab the Makita and start drilling holes, but resisted. Bo's story was likely true, and I didn't want to question his research. I heard wet noises behind me and Brody came up the ladder, this time with the half gallon of rum. "Grab some glasses," I said. "I think we have earned a little celebration." Well, two of us, at least as Grace was too young and in mourning for her lost IPod, laptop and door size poster of Orlando Bloom. I would have bent the rules for Brody, but he's not a drinker and reached in Bo's ice chest for a root beer instead.

I don't really think Bo planned it this way, but when he came alongside the sinking houseboat to rescue survivors and then tied up to the wreck and dove down to retrieve valuables, bringing them aboard the *Captain Morgan* he had just established a legal salvage claim on a sunken vessel and its contents.

Sipping his rum, Bo casually mentioned, looking over at the houseboat. "Well, it's nice to be back in the salvage business." Looking then directly at me. I caught the meaning immediately. I know the laws of salvage. That shrewd old bastard has just fired a warning shot across my bow. I could see a twinkle in his eye and a pirate's smile too. I also know that all that treasure would have never been found had it not been for Bo.

"Bo, you take one of these bars, you deserve it. To boot, you can have your houseboat back if you want to float it and take it back home. I suppose I'll need to buy Rumpy a couple of motors. I guess I can afford it now." I was also thinking that I would soon have to pay a return visit to my Jewish friends in Miami too.

This is getting complicated again.

Bo tossed the rest of his glass of rum back, smiled again and I shook hands to seal a deal with him for the third time in a year. Nothing was ever mentioned again about salvage rights. Probably the easiest half-million he ever made.

Bo's phone was ringing. It was Harry and I almost didn't need a phone. I'm sure if I turned my ears east I could have heard him from the dock across the bay, where I could see his fat ass jumping up and down. He had tried my phone, which was currently swimming with the fishies, and turned his wrath on Bo. Bad mistake. The last time I heard that much profanity was when I watched the unabridged version of 'Scarface'. Apparently we couldn't navigate a toy tugboat in a bathtub, this is gonna be a big problem, when do I plan to start work, yadda, yadda yadda. "Let me see your phone, Bo," I asked, he smiled and handed it over to me.

"Harry, Bric. Let me put this gently. If you hadn't put a gun to my head, my house wouldn't be defiling your bay bottom right now. Let's just say, after further review, "I QUIT!" And with that, threw the cell phone as far as I could into the river.

"Ah, nice toss, Bric old buddy, but that was my phone."

"Oops, well, I guess you can afford a new one. Sorry Bo 'ol buddy." There goes that rum talking again.

The houseboat was grounded in about fifteen feet of water, and the current had pulled it out of the navigation channel, but it didn't stop the Coasties from paying a visit, issuing us a citation a foot long for a multitude of violations. I offered them a taste of rum and that got me one more ticket.

Bribing them with some Spanish Pieces of Eight probably wasn't a good idea either.

Then the Sheriff boat showed up.
Sheesh.

All Things Considered,
I'd Rather Be in Key West

So there we were, without a care in the world, homeless and wet, but theoretically rich. Come to think of it, what if the only one of my three bars that had gold was the one I most generously donated to Bo? At this point I was working on faith and trust, and anyway, I was having too much fun to get off the ride at this point. Once we finished our two hours of "yessers" and "yessmaams", and had the authorities convinced we could clean up our own mess, they left us alone for the time being, no doubt retreating to neutral corners where they could watch us like a hawk. Or buzzards. Now that we were by ourselves again, I turned to Bo with a perfectly honest question. "So how do we float our boat again?" Bo smiled his half Cheshire cat – half Mona Lisa smile and said. "Watch me. I could start this a lot quicker but somebody decided to throw my phone in the ocean. We need to get to a pay phone."

Bo and Tack jumped in my little Zodiac and headed for the port, while Brody and I tried to rescue a few personal items and clothes from the houseboat before they floated away. I also directed Brody to head down a level and see what he could drag, so to speak, up from Scarlet's place. After all, a scarf skirt and lame top isn't going to be that comfortable, even when it dried out. He emerged with capri pants, flip flops and a various assortment of tank tops.

191

I turned to Scarlet. "What's your plans from here my friend? Looks like ours are in a bit of flux."

"Flux," she responded, "is an understatement. For me, it's the end of the road. Get me to landfall and I'll part company for a spell. Not goodbye, but let's just say an adventurous interlude."

After a few hours, Bo returned, new cell phone in hand, which he kept far away from me, and a game plan. He had found the number for a different local salvage company, since I was officially *persona non grata* with Harry's company, and they would be here tomorrow morning.

In the meantime we maneuvered the *Captain Morgan,* backing up to where the two outboards were. The youths dove down and unbolted the two Yamahas. Using the winch on the back of the *Morgan*, we hauled the two motors up. Fortunately they had been shut down before they started drinking water so it was just a matter of a flush, cleanout and some electrical items and they would be good as new. "Bo, can I borrow your phone to explain to my friend that (A) I had drowned his two motors, (B) that I would be buying him two brand new ones and (C) It's gonna be a few weeks before I was flush with cash." "You can wait till you have your own phone. I like this new one and don't want it used as a hand missile next time you lose your temper."

There was a Yamaha Marine store across from the tourist area at Tarpon Springs, so we took the motors over for repair, and gave Scarlet an escape as the day drew to a close. I'm not sure Tarpon Springs was ready for a the likes of Scarlet, but it wasn't an option as Scarlet prepared to step off the back of the *Captain Morgan* as it nosed up to the dock. We were all subjected to being smothered by two massive arms, and some successful hugs and a few dodged kisses. Grace got a few private words, and brief instructions as to what to do with personal effects if and when they were retrieved. "Box them up and take them to Good Will. You can keep the jewelry since it's all fake" and with that Scarlet stormed down the wharf to hail a cab. Traffic, spectators, merchants and the cops more or less froze at the spectacle. It made me think of the scene from "The day the earth stood still", as the cab drove out of sight to who knows where.

What a day this has been.

The cops had been clear we had about eight nano-seconds to get this boat floating and out of their sight or they would take action and send us the bill. We figured we could be gone in two days if we busted our asses, and it wasn't clear that would be good enough. Needless to say, I was happy to see the salvage boat show up the next morning just after sunrise. Per Bo's order, they had a half dozen large airlift bags, a compressor and air hoses. Brody, Tack and I pulled on scuba gear and tools, stepped off the *Captain Morgan* into the lower floors of the houseboat, and started cutting holes in the floors big enough to stuff the airbags inside. We got that part done by the end of the first day and then, early the next morning, we started to inflate them slowly, alternating each bag till the houseboat slowly lifted off the bottom. By noon it was floating fairly level with the first level floor only about eighteen inches below the waterline. From there, we went over the side and worked all the gashes over till there were no sharp edges.

Now came the fun part. The fiberglass treated cloth "diaper" had been sitting in a big bale on the deck of the *Morgan*. All we had to do was drag this big bag under the houseboat, pull it up snug to the bottom, and then start pumping the water out. I honestly had no clue how, but Bo seemed to be completely in control. Backing the *Captain Morgan* up to one side of the houseboat, we tied long nylon ropes to corners of the diaper, and then swam around the houseboat, handing the ropes to the kids at the back sliding glass doors. Then it was "Heave-Ho!" while Bo and Tack slowly pushed the heavy cloth over the side. This suddenly became a very heavy bag of water and it was all we could do to get it under the boat and have some of the material start to show. Then we got a guy on each corner and just hauled till it was more or less under the boat. We fired up the trusty bilge pump with the boat generator and water started pumping out of the pontoons. Straining as hard as we could, and tying ropes up on anything that we could take a wrap around, we still didn't look like we were making any headway.

Finally after about two hours, the black cloth of the diaper started showing up on all sides. With all the corners of the diaper above water level, the boat started rising quickly. A few hours later and we switched on a second pump, this time to empty out the diaper under the boat. Just before dark, the repair was snugged nicely up to the side of the houseboat all the way around. We would wait till morning to attach it to the sides with long screws and two by fours.

The following day we deflated the air bladders and towed the houseboat over to the salvage dock. Stoves, refrigerators, microwaves, carpets, TV's, laptops and all the clothes went into a dumpster. Bo would re-furbish and re-furnish it when he got it home.

"So, Bo, you gonna bolt those motors back on and drive it home?" I asked. "Hell, no. Do I look that dumb?" he replied. "You didn't think it was that dumb when I asked you if I could do it." "As I recall," he said, "I told you that YOU could do it with some work and a little luck. I never said it was something that I would do. I'm going to tow it home behind the *Captain Morgan*."

"So now the *Morgan* is healthy enough for the job?" I asked.

"Let's just say I'll be able to afford a re-build when I'm done this time," Bo replied.

Since I was technically flat broke till I could get the gold out of those lead bricks, I saw little option, being unemployed due to my big mouth, than to head back to Key West. Bo was cool with adding the crew. He had a couple of decent boat jockeys to help him and he figured he could win what little cash I had left on me playing poker on the way. We picked up the cleaned-up outboard motors, got some supplies and headed back out the Ancelotte River with the tide the next day. I offered to send Grace back to Ohio till we got squared away but she declined – said she was starting to enjoy the fun a little.

One thing for sure, it was never dull.

The trip back was nothing compared to the trip up. We still were stuck at about four knots, but without the stress of driving, it was just a leisurely cruise on calm waters. That speed was almost the perfect trolling speed with Tack and Brody hanging out the back sliding doors with rods and lures trailing. Almost every time we motored over any structure or shallow area, we brought a sailfish, bull shark or even the occasional grouper up to the surface. Since we didn't stop it would usually be a short fight, but an exciting one. Tack got a hammerhead on once that had to be fourteen feet long. It ripped off two hundred fifty yards of braided mono before snapping one of Tack's good deep-water rods in two. After that, the fishing was limited to small lures and smaller fish.

The other easier part to the trip home was that we could unhook the houseboat, drop an anchor and take the *Morgan* into harbor for food, fuel and a quiet moment. We did that at Siesta Key, Port Charlotte, Fort Myers and Naples before heading out over Florida Bay for the last run home. It took nine days this time with the stops, and we berthed the houseboat back in its place on Hilton Haven just three weeks after leaving. Bo has two other houseboats that look much more like what you envision a houseboat looks like, the kind you rent for a day and cruise in a lake, and he offered one of those to use while we could figure out which way to turn. I had to get the gold out of those lead bars, find a source to sell them and then, if the money was as good as it looked like, we could maybe take it easy for a while. I would love to see Brody in college, but I may have already lost him to the sea. For Grace Alice, I would make sure she could choose the best college in the world, and pursue writing, music or drama as she pleased. Maybe the day would come that I could get back on her good side. I wasn't going to buy my way in, but I still wanted to give her the best shot possible.

We didn't have much to our names at this point. We were going to try and dry out as much stuff as possible, but most of our personal stuff and collectables were ruined, except for Brody's dive gear. For once his hobby proved to be the right one for the occasion. We had barely got to sleep on the first night back when I heard the dogs barking like crazy. The bell rang at the gate, and I assumed Bo would take care of whatever the visitor wanted. Probably trying to deliver a pizza to the wrong address. Then there was a knock at the side of the houseboat. I slipped on a pair of shorts and walked out to the deck. Bo was standing there with Key West Officer John Russell.

"Hi cuz. What's up?"

"Hey Bric, guess you need to come downtown with me. Some people want to talk to you."

"About what?"

"I'm arresting you for suspicion of the murder of Donald Ray Roberts."

"Itchy? I haven't seen him since just before we left and we just got back today. You've got the wrong guy."

"Bric, that's for other people than you and me to decide. I told them that I didn't need a bunch of people to bring you in and that you would come without an argument. How do you want to do this?"

"No, not a problem. I haven't killed anyone. Let me get my stuff. You can come in if you want."

"No, that's okay, I'll wait out here."

I went inside and finished dressing, then sat down with Brody and Grace. "Look you guys know where I've been and know I'm not guilty, but it's going to take some explaining I'm sure. Brody, call Uncle Karl – his number was in my address book but it's ruined so call information. Tell him what's going on and ask if he can come down. Tell him I can pay, but won't have the money till after I get this resolved. Gracie, I'll ask again. Do you want to head back up to Nick's in Ohio for a while?"

"No. I'm staying daddy. I know you didn't do anything. I'm good here. Brother will take care of me."

I took my ATM card out of the wallet and gave it to Brody. "Use this for food and what you need. Bo's next door if you need anything."

I walked out and followed John to the squad car. Bo walked us out and said he would look after the kids. He knew better than to say anything else in front of John. Cousin or not, he was on the other side right now.

In the Pokey

They booked me into Monroe County Detention. I had only been inside there or for that matter any jail, once before in my life, and for that a playing little joke that nobody else thought was that funny. I was playing years ago in the band out on the Sunset Pier at Zero Duval when I got wind that the wife of the current vice presidential candidate was in town, stumping for her hubby, and staying at the Sunset Resort. We were told she would be out on the pier at sunset to listen to the band so I ran into town and hit the Dollar Store and bought a bunch of these little earplugs like you use for a cell phone, the kind with little black curly wires coming out of them. Then I handed them out to everyone in the crowd before we went on to play, telling them nothing other than it was an inside joke. When the secret service guys showed up to secure the place, they walked into a crowd of 100 people, all wearing ear-pieces like they had on. They freaked and the band died of hysterics. Somebody snitched and off I went to jail for the night. Some people just can't take a joke.

Anyway, this situation wasn't that funny. They brought me into an interrogation room. The kind that normally has a big mirror on one end that Karl Malden can see you from the other side, but this one just had a table with two chairs on one side and one on the other. Two detectives, Silva and Sloan, came in. I knew both of them a little, as cops that like music and they often came to see the band. Nice enough guys off duty, it was all business tonight.

"Russell, do you know what you're here for?"

"Russell is my first name. Bricklin is my second. You can call me Bric. John Russell gave me the quick and dirty. Somebody thinks I killed Itchy. I didn't do it. I couldn't have done it. I was on my way and back to Tarpon Springs in a two story houseboat for the past three weeks. I've had witnesses with me all the time. When did I supposedly kill Itchy?"

"Bricklin Wahl. Ah. Brick Wall," Detective Sloan said, ignoring my question for the moment. "Very cute. What made your parents hang that on you?"

Russell is my Mom's family name. Bricklin is my Grandmother's name on my dad's side. I guess he wanted me to learn how to fight early in my life."

"Mr. Roberts was found late last week," Sloan continued "he had floated ashore on Marvin Key. His body was partially decomposed and had been a feeding station for various forms of marine life. He had been missing for about two weeks and his family was able to identify him from his tattoos."

"I'm sure dental records wouldn't have been too useful," I said, almost to myself. They used to say that the Feds couldn't solve a crime in Key West because everybody has the same DNA and nobody has any dental records. "Well, like I said, I was out in the middle of the ocean on the way to Tarpon Springs during this whole period. I have witnesses watching me leave, my kids were with me all the time, and my landlord met me in Tarpon Springs, and towed us back here. Oh, also one of my tenants was with me too on the way up."

"You see, that's it. Your witnesses are either family, or your landlord. Mr. Morgan is an upstanding citizen, but your personal friend. You don't have much of an alibi. Who was your tenant that came along?"

"Kevin Montclaire. He's also called Scarlet and used to work at Aqua. When I told him we were moving to Tarpon Springs, I was surprised that he up and decided to come with us. Not many drag shows in Tarpon Springs you know."

Detective Silva raised an eyebrow. "Did you know Mr. Montclaire worked for us as an undercover officer? He was a major help with a huge drug sting operation that just wrapped up.

Kevin felt he was in some risk when the bust went down so a change in venue was probably attractive. If you can produce Kevin, it would be likely you could be cleared from this."

I explained about the houseboat sinking and Kevin telling us that he was going to see the country for a while. I had no idea where he might have gone, although somebody matching Scarlet's description shouldn't be that hard to find.

It suddenly came to me. "Why am I a suspect? I don't care for the man but that doesn't mean I killed him."

"There was also a spear in his back with twenty feet of line trailing in the water," Silva continued. "The initials 'RBW' were Dremmeled on the spear. Any suggestions on who might own that spear?"

"RBW? I think that stands for 'Really Bad Week'. Yeah, likely that's my shaft. I mark all my stuff because it gets mixed up on the salvage boat. Everyone borrows everyone's stuff. I'm guessing that Doobie might have lifted that one.

"We're aware of the chain of incidents between you and Mr. Roberts," Silva said. "And we have this deposition." He slid a couple of pages over to me. "It's a statement from one Barbara Peterson, waitress at the Hogfish Bar and Grille, verifying that you had indeed threatened Roberts with an ocean-based death not three weeks ago. There were five other people at the bar that collaborated this story." Looks like his friends and family had more weight than my friends and family.

I started to see how they had this figured out. "So", I said. "I have lots of witnesses see me leave – it was in the Citizen with some sort of sappy headline 'Condo Takes to Sea' or something like that, and an equal number of non-family witnesses that saw my rather inglorious arrival in Tarpon Springs, including Hernando County Sheriffs, Coast Guard, a salvage company and one very pissed-off ex-boss. How can I be a suspect?"

"We figure it's like this. You made your grand exit, got someplace out of sight of land. Anchored the houseboat, had somebody come pick you up in a go-fast – you got lots of friends with go-fast boats - came back at night, bagged Roberts, who knows how? Crabs aren't very helpful with preserving evidence – pitched him in the ocean, and got a ride back before sunrise, then continued your trip. Now that you bring it up, if you can't produce your only legitimate witness in the form of Mr. Montclaire, we may contact Hernando County and advise them we have a person of interest in the disappearance of that individual too."

I knew when I was being end-runned. "I think I'll shut up until my lawyer arrives," I responded.

"Bric, we really want to believe you, but you have method, motive, motivation and a weapon you agree is yours. We don't really even need a murder weapon; we have the whole gulf-of fucking Mexico as a murder weapon, and a whole lot of people that heard you tell Itchy that was going to be how you would kill him. We're going to book you for suspicion of capital murder."

From there I got processed, photographed, fingerprinted, was given a shower and issued some nice blue jail clothes and plastic sandals. They threw me in the holding cell for the rest of the night. I was in with a half dozen deadbeats, winos, pickpockets and assorted scumballs. Gave to mind the order of a downwind venue at the city dump. They must have bypassed the shower offer. They could tell I wasn't a regular and tried to mess with me a little.

"What are you here for?" dirt bag one asked.

"I got a 'D' in spelling at the city college. It's a tough class."

"Hey look guys, a smartass. Everyone loves a smartass. What's your name smart guy?"

I gave a heavy sigh and stood up. Nobody looked like a real thug so I gave my go away speech. "Look guys, I'm not in the mood to play patty cake. If someone wants to come over here and let me help them smack their face into the bars to help them shut up, then get in line. Otherwise, leave me the fuck alone. It's been a long night." I lay back down and turned my back to the crowd. After a very long time I drifted off to sleep, dreaming of Spanish galleons, gold bars and pretty blonde pirates with sky blue eyes.

The following morning I was led back into the interrogation room. My dad's brother, Karl Wahl, was there. The deputy left us alone and we sat down. "I brought you a cup of coffee Bric. You can't believe how hard it was to find a Starbucks in this town. I never understood what my brother saw in this place."

"Well, among other things, my mother," I replied.

"So," Karl said, changing the subject and getting down to business. He never cared for my Mom's side of the family. Thought they were snooty pseudo-Key West royalty. "I've read the complaint, and the deposition. Looks like you're in trouble. Tell me about it."

I started from the beginning, when we threw the cherry bombs and I cut off the air supply. I explained the truth of maritime law is not always the spirit of it. Had I discovered these guys on the wreck, then went and got the cops, it was more of a civil matter than a legal one, at least at the first. By the time I had proved they had no right on my wreck, it would have been cleaned out. Heck, if they had suffered mutual and fatal accidents, it's likely it would have never gone to trial. I figured they were lucky I had just given a warning. Anyway, from there to the sword attack, my retaliation, having my car burned, then my rather inappropriate public counseling session at the Hogfish, our leaving town and then coming back, only to find out that Itchy had become a pelagic food source. Karl knew the rest.

"Let me ask you," Karl continued. "And I'm not going to ask the obvious question. Would it be physically possible for you to do that?"

I had to be honest. "Yep. It's possible, but, to answer that obvious question, I didn't." Karl waived his hand as to dismiss what I said. "So, the detective said you might have a quality witness that would help this not even going to trial. Do you know where this individual is?"

"Not a clue. Scarlet doesn't have a cell phone, doesn't believe in them, and only carries cash, no credit cards. Comes from middle Louisiana, but the family doesn't care much for his lifestyle. He could be anywhere. Just anywhere."

"Well, I'll get my people working on that part. Mr. Montclaire doesn't sound like someone that can stay out of sight forever. In the meantime, I'm going to stay down here till we get this resolved, even if it means going to trial. I can have my staff keep the home office lights burning. And don't worry about payment. It's family."

I mumbled something about being able to pay, but just later. Should have kept my mouth shut. This got Karl curious.

"How? You just told me that your house sunk, your ex-landlord claimed salvage on it and you quit your job. I don't see how you are going to be able to eat, much less pay legal fees. Is there more to this story?"

I gave Karl the Reader's Digest version of the gold bars. He raised his eyebrows at the apparent value of the bars. "Is there any chance this guy would have known about the bars? For that matter who does know?"

"Bo, my kids, Kevin Montclaire and that's all. Heck, I didn't know about the gold till after we got to Tarpon Springs, and that was two weeks or so after Itchy supposedly got whacked. Karl, if I was a guessing man, somebody overheard the conversation at the Hogfish, and figured I was a good mark to lay the blame on for Itchy's being made dead. Round up that pack of low-life's and you will find your perp."

"Back to the gold," Karl said. "Is it legally yours? Does your ex boss have a claim on it? It looks fishy that you went through all the trouble to get your houseboat up there and then turned around and came home."

"Technically yes, and technically no. The gold wasn't part of the treasure we had a permit to salvage, and it was too far from the wreck site to even be included, but I found it while working for Sykas – sort of. I actually didn't put the items in my possession until I was off duty. Maybe a grey area, but it's definitely not part of Harry's treasure ship."

"Well, I'm not here to discuss the legality of that," Karl went on "but you are for sure in a pickle. All you have for an alibi is your two kids, your best friend, an Amazon cross-dresser that has vanished out of sight, and an ex-boss that probably wouldn't piss on you if you were on fire. Unless they can find a real witness, or better evidence, I don't think they can bring it to trial, but they will make your life miserable in the meantime. I'll take a shot at bail and see what we can do."

Three days later I was brought before the judge and arraigned for first degree murder. Karl threw everything he had at Judge Curry but it had the same impression as Joe Pesci did in "My Cousin Vinny." Uncle Karl was fair haired, and his Minnesota tan had left him fair skinned enough to be considered transparent by local standards. The Armani three-piece suit was about as out of place as a nun in a whore-house. Karl threw out a couple of precedents, and the judge calmly advised that he would research them over the next few centuries while I cooled my heels in County. We finally got to the plea and I got to say my whole two words.

"Not guilty."

The judge set a preliminary hearing vaguely for some time in the next two years, denied bail, and off I went to more permanent quarters.

Ain't life just the tits?

Over the next three weeks, Karl kept looking for Scarlet with no success, and Bo brought the kids to see me every day. Maggie appeared to be not interested in a suspected felon, and sort of melted into the shadows. Karen was out of the state on sales calls and anyway I didn't have time for a relationship right now. Besides, Monroe County had no provisions for conjugal visits. My only dates for the time being would be with rosy palm and the five fingers. I'm sure the cops were equally frustrated in trying to find any evidence, since I didn't do anything there *WASN'T* any evidence that I did. Either way, they tore into the soggy houseboat and dragged out box loads of potential evidence. I quietly asked Brody to make sure our doorstops were someplace else and he told me that Bo had already hidden them away the night I got hauled off. He had also been fairly neutral cooperative with the cops, and even let Lucky and the Rots tree a couple of them one afternoon when he accidently left the back door open. I found this funny as Lucky probably just wanted to play catch with them, but the police made fewer exploratory trips after that. If they wanted to sort through waterlogged stinky useless stuff, be my guest. There was nothing there to hide.

I was about to the point where I was either going to start pumping iron for a career or resign myself to getting some prison tattoos and becoming someone's bitch, when I heard some sort of disturbance in the hallway, followed by a very familiar voice announcing, "Baby, you don't let me in that room right now, I'm gonna spin yo lily white ass 'round and yo gonna wake up tomora mornin feeling like you been fucked by da Conch Train!"

Scarlet had come home.

She made a grand entrance into the common area, tastefully attired in black skin tight spandex Capri pants, Halloween orange silk top, the biggest fake boobs created in the western hemisphere and white spike heel cowboy boots. That spandex was tight. I had no idea where the pickle was hiding, and at that point really didn't care. John Russell opened the cell and Scarlett tried to smother me in six pounds of high density foam. I motioned distress with two fingers and she let me come up for air. Karl walked in behind Scarlett with a big smile on his face. "I put an ad on Craig's List looking for any black men over six foot five that could roller skate in a dress. You would not believe that I had six takers, but one of them was your friend here."

It only took two days to get me changed from a murder suspect to a "person of interest." Kevin - AKA Scarlett had huge pull with the department and came forward as a valid witness. "They asked me if I thought you were honest and trustworthy. I told them that I wouldn't leave you alone with a six pack of Icehouse, but other than that, you were a straight player. Guess that was good enough for them."

After giving a deposition and offering to return if there was a need, Scarlett headed to the bus station. "Ain't that healthy for me down here right now," she told me. "People be very pissed off that I ratted on them, but I'd do it again. Drugs ruin this town and especially black people here. It needs to stop."

And back out of my life one Kevin 'Scarlet' Montclaire went.

I wasn't completely off the hook. Just because it was proved I didn't do it, didn't mean I didn't do it.

"You're free go, but don't leave town, check in with the detectives on schedule, and try to stay out of trouble of any kind in the near future," Curry said.

"That shouldn't be a problem, your honor, I can't leave. My murder victim burned my car up and I seemed to have sunk my home all by myself."

"That statement just about earned you another thirty days. Get out of my sight before I throw you in again."

I didn't have to be asked twice.

Two weeks later, they arrested Billy "Scab" Forester for Itchy's murder. Scab was already in jail for rolling a drunk on Stock Island, and while he was in the tank waiting to go before the judge, he started bragging about how he wasted Itchy and made it look like I had done it. Half the crooks in the cell, looking for a good behavior early-out told the cops, and when they put Scab under the hot lights for about ten minutes, he started singing like a choir boy. Seems Scab was mad at Itchy for sneaking around with his wife, and now the heritage of her impending bun in the oven is suspect. Making Itchy dead was the only retribution conceivable.

I seriously doubt you would have been able to differentiate the DNA.

Déjà Vu All Over Again

With all of that excitement behind us, there were a few matters at hand, not the least of, getting the gold out of those lead bars and then find a way to quietly convert them into cash. I was pretty sure my friends in Miami would be players, but I was currently not supposed to even be leaving town. I really didn't want to get anyone else to do this for me, so it was likely I would be breaking the law again while I was committing a crime by fencing gold. Wow. How deep did I want to go?

Since Bo was the owner of one of the three bars now, we decided to collaborate efforts on how to get it out of the lead ingots. We examined the empty bar from the old barn for clues. I would guess that there was only one left because they tried to melt one of the others to turn it into bullets or sinkers. Lead melts at about 850 degrees and gold is closer to 1800, so it's conceivable, that you could melt one and not the other, but that's easier said than done. Playing with thousand degree molten metal is not child's play, and these things were pretty large. There was probably nothing in town big enough to do it. Anyway, it looked like they had figured this out by the time they got to this bar. It appears that the lead ingot was cast with a hollow center – fairly easy with a sand-cast if you knew your business – and then you cast the gold plug the same size as the hole and slipped it in, then poured a ¼ inch cap over the bottom. It appeared the old man had just ground the bottom of the lead brick and let the gold fall out. We decided to do the same with an acetylene torch. I really wanted to get mine opened up and leave the lead with the CSA emblem intact. It would still be a good doorstop, and one hell of a memory.

We sat the ingot on two stacks of bricks and held the torch under it. Slowly the lead started to drip out on the ground, cooling into slugs as it hit the dirt. I turned to Bo and started to say "it looks like it's starting to sag" when the bottom of the lead bar dropped out and a bright golden rectangle fell to the ground. We danced as molten lead splashed everywhere, but most of it missed us except for one tiny piece that caught Lucky in the ass and sent her running for the bay, yelping. Bo took a welding glove and picked up the gold bar. All we had was a bathroom scale in his houseboat and, after soaking the bar in the ocean for a few minutes so it didn't melt the scale, set it on the top.

"Thirty two pounds," Bo said. "And it's probably a little more cause this scale lies to me. But even thirty two pounds at a fourteen point four Troy ounces per pound is, hmmm, let's see, 450 or more ounces, times fifteen hundred an ounce. Yep. That's a goodly piece of cash there my boy!" Having learned from our mistake, we sat a bait bucket full of beach sand under the anvil for the second two meltings and suffered only a couple of sand splashes instead of being shot with melted lead.

We repeated the exercise for the next two bars and they were all three the same size. I wasn't an expert, but they appeared to be pure gold to me.

Finally, maybe, steak today, but I had to sell them to someone, and do it fairly quietly. Back to Miami I go.

I still had Harry's Amex Gold card and I suspected it never occurred to him to cancel it. The next morning, I threw the bars in a couple of backpacks and had Bo drop me off at the Key West International Airport. I went into the Hertz counter and rented the nicest convertible they had on the lot. Bo was waiting at the East Martello parking lot and I hoisted the backpacks into the trunk of the rental. Bo's lack of desire to go up the Keys was only slightly outweighed by having me become a fugitive by leaving the island without permission or knowledge of the cops.

"Hakuna Matatta, Bo," I said. "No worries, I'll drive forty five, not hit any dogs, women or children and promise to not flip the bird to the FHP guys in parked at the Denny's Florida City. I'll be home for dinner."

I reached in my bag, pulled out the "*Meet me in Margaritaville*" Jimmy Buffett CD and headed up A1A, singing '*Tin Cup for a Chalice*' at the top of my lungs.

Let's see where this road takes me today.

It seemed like a hundred years since I parked in this lot and went up the elevator to see my Jewish friends, but it had only been about eighteen months. Last time I thought I had something. This time I knew.

"Ah, my treasure hunting friend," Mordecai said as he opened his door. "Have some more exotic lead for us to examine?"

This time, I turned and closed the door myself. I then told them the Reader's Digest version of what had transpired in the last year and a half, and what we had uncovered. "This," I said, reaching in the backpack, "is what was inside the lead ingots." And I brought out the gold bar.

"Well, this looks more promising," Mordecai said. He reached for the bar. "May I?" I nodded okay and he hefted the bar. "We still don't have a scale this large. Yehuda, see if you can find something we can weigh this with." His brother walked down the hall to look for something that would weigh the gold. "So, my friend, I'm sure the story is the same about how you came about this gold, but I suspect you are still looking for a discrete way to divest yourself of it. I recall you had three lead bars. I can assume you have three gold ones now?"

"That's correct. The other two are in the trunk downstairs. You're right. I found these and it's obvious that they are not part of the wreck we were working, but this guy has lots more lawyers than I do, and the state of Florida will take a quarter of the value right off the top if I go public. I could win the battle and lose the war. One thing for sure. I can pretty well guarantee that nobody knows I have them. After all they sat on my living room floor for a year and a half and had no value to anyone other than to stub my toe occasionally."

Yehuda came back in the room rolling a floor scale. "It's not going to be perfectly accurate, but it will be pretty close." He sat the bar on the scale and tapped the weights to balance. A touch under thirty one pounds. Say close to four hundred twenty five troy ounces" Mordecai said, calculating in his head. "And you say you have two more like this? That's almost thirteen hundred ounces of gold. Current market value at one thousand, five hundred an ounce - ah, one point nine million, give or take a hundred thousand."

Mordecai sighed and looked up at me. "My friend, we are honest people and work according to the law. We are not 'fences'. That being said, I'm quite certain your story is valid. After all, I saw the lead ingots, and your story is too strange to make up. Can you bring me the other two bars? I need to get an accurate weight, and also see how pure this gold is. I also need to consult with my associates."

I lugged the other two bars up to their office, was told to come back in the afternoon, and then jumped in the rental and headed up Brickell road to find a nice outdoor Cuban restaurant, where I enjoyed a Cuban sandwich, had a few beers and finished off with a Cuban coffee. The waiter brought out the tiny cup that looked like it belonged in Gracie's toy tea set I bought her when I was in London. Those tiny cups contain the most delicious two ounces of concentrated caffeinated wake-up juice on the face of the planet. Two of those and you couldn't comb your hair.

So I ordered a second one. I don't have that much hair left anyway.

As requested, I came back at two, inwardly shivering like the guy that was having his lottery ticket verified. I tapped on the door and entered. Mordecai was alone.

"Your story has a few more twists than you know," Mordecai started. It's almost pure gold. If I was a betting man, I would say it could be Spanish Gold from South America. But you say it most likely came from the Confederacy. I have no idea how Spanish gold got inside of a Confederate lead ingot in America. There are tests to determine where gold originated. It's not perfect but can be helpful, anyway, it really doesn't matter at this point."

Mordecai removed his glasses and slowly cleaned them. I could tell he was mulling something over. He seemed to come to a decision and put his glasses back on. "I told you we are not here to fence stolen merchandise, but I think you are a good man that saw an opportunity. I'm an opportunist too, and a businessman. I'm prepared to buy your gold. He reached down and sat my two knapsacks on the table. "I will pay you eighty cents on the dollar. There's a million, five hundred fifty six thousand dollars in those two knapsacks. You are free to count it."

"Ah………."

That's all the words I could get out of my mouth. It meant I could walk out of there with a million bucks to my name. It's possible that I could take my gold back, melt off little pieces, and eventually end up with more. I could also get mugged in the parking lot and die. For that matter that could happen to me with two knapsacks of cash. It didn't even occur to me that I should consult with Bo. I nodded and reached out to shake his hand. Instead Mordecai just picked up both knapsacks and handed them to me.

"I will ask that you not remember where this happened. And I will respect that you not return to this building ever again. I don't care if you find King Solomon's Mine. Good bye." And with that, he sat down, put his glasses back on, turned away from me, and went back to his work.

I slipped a backpack over each shoulder and took the elevator to street level, then walked back across the street to the car. I tried to act as nonchalantly as possible, but looked at any person within two hundred feet as a possible robber. Reaching the car, I threw the two bags in the trunk and headed south.

Heaven knows I obeyed every traffic law known to man for the next three hours. I thought about stopping at Alabama Jacks for a beer, but didn't want to risk a DUI, and honestly, my hand would have been shaking so hard, I guessed more beer would have been on my shirt than in my mouth. I did make a stop at Boondocks for a Mahi sandwich, fries and a coke, and slipped a crisp hundred under the glass to cover the check when I left. Figured it was reasonable interest on that meal we walked out on before the hurricane. I got home after dark and tapped on Bo's door. My shit-eating grin gave him a hint the trip was successful.

"Those bags look lighter than when you left," Bo said.

"Less gold, more cash," I replied and threw one backpack to him. He unzipped one, looked inside and his eyes got wide.

"How much?"

I explained the eighty cents on the dollar deal, and then

realized I should have called and given him the option of turning down that deal, but Bo realizes the difference between public, taxable income and clean, off the record cash and had no problem with the arrangement. We opened the bottle of Appleton's and a couple of cokes and cleared the dining table to divvy up two-thirds, one-third. It was quite a pile of cash, likely more than I had ever seen in my life and most of it was mine. I decided to start investing some of it immediately.

"I want to buy my houseboat back from you. How much?"

Bo the friend immediately turned into Bo the ruthless businessman as I watched. He squinted his eyes and consulted the hidden instructions on the ceiling.

"It needs a lot of refurb – damaged goods now, but you can make it nicer now. Let's say thirty grand, and two grand a year for dockage. Good with you?"

I counted over three hundred C-notes to his pile for the houseboat, and twenty more for a year's dockage. "I can live with that. I owe you for the diaper too. I never paid for it."

Bo scooped his pile to one side. "I think we can call that square. By the way, plenty of room in my floor safe for your cash if you need a place to store it."

I didn't even know Bo had a floor safe. He opened it up and you could have probably put a body in it. We scooped the cash back into the bags, except for some walking cash, and I went down the steps to the temporary houseboat.

"Okay guys, ready for this? I just bought the houseboat back, but this time, no tenants. We will convert it into a two story, three bedroom house. All new furniture, appliances and fixings. We good with that?"

Brody gave me a grin and a high-five. Grace sat quietly for a moment, and then asked if we could go someplace to talk. I took the leashes out from behind the door and both puppies started dancing in circles, knowing they were going someplace. I borrowed Bo's pickup, let the puppies jump in the back and we drove toward town. On an impulse, I went to the Key West Cemetery and we got out. The cemetery is fenced and there was nobody there on a Tuesday afternoon, so we unleashed the puppies and let them go ape while we walked. This cemetery is 150 years of history. Many of the headstones have just melted away with the salt air and summer rain showers. We found the Russell family plot, and walked by one of the dozens of John Russells that have lived throughout the years. We found Joseph Russell's, my great grandmother's brother, and sat down on the edge of the concrete slab. 'Josie' Russell had been a close friend and fishing skipper to Ernest Hemmingway, and opened a bar called Sloppy Joes in 1933, ironically, on the sight of the present Captain Tony's. Grace took my hand, the first time since her mother had died.

"Daddy, I'm sorry I've been so much trouble. I don't mean to be, but I really miss mom. It really hurts. I miss her so much."

"I understand Gracie. I know it wasn't about me. It's all behind us now. We're cool?"

"Yeah, we're cool. But I have something else to talk to you about. You came home in a really good mood so I take it you got some money for that gold?"

"Yes, I did. We're not poor anymore. That's why I bought the houseboat back. And I can take some time off for a while too and maybe get you some new things, even a car if you want one, down the road. I'm not going to make a lot of noise about it, not because it's stolen on anything but just need to be a little discrete because it's quite a bit of cash."

"No biggie, but here's the deal. There's a school up in Washington State. Performing arts school north of Seattle. I want to do my Junior and Senior year up there, and then go to college up there to major in journalism and music. Can I go?"

I stopped. I just got my daughter back, and now I'm losing her again.

"Is this what you really want to do?"

"There's no future for me in Key West. I want to write, sing, and act. I need formal training. This school is the best place in America for what I want, and there's trees and rain, and it's cool. I want to be where the weather is more temperate."

"You sure you're my daughter?" I asked, grinning.

"Daddy!"

"Okay kiddo, I'm good with it. You gotta come see me occasionally though. Deal?"

"Hey, it's the same distance my way as it is yours. And I think you will have some time on your hands."

We rounded up the pups and drove back to the boat in silence. For the first time in what seemed like a million years, I was at peace with the world.

The following day I went car-hunting. Since the late Itchy Roberts turned the only VW Thing in Key West into a crispy critter, it appeared I needed to trade up. I've always wanted a Jeep so I hit the local dealers to see what I could find late model and not trashed. The Nissan dealer had a nice Wrangler in black, automatic with a removable hardtop for a decent price. I negotiated and ground them down till they were ready to crack, then signed the contract. They handed me a credit application and I reached in my bag and started counting out hundred dollar bills. "Hey, you didn't say you were paying cash," the dealer said. "You didn't ask," I answered. The dealer sunk in his chair and shook his head, knowing I had him. The kickbacks on financing sometimes are more than the profit from the sale, and I had just aced him out of half his money. He didn't know that I knew what I knew. There was more than benefit to my job selling used cars a long time ago.

My first drive was up the Keys to Marathon and the Home Depot, where I bought all new appliances, carpeting and fixtures. The A/C units had never hit salt water but darn near everything else had. Some of this I would do myself and some I wouldn't. I threw them cash for a deposit and back down the Keys where I bought some furniture and beds. I turned Brody back to the Internet to re-decorate his part in early American survivor. For Gracie, it would just be a guestroom that she might occasionally use, but I would let her pick out the pieces.

Spending was fun, but it was like eating your way to the bottom of a fifty five gallon barrel of ice cream. Eventually your arms get tired.

I still had some of my personal stuff left in the warehouse and I drove over to see Tack to pick it up. He had the job of boxing everything up to load in the truck and haul up to the Tarpon Springs offices. He was still working for Harry, but planned to say sayonara after he got his final bonus payout. Spending six or eight hours a day in the water will make you old.

Just look at me.

Tack had my stuff in a box, mostly some notebooks, and a few of my own tools, plus a bag of dive gear. There was also an envelope of 8x10 glossies in the box.

"I thought you would like some memories of the event," Tack said. I pulled out the pics and thumbed through them. The *La Brisa*. A group shot of some of us holding up silver bars. A color glossy of me with a big gold chain around my neck, and other shots of items we had brought in and cleaned up or restored. There was the "big clue", that eight pound cannon that I fell over almost two years ago on Boca Grande. I had shipped it north in a salt water bath and never saw it cleaned up. There was a close up of the scratches on top of barrel, likely put there to remind the salvagers that the cannon pointed toward the wreck, although the whole gun would have likely sufficed. The "shaft" and the arrowhead that was pointing toward the end of the cannon were deep scratches, almost gouges. The scratch on the other end was not as deep and ragged, almost like it was done later, or with a tool that wasn't as sharp. I don't know how familiar Spanish sailors and soldiers were with arrows, but this one had the fletching pointing the wrong direction. $\longleftrightarrow$.

I almost moved to the next photograph and then stopped. I starred at that image for a minute before the light came on.

Holy Shit.

No Fat Lady Singing Just Yet

Without looking up I said; "Tack, get dickwad on the phone. I need an exit interview."

"Not a good idea, boss," Tack replied. Harry is big-time pissed off at you, especially after he tried to close out your Amex card and saw another four hundred in expenses from last week. Think you better leave that sleeping pig lie."

"Call him. Tell him I regret that expenditure and want to make arrangements to reimburse him, with large interest."

Tack shrugged and called Harry's cell, and told him who wanted to talk. I could hear his squeaky voice over the speaker from where I stood. When Tack told him that I wanted to give him money, he shut up. Tack handed me the phone.

"This better not be another fucking jackoff, Bric. What's this about paying me back? You better do it quick or the Key West Police will be back on your doorstep. Yeah, I heard about the trouble you are in. Spill it."

"Harry, I know where the rest of the treasure from the wreck is. I could probably just go get it and you would never know, or I could file a separate claim, and likely beat you in court, but I woke up in a charitable mood. Give me permission to salvage under your license for this, we will give the required twenty five percent to Uncle Sugar and split the rest seventy five-twenty five."

"I get the seventy five?" Harry asked

"No asshole. I do. Listen, I can just sit on my hands and you get nothing. It's still there and will be there forever. It's not near the wreck and you could look forever and not find it. That's my deal, take it or leave it."

"How much is it and how do you know where it is?" he asked

"Where? That's for me to show you, after we have a contract. Maybe. Let's just say it's a place called Treasure Key. Don't look, it's not on a map. How much? Well, just look at the cargo manifest of the *Capitana* and see how much

215

gold she was hauling."

"Gold? There was almost no gold on our wreck. What makes you think you know where it is?"

"Let's just say the clues were under our noses, and sharp as an arrow. I won't know till I go look and I won't look till I get a nice, original piece of paper in my hot little hands via Fed-ex. Deal or not?"

I could almost smell his garlic breath over the cell phone as he gave a heavy sigh. Silence for ten seconds, then the greed gene took over.

"Deal. But...."

"No 'buts' Harry. Get me that piece of paper, and re-activate my Amex card too. I need to order a couple of grand worth of stuff. You can make Tack my sidekick to make sure I play nice. He will be handy for what I need to do anyway. No more questions just get that paper here and let me get to work. I gotta run. Talk later." And with that I flipped the phone closed.

Tack was standing there with his hands on his hips and a big grin. "What did you see on those pictures?" he asked.

I smiled at Tack, but changed the subject. His dad taught me well. "I'm going to order a good metal detector as soon as that Amex card comes to life. Soon as it gets here, we will go find out."

Three days later Fed-ex arrived with a Nokta professional metal detector. This product is guaranteed to find a gold nugget a foot under the ground. I was hoping it would find a couple of hundred pounds deeper than that. At about two grand, it wasn't cheap, but if we didn't score with that unit, we would have to get our hands on some seriously big stuff that would look much deeper.

We loaded up in Tack's flats boat and headed out to Boca Grande. This project might take six months, but I bet I can find what I'm looking for in a day or two. I was banking on the short version so we just decided to daytrip it and see if we could get lucky. The *La Brisa* was still anchored over the wreck and the crew was still bringing up loose coins and other items. Archeologists determined there weren't enough ship's timbers left to try and recover any of the hull intact, but the huge pieces of wood were still being removed and would undergo a lengthy preservation process as they chased out all the water and eventually replaced it with a plastic polymer.

Using the GPS we were able to go directly to the site of the cannon, where we beached the flats boat and unloaded. All signs of the find and the golf course flags were long gone, but with the GPS we could easily stand on the spot and then point directly to *La Brisa* parked over wreck site. The cannon had not pointed directly out to sea, but southwest, so I marked a line from there to the northeast and then put up a wooden stake way up the beach. Tack didn't have a clue what I was doing, but he loved a good mystery and was going along for the ride at this point. How far away from the shore that I needed to look I didn't know, but I would have to guess not that far, probably less than a few hundred feet. I also didn't know how deep what I was looking for would be, and also didn't know how straight a line the sailors kept. My first thought was they would have to keep line of sight, and too far inland the ground got low and marshy.

"Care to share your theory?" Tack finally asked.

"Spanish soldiers knew very well what an arrow looked like. They were still using crossbows in the eighteenth century. That scratch on the top of the cannon wasn't a bad drawing. It was a mark that was pointing in two directions."

"You mean inland?" Tack asked. "So you think the reason we only found one gold bar was that the rest was brought ashore and buried? Oh that's rich. Buried pirate treasure on an island. Welcome to Treasure Key. You better find something here or you will be laughed off the rock. "

"It would fit," I replied, ignoring his remark. "There are no records anywhere of a salvage ship from the 1733 ship wrecking and then being recovered, even in part. I'm guessing before they scuttled the boat, they took the most valuable treasure off and brought it to shore. After all, they took the time to drag that cannon out and point it at the wreck." I had the picture with me. "Look at the picture of the barrel. A very crisp line and 'arrowhead' pointing at the wreck, and then it looks like the other point was scratched on crudely, like with a rock or piece of coral or an iron nail. That second part was done by someone else, and not at the same moment I guess."

"And you just figured all of this out?" Tack asked.

"I've always wondered why we didn't find any gold. It would have been the first thing salvaged, and there would have been quite a bit, based on other treasure found from other ships in the 1733 fleet. I kept thinking we would eventually find some gold on the wreck but we never did. Honestly, I had pretty well forgotten about it till I started cruising through those glossies. Then it hit me like a shot. The cannon was pointing in two directions."

We put the last stake at the highest part of the beach, about a hundred feet from shore. There was no way to tell for sure, but, with sea levels rising and just the normal way the Keys terrain changes, that cannon could have been as much as forty feet or farther from the shore when it was originally placed there. Assuming all else was the same, the treasure, if it was there, would likely be someplace between the shore and that stake.

I broke out the metal detector, and fired it up. I tested it first by dropping my gold-bezeled four reale pendant on the beach. It gave off a satisfying "wheep" when I passed the business end of the detector over it. I put the pendant back on and started sweeping up the beach. This was the kind of detector that would usually tell you what it was hitting on, but any artifact might be valuable, so Tack dug with a camp shovel every time it "hit" on something. This beach, as I mentioned before, had been a popular camp, lunch and party spot for a long time. In fifteen minutes, we had dug up a dozen beer cans, pop tops, tuna cans, old roach clips, a pair of glasses, three sets of car and boat keys (bet somebody was really unhappy they had lost those), fishhooks, some not too old nails, and a very rusty old iron spike, that might be period. The farther we got from the beach, the fewer the hits, and by the time we got to the top of the beach, it was fairly quiet. I started working my way back down, sweeping the metal detector in a wide swath as I slowly walked. More junk. The good thing was this detector, as claimed, would find small chunks of metal, either ferrous or non-ferrous, as far as a foot or more down. The bad part was that Tack was getting a workout digging up old alligator clips that had held countless joints in days of future passed. After three hours, we had made it back down to the beach.

No joy. I didn't think it was going to be that easy, but there was always hope.

Next passes were four feet to the left and right of the original trail. Again we had to wade through a ton of "hits" near the beach. As much as I hated wasting the time, we needed to make sure we weren't missing anything. I got a good hit and Tack dug. He came up with a very rusted, broken cutlass complete with the remnants of a bell-shaped hand guard. Almost definitely 17th or 18th century and probably Spanish. That was encouraging. We dug around that area for an hour and did uncover the very old remnants of a fire-pit, and what looked like pork bones, but nothing else. It would have probably been smarter to be a little more scientific, but we were on a mission. I started moving up the hill again, sweeping the detector left and right. Just like last time, as we got away from the beach, the detector got quiet and stayed quiet. Was my guess just wrong, and there was no gold?

The third pass was about fifteen feet from the centerline. I was starting to get a little discouraged as this was far from the line of the cannon. The cannon might have moved, but then it wouldn't have pointed at the wreck and we found it pretty quick. We went to the top of the hill and then back down to the shoreline again without a serious hit. That pretty well wiped out the day and we returned home to re-group.

Back in the little houseboat that night, I looked at my portable waterproof GPS and checked my original numbers. It looked like the actual compass reading of the wreck site was a few degrees to the left of where we lined up the two golf flags at the beginning. That, combined with men just walking in a general direction could result in a fairly large margin of error. We would return tomorrow and concentrate to the left of the line. Karen joined us at Bo's next door and shared a rum drink while I went over the plan. There was another concern.

"I'm really worried that we're digging around on a wildlife preserve. If Fish and Wildlife happened to stumble on us, we could catch major Hell. Got any bright ideas?"

"Sure," Bo answered with a grin. "Coconuts."

"This," I said, pouring another boat drink. "I gotta hear."

Bo explained, "back when I was hunting treasure full time, we used to camp on Boca Grande all the time. We called it the Palm Tree Anchorage, because there was one lonely palm tree that leaned precariously out over the beach. It was the only palm tree on that island. Eventually it fell down in a storm. After that, every time we were around there, I used to bring coconuts with me and planted them in the hopes there might be some trees on the island again. It doesn't take much to plant a coconut. Just scoop out enough sand to make them half buried and some of them will grow."

"Touching story Bo. You tried to play Johnny Palm Tree, but how does that fit in our plan?"

"Just bring a bunch of coconuts with you. Every time you get a mag hit, you dig a hole and then plant a coconut. It's still illegal, but will probably get you off the hook."

"And the metal detector?" I asked

"Hey, I can't solve all your problems," Bo smiled.

Goin' Coconuts

Tack had to work the next day so Karen joined the adventure. She's a good helper, doesn't mind getting dirt under her nails and a hell of a lot prettier than Tack. Besides it was a beautiful day and good opportunity for her to work on a tan. My new revelation had converted a straight line into a half acre area of undefined sand and I still didn't know how deep the treasure might be buried. These detectors promise to find a gold coin a foot deep. I'm hoping that a much larger cache is findable deeper. I decided to start at my theoretical farthest point, the top of the beach line, about two hundred feet from shore, and work my way back and forth down. If this didn't work, I would have to convince Harry to hire some big equipment, and that would likely draw a lot of attention with the Fish and Wildlife people as the whole island is part of the Key West National Wildlife Refuge. I can attest that the beach has been a frequent location of wild life, but not the kind with fins and feathers. We really needed to get lucky quick.

I tested the unit with my pendant again to make sure it was hunting gold and started working my way back and forth down the beach. Karen was right behind me with the shovel and a bag of coconuts, wearing a twelve-inch wide electric green knit tube-top and tattered super-short Levi cutoffs, ready to dive in and dig up a pile of gold bars the second the detector went "wheep", or drop a nut in the hole to make us look like Audubon award winners.

Treasure hunting isn't glamorous work. Its hours, weeks, months, or even years of agonizing disappointment, sometimes followed by one magical instant of glorious success.

We were in that disappointment stage right now.

As we walked along in the morning sun, I took off with my best radio voice. *"You too can have an exciting career in the treasure hunting business. Yes folks, in ten short minutes with the Acme Galleon Finder, you are guaranteed to find at least ten pounds of Spanish Gold. But wait, there's more. If you call in the next ten minutes we will double your order. . . . .*

"

"WHEEP!"

I froze in my tracks. I passed the finder over the spot again and it went ape shit. It screamed for about three feet to the left and right, which means it thinks something really big was down there. This detector was the kind that tells you what you are hitting on and this one was saying;

GOLD.

"Karen," I whispered quietly. "We might want to consider digging here."

"Good idea," and she dropped her coconuts and started moving sand. I was focused 'down' while Karen dug and I cursed myself for not bringing a second shovel. She scooped for five minutes and I took over. We were both looking in the enlarging hole and never saw the Fish and Wildlife boat cruising around the tip of the key. The portable boom box sitting on the deck of our boat was tuned to US1 Radio with Aerosmith wailing "Dream On" at volume ten so we didn't even hear the motors. We both jumped about three feet in the air and the sound of the siren, just about the time they beached next to our boat. Three officers stepped out. I was standing behind some low scrub and I quietly dropped the metal detector.

"Afternoon folks. Please stay right there and I'll come up to talk to you." I recognized two of them. One was Brody's nemesis Joe Clark. The other was the regional dickhead in charge, Andy Skippenburg.

"Hey Skippy, what's going on?" I called.

"You guys are digging around in a National Wildlife Refuge. That's a big fine and some quality jail time."

"Don't you dare come up here! I'm not decent!" I turned and saw that Karen had kicked off her cutoffs and pulled the tube top down to her waist to make a tiny skirt. She stepped out from behind the bushes, covering her tits, sort of, with both hands, the tube top well below her navel and still barely covering her privates. The cops froze in their tracks, accomplishing Karen's goal of keeping them away from our site. "Gentlemen please turn around for a moment so I can get some clothes out of the boat." They obliged and we quickly retreated to the shore, bag of coconuts in hand. Karen reached in the boat and threw a thin wife beater tank top on. Decent, but barely.

I threw our island beautification concept at them. They consulted back and forth for a moment and then came to a consensus.

"Sounds like a noble cause, Bric, but it's still against the law. There ain't no organized beautification project, and you're not going to bullshit me. Either way, I don't really care. You guys come with me. You are under arrest for violating Section Two Hundred Fifty Eight, Part One Hundred Fifty Seven of the. . . . ."

"Oh, shut the fuck up Skippy. I know the rules. Skippy, can you let Karen go? She can take the boat home."

"No Bric, she's coming too. I should write her up for public nudity while I'm at it."

"Thirty miles from the nearest public anything else? Now that's rich."

"Just get in the boat, sit down and shut up. If you guys promise to play nice, I won't put cuffs on you. Not like you're going to make a run for it." He leered, looking at Karen. "We good with this?"

"We will be good children, I promise," I replied. We jumped in the FWC boat and it backed out into deeper water, as we pulled away and got up to speed, Joe stepped into the flats boat and followed us.

I just had to hope nobody cruised up that way and found our detector, shovel, and for that matter, Karen's cutoffs.

Fish and Wildlife has a deal with Monroe County Sherriff to lock up their hardened criminals for them. Skippy is a dick but was cool enough today to know I was just feeding him a line about the beach cleanup. They ran our wants and warrants and saw that I had been afoul of Key West's finest a few times in recent past. Skippy was also aware I was a contracted treasure hunter.

It was a slow day and we got walked into the judge's chambers before closing time. This judge was a tough guy. I knew him and he would likely not be as kind as the city judge, who merely tried to throw me in jail for a week for being a wiseass.

"Mr. Wahl, and Miss Murphy, you are being cited for trespassing on, digging in, and disturbing a National Wildlife refuge. If your FWC buddies decide to file a complaint, I can book you and put you behind bars. You could be here for quite a while. What's this about a tree planting project? Something tells me your story isn't going to hold much water."

"Okay your Honor, here's the deal." And I told him Bo's story about planting coconuts so the island would have trees as if it were my first-hand experience. I even tried to leak a little tear out of the corner of my eye. Karen was looking as forlorn as possible. Thankfully they had scrounged up some prison blues so she wasn't dressed like a hooker.

The judge looked at me, then he read the complaint, and then back to me. I felt a little like Dustin Hoffman in 'Little Big Man' I didn't know if I was going to walk or swing.

"Mr. Wahl, it would give me pleasure to throw you in jail so deep they wouldn't be able to pump light to you, but it so happens that your ex employer, along with dutifully reporting all the treasure they have found as required by law, also made several generous donations to two of my favorite Greek charitable organizations here in Key West, along with funding a Tennessee Williams play at the little playhouse. He just bought you a 'Get Out Of Jail' card. You are both free to go. I strongly suggest though if we ever find either of you near Boca Grande or any of the nearby Keys in the next three hundred years, you better be washed up on shore, face down. Five hundred dollars each and time served, all three hours of it."

I forgot that Judge Stanos Stefanatos and Harry were buddies. For almost ten seconds, I liked Harry, and then came to my senses. I called Bo and told him to dig in the cookie jar for some cash and come get us. We got home after dark.

After I got home, I got Harry on the phone and I explained what was going on. He got hot and then calmed down when I told him how I got sprung, and that my search area was going to be a hot zone for a period about equal to the half-life of Plutonium. I also told him I would send him a check for the metal detector, which made him happier.

"So you think you found gold?" He asked. "Where do we go from here?"

"Fish and Wildlife will be watching the whole area and especially me like a hawk. That mark, whatever it is, won't be going anyplace, so I think we should just let the scene cool off, then dig it up some night and 'find' it later in the ocean, report it to the State of Florida, let them take their 25% and walk away with the rest. We never sunk a shovel within fifty yards of the site, so even if our FWC guys get a hankering to create a retirement fund, they won't know where to look. We're cool. (That was a lie but Harry didn't know that. I would figure out a way to clean the site in a hurry)

"How much do you think is there, and how long do we need to wait?"

I gave a weary sigh. "Harry, the manifest on the *Capitaina* said fifty gold bars. We found only one on the wreck site. There could be a hundred to a hundred-fifty pounds in gold in that hole, plus maybe some jewels and gold coins. That's huge. How long? I would wait six months or more. Maybe a year. The value is almost too much to consider. The one bar we pulled off the wreck was seventy-two troy ounces. That's over a hundred grand in just gold value. That one bar, if I remember, has a historical value of over half a million dollars. We're talking about more than five mil in that hole, face value, maybe."

Harry didn't like that scenario, but knew he really didn't have a choice, and the upside was huge. Screw up and nobody gets anything. Before hanging up, I told Harry that we were going to travel a little, and that I would be back in touch. He asked one final time if I could give him the exact GPS on the location of the hit.

"No, Harry. For one thing, I don't trust you or your Greek hoodlum friends. If you didn't need me I would have a good chance of helping up Key West's murder count for this year, this time as a victim. Also, I don't know it. I didn't have my portable GPS with me, and when the cops showed up, I had to dance a bit, so it never came to mind. I'll draw a map, and in case of my death by means other than murder, I'll make sure it gets in the right hands."

Harry was beyond unhappy with my position of power, but didn't know any way around it. I couldn't get him to shut up, so eventually, I just hung up. Not the first time this year that I've had someone by the nuts.

All The Time In the World

One month later.

I was in no real hurry. Gracie was off to school, Brody was working for Tack, living in the houseboat and taking care of the dogs till Grace had a place she could keep them. The very night after we got out of jail, Brody did a morning flats fishing trip, casually dropping by our little Treasure Key and rescuing the detector and other evidence, and bagged two nice Cobia as a bonus. The secret is secure. As I sit here, sipping my third Mai-Tai on the beach at the Coconut Palms Resort in Kauai, I contemplated my bucket list. Time to see more of the world and burn up a few of these shady dollars I had. I wanted to motor down a Klong in Bangkok, see the Great Wall of China, have a Singapore Sling at Raffles Bar, spin a prayer wheel in Katmandu, race the Baja 1000, go see this certain young lady in Seattle, look at the northern lights in Alaska and the Southern Cross in Tasmania, have a Caiparina on Ipanima Beach in Rio and sit next to a Mountain Gorilla in Africa. I had a nice virtual safe deposit box, sitting a few feet under the sand on a very unpopulated place with an inconceivable treasure just waiting to be dug up when the time was right. With the economy like it is, that stash of gold is gathering interest faster than pictures of dead presidents in a bank.

So, in the meantime, time for a little kickback R&R. Karen rolled onto her stomach and undid the back of her swimsuit top. "Put a little SPF 30 on for me, would you?" She asked. I complied by dumping a full glass of ice water on her, causing a momentary full frontal nudity opportunity, much to the pleasure of the nearby tourists. My reflexes were good enough to miss the left hook but the kick in the balls couldn't be avoided. I pitched her a towel so she would be decent and legal, and gathered her into my lap for a 'forgive me' kiss.

"You're a rat and a pig, but I do love you" she said, kissing back. "Where are we going next?"

"I think someplace that has a legitimate nude beach. My

227

nuts are going to be too sore if we keep this system up. How about the French Riviera?"

"Nah, all those Botox, collagen tits on sticks are far too much competition for this old body. Let's just find a secluded beach in the Caribbean on Saint Somewhere. Do we have time to change our schedule?"

"Yeah baby, we have time. That's one thing we do have."

Right now, we've got all the time in the world.

Also Available on Amazon
By Wayne Gales

The Sequel to Treasure Key

Key West Camouflage
Hide in Plain Sight

Made in the USA
San Bernardino, CA
18 December 2013